What othe

I believe this may be a first – Mark V ... and Amy Turner have ... to write a book that's both an incredibly helpful dating manual and a sexy romantic comedy. This book makes you feel as if you're getting to eavesdrop on the most intimate and hilarious conversation about dating, sex and looking for true love – while rooting for Amy and Mark every step of the way.

– Liz Tuccillo, co-author of He's Just Not That Into You and executive story editor of Sex and the City

Amy Turner and Mark Van Wye have come up with an hilarious, poignant, hip and sexy glance at flirtation in the age of instant-messaging.

– Aaron Sorkin, creator of The West Wing

He Typed. She Typed. is a funny, heartwarming page-turner that gives you a painfully honest glimpse into the love lives of Mark and Amy: two witty, charming, and eloquent souls and mates who attempt to platonically bridge the gap between men and women one e-mail at a time.

– Cindy Chupack, author of The Between Boyfriends Book and writer/executive producer of Sex and the City

Move over Bridget Jones, here come Mark and Amy, typing their way into the modern consciousness with their pitch-perfect take on the mating and dating habits of the 21st century homo sapiens. I couldn't believe a book of letters could be such a nail-biting page-turner. It had me racing to the end to find out if these two emailing romantics would find the true love they so clearly deserve.

– Stuart Blumberg, screenwriter of *Keeping The Faith* and The Girl Next Door

What a funny book. I found myself laughing out loud, which I've never done in a two-dimensional experience (I need sounds and smells). Amy and Mark have an insightful take on the terrifying black hole commonly referred to as modern-day dating. With such attention to detail, I actually felt like I had dated Amy before... (Oh wait, I did!)

– Mark McGrath, co-host of Extra and lead singer of Sugar Ray

When Harry Met Sally meets Anaïs Nin and Henry Miller in this true comic gem. An indispensable addition to the dating arsenal.

– Krista Smith, West Coast Editor of Vanity Fair

He Typed. She Typed.

He Typed. She Typed.

by: Amy Turner & Mark Van Wye

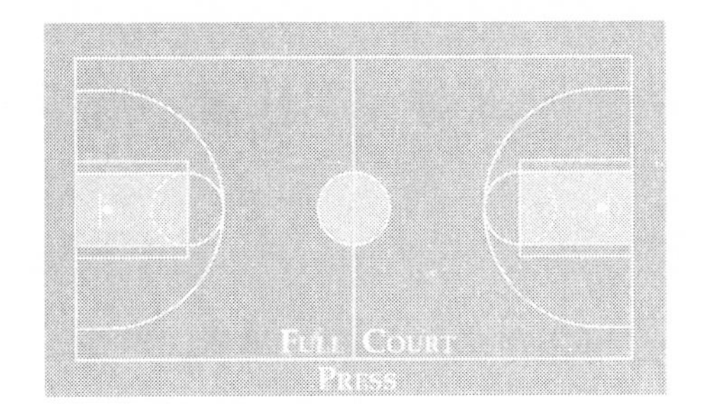

ISBN: 978-0-6151-4839-7

First Edition published in 2007 by Full Court Press, Los Angeles.

http://www.HeTypedSheTyped.com

10 9 8 7 6 5 4 3 2 1

Printed in the U.S.A.

He typed.

From: Mark Van Wye
To: E.A.G. and E.A.T.

She typed.

From: Amy Turner
To: Gutsy women & other outlaws:
J.H., L.F. & M.R.

February 14
To: Amy
From: Mark
Subject: Knock knock

Dear Amy,

Remember me? The newly single guy with the Nat Shermans who completely monopolized you at Geoff & Melinda's wedding last Sunday? The one who tear-stained your taffeta sleeves with his tales of heartbreak and sorrow? (I know, it probably wasn't taffeta. Not good with fabrics.)

If you haven't guessed, it's Mark. Remember at the end when you said to keep you posted? I'm not sure if you were in earnest, or just being nice to the sad sack with the red-rimmed eyes, but even if I don't hear back, I want to say thank you. Talking to you about Diana lightened my load (a little, I'm still stunned). You're good.

Best,
Mark

February 14
To: Mark
From: Amy
Subject: Hey Sack

Hey Mark,

Of course I remember you. You're the guy who had been dumped the day before by the love of his life but came to the wedding anyway (and didn't even get that drunk).

You looked pretty destroyed on Sunday. I'm glad you wrote so I could call off the suicide watch. The last time I got dumped I ignored it for two months. (It was long distance, I rationalized that Jeremy the Trust Fund Cowboy's disappearance involved kidnappers and a loading dock and not his fear of adulthood.) Then I was frozen for about two years. Too much time to grieve? Perhaps. I thought about writing Peter Pan a letter and telling him he left his green tights behind my couch but ultimately wound up going to therapy.

I was so low I grabbed an LA Weekly and found some wacked out chick who worked out of her condo in Culver City. She and her Shar-Pei ("Romeo") were chubby, white and single. How was this agoraphobic albino going to help me, I wondered? Sitting on her white couch surrounded by crystals I would weep and tell her about pulling up to stoplights crying, how people in the next lane would give me the 'buck up camper' smile and I would feel even worse.

One session she told me I needed to connect with my spirit guide and that I could not proceed to heal until I gave him a name. "Hector," I replied. Hector was the name of my favorite bartender.

"Let's talk to Hector and see what he thinks," she said. And then I left and remembered that a free newspaper is not the place to seek medical help.

That wedding was fun and I apologize for making you do the chicken dance with Melinda's mother.

I hope you are doing something jovial for Valentine's Day.

Amy

P.S. I'm sorry you're sad. But sad is okay (I learned that in project self-esteem in third grade, 'feelings aren't good or bad, they just are.' I also learned long division, and don't use either concept on a daily basis.)

February 14
To: Amy
From: Mark
Subject: Misfortune Cookies

Dear Amy,

Yes, cruelly, it is Valentine's Day. I had tickets to an Al Green concert tonight, for me and Diana. Gave 'em to Geoff & Melinda as a bonus. Diana. Shot me with that arrow. And not the good fat pink cupidy kind.

Last night I went over to my buddy Dean's. Helped him make dirty fortune cookies for this big secret party tonight. Turns out there's this swank Kissing Party every V-day for the past 10 years or so. This is the first year I'm invited (thanks to Dean).

Or I should say, thanks, but no thanks, Dean. Even thinking about some lip-locked orgy is more than I can bear right now. No, I will stay home and play a little game in which I try to find a single song or movie or book that DOESN'T remind me of Her.

Sorry things didn't work out with Jeremy. I'm sure Mr. Right is still out there if you assemble the Right search party.

I wonder if I've met your "therapist." When I was house-sitting in the Hollywood Hills last year, there was this lady with a Shar-Pei at the same dog park where I'd walk Stella. She always stationed herself next to the gate, and tried to realign everyone's chakras before they entered the park.

I wish to God (or Hector) I were making this up. Sadly, I'm not.

Best,
Mark

P.S. I highly recommend naming a dog Stella. Every day you get to take a deep breath, hunch your shoulders, and belt out her name in your best Brando.

P.P.S. What do you do that allows you to play hooky and e with me?

February 14
To: Mark
From: Amy
Subject: No Search Party Needed

Hmmm. Maybe I didn't make myself clear. I'm not out looking for Mr. Right, I'm looking for Mr. Right as in I've got my own life and bring stuff to the table and am sexy and passionate and not interested in sucking away all of Amy's time but am interested in screwing prolifically and loving fearlessly for as long as it's real. See, I'm not sold on the soul mate theory. I've seen some of those nature shows and though some species mate for life (species such as Geoff and Melinda), I think partners show up at certain times to teach us certain things and I am a lifelong student. My weakness is mythologizing men. I'd love to stop falling in love with my images of who I want them to be and just, well, you know, let them be real people.

I love that it's Valentine's Day (sorry). Think of it as an overall love day, not just a 'why does no one love me I am going to die alone' day. Last year my landlady Idina gave me a Whitman's Sampler and despite the chocolate smelling like her rancid Pall Mall smoke, I was touched by the gesture. So this year, in addition to getting myself one very sexy fire engine red mani-pedi with toe rhinestone, I bough Idina a purple cigarette lighter and a lemon tart.

Kissing party? That sounds like watered-down wife-swapping. Gross.

Thanks for keeping me posted. Wow. A guy who does what he says he's gonna do. Weird.

I work at night. Restaurant. You're a nine to fiver huh?

– A.

February 14
To: Amy
From: Mark
Subject: Pact Romantus

My hours are quirkier than 9-to-5. I'm an art consultant.

So you're not out for Mr. Right. Know what I'd like? A new friend, a gently sloped shoulder to sometimes make a fool of myself on... If you're game... And I listen, too. (Weird genetic defect in my male chromosome.) So I'm going to go out on a limb and propose.

How about we keep up this e-repartee? Just sort of hold each other's electronic hands, laying bare our respective romantic lives. I'll show you mine if you show me yours.

Me, I want it all. First things first, a lessening of this pain. But eventually? Someone perfect for me to spend the rest of my life with. And whenever you need the guy's perspective – or at least this guy's perspective – you know where to find me.

You know, Amy, I almost didn't show up for that wedding. When Diana gave me my walking papers and I learned that I'd be attending the nuptials stag, I'd already picked out which re-runs to stay home and watch instead.

But at the very last minute, I dusted off those cufflinks and... All I can say, Amy, is I'm glad I did.

Your new friend?

Mark

February 14
To: Mark
From: Amy
Subject: You're on

I don't know, Mark. Most boys are afraid of commitment. Are you really ready to get into some sort of long-term letter-writing show and tell?

Tell you what: show me that you can do this over a year – say from this Valentine's Day to next – and then we'll see where things go. I mean, a year. Have you thought about how long that is? Most guys would evaporate after about six weeks.

Can you handle it?

I guess that I would be game to try, but you're gonna have to convince me, Sparky. Play your cards right and you can be the man-microscope, helping distinguish the good germs from the bad.

By the way, I do have great shoulders for crying on (even though you didn't see those, since the purple bridesmaid dress had that nifty Victorian style neckline that made me look like a Little House on the Prairie extra).

That said, the whole Jeremy tragedy now seems so melodramatic and silly. I didn't need to hide for two years or consult a spirit guide, I just needed to understand that his leaving wasn't about me. And that my identity wasn't tethered to his feelings for me.

Took me two years to get clear on those two sentences. I know I'm supposed to be wanting to get married and all that stuff but really, I look around me, I look at my parents, I look all over and relationships seem, well... dull and tedious. Destructive growth-stunting commitments based on real estate.

Oops, did I say that?

I always thought it was either/or (soup or salad, east or west, career or relationship). I am still confused. All I know is I'm tired of trying to snuggle up with my ambition.

Just think, by this time next year, you and your lady could be fighting about where to spend your spring vacation and I could be dating a real live human being (as opposed to a mythical fantasy figure).

Yeah. Let's commit to that. I dare us.

Onward Love Soldier,
Amy

February 14
To: Amy
From: Mark
Subject: Almost forgot to ask...

What are you doing tonight to celebrate?

February 14
To: Mark
From: Amy
Subject: Gnawing Man Jerky

What am I doing tonight? You're wondering who gets to look at my trampy Vegas toe cleavage?

My Valentine's date is Ted. Ted is a very handsome, very nebulous, vegan "mactor" (model-slash-actor-slash-waiter). We had dinner last week and he ordered the 'brooley.' Upon further menu inspection I realized the man wanted brulée, as in crème. He doesn't know how to say it or that it has dairy. No judgment, some people are still phonetic, that doesn't make them bad people, it just makes them people who can't travel overseas.

Okay, so he's not my dream date but he's sinewy in that sexy rock 'n' roll beef jerky sort of way. I'm not exactly sure what we're doing but it begins at eight, so I should pick out a nice bra (but not nice panties as it is a second date and he will not be seeing those).

February 15
To: Amy
From: Mark
Subject: Hector

Dear Aymee (as your rock 'n' roll jerky might spell it),

Whether you meant it to have this effect or not, your cautionary tale of two-years-for-two-sentences galvanized me into action. (I'm a quick study.) I thought of seeing you at a stop light, and decided I don't want to spend a life sentence just to learn a life lesson, one life too late. In other words, your object lesson arrived in my inbox and hectored me off the divot in my couch, into my lean-in closet, and into my best pair of jeans.

Yes, Virginia, I did go to the Kissing Party last night. Will wonders never cease.

Just remembered this scene in The Apartment. Jack Lemmon is at his office party. I think it's New Year's. And he finds out things with Shirley MacLaine are no go. He's all alone in his cubicle when he gets the news. His eyes fill up with stoic rivers. God, I just want to die. Because that's just it – if he'd been home alone, it would've just been bad news. Guy loses girl. But there at a party – everyone around him literally dancing on the desks, dipping in dances, necking by the cooler – it's true tragedy. He could not be more alone.

And that, my new friend, was yours truly last night. I wore a white cashmere hoodie, hoping every girl on the block would rush over for a stroke. But in spite of the sweater and the old college charm, I kissed: nobody. And nobody kissed me. Even Dean (picture Danny Bonaducci with wolfman sideburns) was lip-locked with at least five at my last count. There were kissing games, kiss-dollars, our lewd fortune cookies (i.e. "whisper in someone's ear something you've never done," or "take a stranger's hand and with your finger draw your favorite position on the inside of his/her arm"). And... bupkis.

I was trapped in my turtle shell, having dragged my baggage with me. I've always sworn that no man is an island, unless of course he wets his bed. But I proved myself wrong. I was an island – like poor Jack Lemmon – and you could hear my lips chap. My sweater might as well have been a polar bear in a snow storm.

Enough about me. As to Ted, I say do not pass Go. Do not collect $200, or more likely the 42 bucks he picked up in tips last week. An actor/waiter? Really? You've lived in L.A. long enough to know better. A man-child waiting to act is no man for you.

More importantly, which bra did you settle on?

Only 364 days 'til next Valentine's Day, Amy. Let's do it. I'll race you.

Dry lippedly,
Mark

February 16
To: Mark
From: Amy
Subject: Fuzzy White Sweaters Belong on Kathie Lee Gifford

Dear M.,
As your new female pal trying to navigate and lead you to a turbo bitchin' chick, I must tell you, girls don't like white cashmere on anything but themselves. Just trust that I care about you and that I am right. Next party we're going navy, forest green, a happy neutral that says, "I could chop wood or order a fine bottle of wine."

I'm sorry you didn't swap spit but I think just the action of going was enough. Those games sound horrible to me. Whatever happened to mutual attraction and awkward small talk about the weather/hors d'oeuvres/latest Court TV re-enactment? Did you approach anyone? Girls like boys with balls.

Have you talked to Diana the ex? I mean is it over over or 'I just need a new job or a new hobby but I'm going to declare it a Relationship Problem' over? How long were you together?

As for my holiday – after dinner at a little bistro (I rationalized his long-winded Burning Man stories while thinking about his abs), Ted said he had a surprise for me. He then pulled into the parking lot of Jumbo's Clown Room. That's right, the creepy Hollywood strip club known for hiring plump girls and Courtney Love in the nineties. I refused to get out of the car and cursed myself for spending forty bucks at Fantasy Nails.

He apologized and said he thought it was funny. I told him he ought to research the word 'comedy' and that I did not consider pitching pennies at zaftig girls in clear high heels high comedy. Perhaps he should've gone for something a little more romantic, like a rubber chicken, a whoopee cushion or a book of Mad Libs.

After the fight we were kind of worked up so we went out for a drink. (Did you know that vegans can drink whiskey?) Then we came home and did it. Oh Mark, am I a bad person? He's so cute and dippy and tall. So tall.

I wore a white cashmere bra. (Joking. Black lace, demi cup.)

Amy

P.S. My landlady Idina is single! She wears mad housecoats, lives on ground beef and generic brand bourbon and has lots of hair (under her nose, in her ears).

P.P.S. You know what's silly about me and Ted, we're both trying to pretend like this is a really great match, when we're just horny. I wonder if it's possible to have a relationship with someone based on like two qualities, say, hot and uhmmm, good penmanship.

February 20
To: Amy
From: Mark
Subject: I'm a Lumberjack, but not so okay...

Dear Amy Eye for the Straight Guy,

Even though I hail from the neon streets of Miami Beach, I can chop wood just fine, thank you very much. Even used to own my own Swede saw. (Though by now I forget what that is.) So fine, I'll stick to the manly plaids. I've been told "Intellectual Marlboro Man" is my best look.

Did you know vegans can't eat Altoids? Gelatin. I think you're being too hard on Ted's comedic sensibilities. So what if you've "heard the joke" before? He meant well. And word on the street is that the gals at Jumbo's are always good for a chuckle, especially with those little round band-aids on their nipples to comply with the liquor laws.

Was it the most avant-garde date idea? No. But you know what? Learn to laugh twice at the same joke. When you hitch your wagon to a guy, you're gonna hear the same stories over and again, so think of this as practice. Practice being a good sport. (But if he wants to go to Jumbo's every Friday night, move on with my blessings.)

I'm going on about your date, because I'm frankly scared to answer your questions about Diana. Don't want to open that door. I've mixed a paste out of humor and daily routine to spackle plaster over that wound.

But yes. It's really over. And I thought she was the one. In my eyes, all the turbo bitchin' chicks of L.A. look like rain-squiggles on my windshield as I drive home in the night, alone.

Sad-Clown-on-Velvet-ly,
Mark

P.S. I'll pass on the landlady. But thanks.

P.P.S. You mentioned that girls like guys with balls. Speaking of which, remind me to tell you about my first date with Diana. (It involves leather pants and an Emergency Room.)

February 21
To: Mark
From: Amy
Subject: Accepting What Is

Oh Marky Warky,

You must divulge the leather pants story immediately. And you also must come clean about Diana. Guys who can't be clear about the last gig usually screw up the next one. How long were you together? I know you are still tender, so take your time and curl up fetal with your blankie.

Ultimately, you've got to be clear about what worked and what didn't.

Okay, my apologies if I sound like a therapy nazi but people who just lovingly bumble along making the same mistakes break my heart. Speaking of bumbling along...

Ted and I went to dinner and I looked at him across the table (at a restaurant managed by a guy in his acting class, so we got a free artichoke) and thought things would be perfect if he just didn't talk.

AND THERE IT WAS! MY MOMENT OF GENIUS AND CLARITY!

"Ted," I said, "let's play a little game."

"Okay." He gave me his deviant James Spader face.

"For the rest of the night, no more talking."

"No more talking?"

"No more talking." Oh Christ, this was starting to sound like a Meisner exercise.

"No more talking." The eagle landed, he got it.

We pointed to our selections on the menu, and the waiter nodded. We just watched each other drink and eat all sexy and mute, played some footsie. We had a silent exchange with the valet and by the time we got to my door we were so in touch with the breath and eyes of the other, oh my God, Mark – I am never letting a man talk again.

It was so fantastic, there was this whole communication, this giant flesh ballet choreographed as a result of the freedom with this new singular rule. The push and the pull, the inclination to speak that was stifled and communicated with hands and eyes, and the build-up, the long deliriously mute dinner, all the pressure to be interested in words, gone.

Till dawn Marky, till dawn I sing the body electric.

Morning. "Babe, ya wanna grab some breakfast? There's some dope organic grub on La Brea."

And the spell was broken.

What did I learn? Never be afraid to ask for what you want. That and what it must feel to be Maria Shriver.

What did you love so much about Diana?

Happy Child of A Lesser God,
Amy

February 24
To: Amy
From: Mark
Subject: The Way We Were (and the pants I wore)

Dear 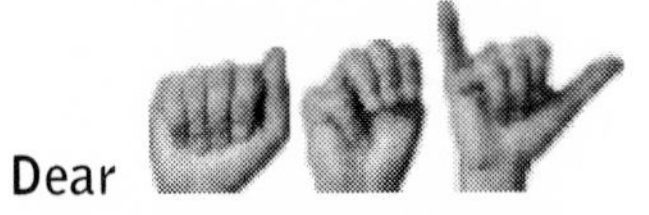

Diana's eyes were deep with sweetness, voice honeyed, laugh infectious, punctuated by a spitfire temper. She'd stomp her feet when she threw a tantrum, and still I thought her the most gorgeous being – the fire and sweetness crackling to molasses I gratefully gulped. She could curl up on sand or sofa and do absolutely nothing for hours on end, the world's happiest piglet in the world's warmest shit. Then she could snap into action and dance a frenzy for five straight hours, sweat in rivulets down the back of an always kicking ensemble. And also, she spoke seven languages, a talent that never fails to pop my socks off. And also, she was the first to make me feel loved. I'd loved before. But never been embraced. Not like that.

Needless to say, I pursued her doggedly for weeks until I finally rated a date. And that's when I wore the fateful leather pants. We drank at the bar while waiting for our table. She asked me to play a game, to act as if we'd never met. I turned my head, took one look at her, and magnetized, I glided unstoppably toward her lips and kissed her then and there.

Dinner's a blur. We went for a drive. I parked. We necked. And then it happened. A strange qualm spread through me. She asked if I was ok. I smiled, acted cool. (As you're sposta in leather pants.) I suggested I should take her home. It was late. Halfway there, I'd stopped talking, stopped listening.

I was doubled over the steering wheel, curved into a comma. "Are you sure you're ok?" This time I couldn't smile. I pulled into a gas station under construction. And here's where I have to remind you – this is our first date.

"Diana, this is going to sound weird, but I have to take off my pants." "Umm, ok..." And I got out. Traffic was whizzing by. And I yanked them off, tossed them in the back seat. No matter that this woman was the stuff of dreams. It was all I could do to keep from puking. Think of every dumb comedy you've ever seen where a guy gets winged in the nuts with a softball. That stricken pruned-up face. That was me.

We drove to her place in silence. Our silent date was not sexy and electric like yours and Ted's. Ours was excruciating. Or at least mine was – I have no idea what Diana was feeling except, "Ok. First date. He pulled into a construction site and took off his pants. Ok."

She stared straight ahead, trying to be polite I guess. Bare-legged, I opened the door for her and gave her a friendly hug – one of those ones where you lean your body away. Back home I sat on ice for an hour, then slipped on some shorts and drove to the E.R. Four hours later I learned I had prostatitis. The leather pants were innocent.

Two weeks of antibiotics and I was good as new. It was a year before I could bear to wear the pants again – not for pain's sake, but for shame. It was a month before Diana and I were officially dating. As you can gather, she is an incredibly good sport. And it was four years later that I got handed my walking papers. And then I met you.

Am I nuts coz I can't let go of her?

– M.

February 25
To: Mark
From: Amy
Subject: Dear Michael Hutchence, I mean Mark

Honey, I think you're nuts for wearing leather pants in the first place but that's neither here nor there. I'm sorry you contracted prostatitis, whatever that is. (We could still let go of the leather pants though.)

Why would you be nuts? You fell in love with some sexy linguistic savant, had a relationship for four years and now she's gone and you're sad. Seems normal to me. I have a theory though, that first dates define relationships, like every relationship I've been in I can look back at the first date and the context defines the next few years/months/weeks whatever. Diana was playful and sexy and you were diseased. (Joking darling, joking.) Honestly, on your first date she wanted to play games and you were willing to hide deep physical discomfort until you could no longer bear it, and then you exposed yourself and she took you anyway. It was a good thing.

I'm still not sure what you loved about her besides the language and the bipolar friskiness (this is coming from a girl who should get a t-shirt that says 'mercurial' in rhinestones, according to one male friend). If we can isolate the qualities we like about people then we can save everyone time. Maybe you like dramatic and damaged. What are the qualities? Or is it all just a mystery? Like, you'll know it when you see it. The right girl is out there waiting to write your last name next to hers on her doodle pad but she will not come to your door via the FedEx man (unless you are into mail order brides).

I have to take a shower, as I am going to a Tibetan Film Festival with Ted.

Namaste,
Amy

P.S. Your assignment – go out for coffee and smile at a few strange ladies. I can feel you festering in a 'what we would've been' Diana cave.

February 26
To: Amy
From: Mark
Subject: The Alone Ranger

Hello Dalai,

Those heels (what were they – titanium?) that you wore to the wedding belied your new age side. That's what makes horse racing. You're having lotus and lettuce with Teddy-san, and me, I could never date a vegan; in fact, after the horse race, I'd be game to eat the horse.

Speaking of horses, I confess I am tempted to come galloping to Diana's rescue, defending her honor by insisting that she's not at all as you describe her, but that just means somehow I failed to do her justice.

I know, I know. You're not dissing her. You're asking me to let go for my own sake. You're looking out for me.

And Amy, that feels spectacular.

I got your e-mail too late last night to go and scope out the caffeinated lovelies. But I'll try tonight. And I'll dress like a man. (Minus the black half-mask.)

Oh, and speaking of mercurial, I'm a Gemini, in case you wanted to know.

Peace out,
M.

<<In a message dated 02/14, Amy wrote:>>
>am interested in screwing prolifically and loving fearlessly
>for as long as it's real.

So... Ted? Is it still real?

February 28
To: Mark
From: Amy
Subject: Leggo My Ego

Dear Mark,

Fuck Ted and the Nehru jacket he rode in on. We were having tea at the Bodhi Tree after the film festival and he was smiling at me and I was thinking, I've got to stop this, I'm tired of hearing about the I Ching and the indie film (i.e. student) he shot last summer. But then I think, one more roll in the hay won't hurt.

We get back to my apartment and he goes, "Amy, I really love hanging out with you," and I thought, "Oh cripes, he's gonna give me a promise ring or something." And then he says, "but I'm kinda going through my rock star phase right now."

I sat frozen in his swirling patchouli oil cloud and acknowledged, I am getting dumped by Ted the Phish tailgate party king.

"That's totally cool," I said. I wanted to say, "You know what, I'm going through my groupie phase right now." But I didn't. He burned my ego and frankly, I'm still in shock. I thought he was really into me. He called all the time, he took me to his favorite surf spot in Malibu, he did the whole sensitive guy, kama sutra love-making routine.

I'm not talking to boys anymore except you.

– A.

P.S. It's okay that you're still in love with Diana.

P.P.S. Maybe I am a little sad that Ted wasn't smitten with me and begging for a one-way ticket to commitmentville.

February 28
To: Amy
From: Mark
Subject: Flattery will get you everywhere (and in the long run, flatware)

Dear Amy,

I know you meant it in a "boys suck" way, and not in a "Mark you're so groovy" way, but reading that I'm the only boy in your life totally made me smile. But didn't you say that you're not looking for a long-haul commitment, only meaningful-and-giddy-while-it-lasts experiences? So big whoop if Ted wasn't begging for that ticket.

Let me say this. I've dated people for weeks or months and never had as lucidly electric an experience as you had that one Silent Night with Ted. That is a treasure no one can take away. Not even Ted. Not that it's a bedtime story you'll tell your grandkids. But a true treat, yours forever. And if it's not about Mr. Right right now, then what it is about is starring in a story. Living a tale, then living to tell.

I feel really good today. No idea why. Maybe it's you.

Cheers,
Mark

P.S. I can't believe I'm doing this via e-mail, and in a postscript at that, but would you like to grab a drink some time? As you saw at the wedding, I clean up good.

March 1
To: Mark
From: Amy
Subject: My Friend Asks Me Out

MARK!!!!! What are you? A MAN. That's what you are.

I go and pour out my sordid silly private life in the hope that it will be some kind of mutual purging that will lead us to better male/female relations and you go and ask me out for a cocktail?

Listen mister, I know what I signed up for in this relationship and it was to be the electronic shoulderer and shoulderee. Is that how you're gonna lighten my load, Sparky?

I thought we were doing this to serve as counsel and insight and then, a long way down the road, you would tell funny stories about me at your wedding and I would invite you to me and my boyfriend's dinner parties.

Talk about kicking a girl when she's down.

Amy

March 1
To: Mark
From: Amy
Subject: Modern Love

Read over your note again and just want to clarify. It's not that I'm NOT looking for a long-haul commitment. If I came across a person who was lovely enough to commit to, that would be great. I have trouble imagining that he really exists, but in my teeny weeny secret heart I hope and believe he (or what's the plural for he) does.

You think I want to spend the rest of my life justifying cute dumb boys? Or chasing after ones who can't commit to car insurance much less me? You think I want to wake up and be 52 years old, wearing a billowing purple peasant blouse and comfortable shoes and celebrating the holidays at a friend's house where the kids have been instructed not to call me "Weird Aunt Amy" to my face? Hell no.

It's just that the engraved invitations and registering at Pottery Barn and the fallacy that one person is going to serve all your needs forever and ever gives me hives. Do you get it?

March 1
To: Amy
From: Mark
Subject: UNSEND would be a Godsend

Dear Amy,

(Picture me prostrate. No, not prostate. Got that taken care of.)

My index finger quivered before I hit SEND. And then it was too late. I'm so sorry. STUPID! STUPID! STUPID! I wanted to call you and tell you not to open it, then realized I don't have your number! We only exchanged e-mail addresses. But you know what? In the spirit of all this – of this undertaking – let's keep it that way.

Not only am I a man. But one on rebound. And thus my nose is finely attuned to the merest whiff of insta-relationship. Comfort zone as comfort food. So, sorry. Won't happen again.

BUT... I'm hoping that I might redeem myself when I tell you this – no sooner did my blood start pumping than I tossed on a coat, checked my breath, and headed out last night to Insomnia Café on Beverly.

A high-cheekboned brunette with slender fingers and a dimpled chin caught my eye, or I caught hers. I sat outside, and she inside at the front table, on the other side of a tenuous pane. We played a game of "who's going to look away first" for what seemed like an hour.

She was reading a book. Couldn't see which. There was no open seat beside her. If she'd been looking for a sugar-shaker, I'd have run in and fetched it. But no such luck. So I sat there staring and stared at, unable to figure out a reasonable entrée. Then it hit me. This was a baby step. And in the right direction.

I drove home with a smile on my face – picture Ralph Malph with his "I still got it!" grin. And that, my friend, was good enough for me.

And if this time you can't tell how friendlily and benevolently I am thinking of you, keep in mind that I restrained myself from addressing this note to "Dear Weird Aunt Amy." And that's no small potatoes.

– The Mark-formerly-known-as-Jerk

P.S. Thank you for qualifying what it is you are seeking. I figured that was the deal, but was wary of reading between the electronic lines.

March 3
To: Mark
From: Amy
Subject: Your Bad

All right. So we agree that our communication is in the name of education, not rebound cuddles.

Next thing, I am confident that after addressing the possible humping of you and me as a no-no, we CAN move on and be very helpful friends to each other.

Tell me you wore something butch to the coffee place.

I can't get over Ted referring to his own 'rock star phase.' I wish he would've said that in the beginning. Saves everyone time. Time is money and money is lip gloss. Welcome to my paradigm.

I despise the idea of sleeping with more than one person. I've never done it. I'm not interested in having my personal life look like an Aaron Spelling program with shittier haircuts and studio apartments.

Where do you meet girls? Where did you meet Diana?

A.

P.S. Good work Ralph, smiling and flirting and all.

March 7
To: Amy
From: Mark
Subject: Mark Goes World Wide

Hey A.,

When you say you despise the idea of sleeping with more than one person, did you mean literally at the same time? Or, like, in the same epoch?

Why do women assume that all men have the same fantasy of two women? It's nonsense. For me, it's all of the Rockettes.

Did you ever read Mark Twain's *Letters from Earth*? There's this great passage where he pooh-poohs the notion of a man having more than one woman, since a man can rarely fully please a single woman, let alone two or a harem. Women, he argues, are the ones who should have harems – nature dictates it. But still, I hear what you're saying. Look how gross movie theater seats get after a mere week of different people sitting on 'em. Nasty.

I've met the odd person in the odd place, but the three LTR's in my lifetime – funny, I never realized it 'til now – I met in high school, college and grad school respectively.

And grad school is where I met Diana. She, however, was younger, having gone high school → college → grad school without a visit to the non-MTV set of Real World. And that proved the fate of our unraveling. On the verge of sanctifying our union, her toes froze. And she bolted for a taste of independence, with a vow to never look back.

But it's funny to go on about that now. It's been almost a week since I wrote, and what a week it's been. Flew to Kaua'i with Dean where I surfed for the first time. (You'll have to tell me about Ted's hotspot in Malibu.) In between drinks, he sang me the praises of online dating. I was so skeptical, my eyebrows lifted a full foot from my face. But he wouldn't relent.

Got back last night and posted my first personal, pictures and all. For a lark, I thought I'd try something really wild and crazy: in my ad, I told only the truth.

And now, I sit back and wait (and in the meantime try to overcome the stigma).

Where do you go to meet guys? I can't see you going to bars. Do your friends proffer setups? The gym? AA meetings? Is the myth of the Grocery Store a real phenomenon? WHY is this so mysterious? Apart from college, how on earth do people ever meet in this world? What did people do before online personals?

Fully ensconced in the 21st century,
Mark

March 10
To: Mark
From: Amy
Subject: Location Motivation

Duh, Haole –

That's why I was asking where you met Diana. So it was in a class? I'm looking for geography here. If we are going to be the Lewis and Clark of love we've gotta establish some territory.

Wow. Online dating. I don't have enough faith to purchase a pair of shoes online. Which service, INeedaDateRealBad.com? I tease, but I have some girlfriends who have had some good luck. Marla, the bartender at work, met her boyfriend of one year online.

I guess I meet people at parties. That's where I've met every significant other. Maybe that's my problem, all we have in common – vodka and a guest list. My mother always said, "You've gotta find a man in college, once you get out it's all shit." I'd like to think she's limited.

Now I'm imagining what my mother's online personal would read like, "Blonde Home Ec. teacher seeks professional man in jeans with good genes. Interests include country line dancing and hypochondria."

I miss Jeremy, my absent Trust Fund Cowboy boyfriend. At least I could get aroused when watching televised rodeos at the West Hollywood gay boy gym. (We all love the televised rodeo.)

I will ignore the double-teaming comment. Men also go to donkey shows, I don't hold it against them. I also don't bray or sit on Pepsi bottles for large groups of strangers.

Wanna hear the grossest thing ever?

Amy

P.S. Remind me to tell you about my grocery store affair.

P.P.S. Tell me you put a picture online of you and not Lorenzo Lamas. You must write as soon as you have your first inter-date.

March 12
To: Amy
From: Mark
Subject: Fresh Meat

Dear Huki Lau,

Hey! If you'd seen me get up on the board on my first try, you wouldn't be callin' me haole!

Then again, what are the odds I'll get up on the broad on my first try at online dating? Too soon to tell. I'm still in pre-production.

But my new name has got to be Fresh Meat, judging by how many responses I've received in just under one week. Yes, I now have a full-time job: reading (70% misspellings, including the occasional "sorry for the mispellings"), clicking to see the pictures (the busty ones cropped from the chest up are the most common; do they really think this fools anyone?), scanning through the myriad predilections and dietary restrictions. And, very rarely, responding, though I've yet to initiate any contact myself.

Want numbers?

87 messages in 6 days. But if we continue the math, the number shrinks. A full half are from the Philippines or the Ukraine, trying to land a green card and a MasterCard with one cut-and-paste hook of pidgin English. Another 15 or so are just "winks," which to my mind is tantamount to the half-grunt one makes when reading a mildly interesting article in the morning paper. Ten of them exactly read "nice pic" and nothing more. Seven were in other states. Which leaves 12 viable candidates, averaging two per day. So I'm not quite the stud my overstuffed inbox implied. (Nor the one in my pho**To:** Lorenzo Lamas-esque; taken early in the morning, hair tousled, a touch of stubble, a hint of a smile, looking like I just got laid.)

I'll bite. What is the grossest thing? This isn't the same as the grocery store story, right? I want both of them.

I'm sorry you miss your cowboy. Me, I miss the Marlboro Man billboard on Sunset Blvd. What kind of parties do you get invited to? I'm feeling three steps below wallflower these days.

By the way, don't worry about my missing one of your missives. All of the online dalliances are routed to a different address.

Ok, back to work (aka the wheat-from-chaff game).

– M.

P.S. I am not neglecting or forgetting your Diana questions. I'm pointing my feet forward and willfully ignoring them – every time I try to answer them, I drift back in my mind, tumble down memory holes and then struggle to climb out intact. I still love her. But that door's closed, and I need to look ahead.

March 15
To: Mark
From: Amy
Subject: Physiological Caller ID

Stop ignoring my questions you ninny. Where did you meet her? Student store, cafeteria, grad student coffee klatch? I'm not asking you to slip into an emotional coma of despair, just tell me where. Crikey. Sensitive new age internet guys.

Twelve candidates eh? Your very own jury. You're essentially 'picking' (and 'picking' based on trivia and a usually misrepresented photo). You are the Cesar Chavez of love. I want to be the Madame Curie of Love. On an obsessive search for radioactive chemicals in Paris, I stumble into my hot Pierre. We are magnetized to each other and Nobel-prized. Something like that.

This is the grossest thing. So yesterday I was, uhh, uhhmm, having a little one on one time with myself (that's right Mark, masturbating) when the phone rang. That in and of itself can break a mood (the ring on the phone is shrill and violent and reminds me of my elementary school fire drill). My answering machine picks up and the voice on the other end is a writer I dated a few years ago, Richard.

Now I dated Richard for about a year and the last six months were terrible. I'm still not sure why it happened (maybe it was because he was borrowing money from me, maybe it was because his futon smelled like that spongy Pirates of the Caribbean ride at Disneyland, maybe it was his puppy dog Snowball, I don't know) but I developed what my then therapist called "vaginismus," a condition in which the female organ scrunches together and screams, penis stay away. The physical sensation being a closed flesh door to which there is no key.

It was so awful. The sound of his voice turned my body from a Slip 'N Slide to a deserted mine shaft. It ruined everything.

Do I have to call him back? I don't want this to happen again. The message was a "Hey, what's up, just found an old picture of us together and wanted to say hi, call me." Please give me permission to ignore.

I'm going to go eat lunch at Whole Foods with my pal Susan. We like to watch the supermodels buy broccoli.

Best of luck sorting the laundry list of future paramours.

– A.

P.S. I'll save the super-erotic supermarket story for the next rainy March day.

March 16
To: Amy
From: Mark
Subject: Kiss and Tell

Dear Self Serve,

Do the models ever eat the broccoli? Or just use it to apply rouge?

Between your scrunched up vagina and my infected prostate we make quite the couple. Good luck with that.

No. Do not call him. If you're going to listen to anyone, listen to your own body.

Why do you still want to know where I met Diana? Wouldn't you rather hear the gritty details of my very first online date (not to mention my first, post-Diana)?! That's right, I cracked my shell and stepped blinking into the light last night. But I have to be honest. You might not know how special this electronic confidential we've got going is to me. I'm about to break a deeply-ingrained rule of not kissing and telling. Best thing my mom ever did.

October 1983. My first time with a girl. Neither of us had ever done anything with anyone. Lisa. A skinny thing I'd never paid any mind, 'til we went on a school trip one summer, and through the sleeve of her T-shirt I caught sight of her left nipple – and was instantly smitten. We ended up dating for the next four years.

That fateful October night, she came over, and alone in my room we listened to Bat Out of Hell on 8-track. It looped over and over – eleven times. We had no idea what we were doing, but we did it all (all except the biggie).

Example: I'd heard there was this thing called a clitoris. I knew it was a little bump. I knew touching it was supposed to make a girl happy. So, after much searching, I found it. Touched it. She wriggled, seemed happy. End of story. Or not. Later, much later (too embarrassed to say HOW much later) I learned that in fact that was not her clitoris. It was her cervix. Swear to God. Don't worry, I've learned a lot since, in case you were ever thinking of recommending me to a friend...

Anyway, half-way through, my mom walks in. Lisa didn't see her, but I did, and my mother exited without saying a word.

A lifetime later, after Lisa left, my mom sat me down and said she wanted to talk. Oh God, I cringed, ready to die. And then she said, "Mark, what happens between a man and a woman is their own business and no one else's. It's only for you and Lisa to know. A gentleman never tells."

Extraordinary. No wonder my standards are so high for a life-mate... My mom rocks.

Ok. Twenty years later. And Bernice (ugly name, hot chick – strawberry blonde and busty) e-mails me her phone number. We chat for a bit. The funny thing is, I'd expected we'd be doing the get-to-know-you talk. You have brothers and sisters? Where'd you grow up? Have any pets? Ever been married? Instead, we just chatted as if we'd been buds. What're you up to? Didja catch that show on TV last night? So it was mundane stuff. She was at work – "sales" (whatever that is) – and her fax was jammed. Me, I was at home, prepping dirty laundry for the washer. I had no idea I was being provocative, but she replied, without missing a beat, "If you like, after work, I could come over to your house and do your laundry for you, and then you can bang me between the loads."

Strike me down if I'm lying. My closet now has three clean loads of laundry, and my drawer two fewer condoms.

Amy, I think I've stumbled onto something new. Just what the doctor ordered to fully get over Diana. Medicinal Dating. I've had my first dose and I feel great. So while you're taking care of yourself in your own sweet back-arched way, me – I'm self-medicating, too.

Mark

P.S. So I don't get balled out again: I met Diana on the first day of class, but when I went to say hello, I got button-holed by a T.A. and missed my chance. Three hours later, I stopped at a café in town and she appeared at my side to ask how I enjoyed class. Before I could answer, the barista stacked two orders on the counter and bellowed, "Mark and Diana." And the rest is history.

P.P.S. It's raining here on the West side. Is it raining there? Raining men? Either way, it's time for the grocery store story. And if you feel an urge to call that allergen Richard, write to me instead, ok?

P.P.P.S. Careful. Madame Curie died from her own experiments.

March 17
To: Mark
From: Amy
Subject: Kissing Blarney Stones and Boys in Parking Lots

Dear Mark,

It's interesting that you would go for that, a mystery chick who offers her domestic and vaginal services in the first conversation. Not really all that challenging or mysterious. I bet Bernice doesn't last two weeks, unless she does windows.

Of course models eat broccoli, it's 25 calories a cup dummy. And models don't apply rouge, people with patience and endless trivial stories about celebrities do. They're called make-up artists.

Your mom tells you not to kiss and tell and my mom tells me "Nobody likes an Easy Marie," (stage whisper) "damaged goods." No wonder this is so confusing.

It's raining buckets... so I knew this guy Mike. I used to wait on him at a breakfast joint I worked at on Melrose. I always thought he was charming in a Star Trek watcher kind of way. So coming home from a silly party with gift bags and all sorts of Hollywood nonsense, I was starving, had not eaten and was, ahem, a little next door to drunk. I walk into Gelson's, grab a mini-baguette and Laughing Cow cheese wheel and see Mike. I haven't seen him in years, and now I am totally embarrassed that I'm drunk and rifling through the deli aisle at 11 o'clock on a Thursday night.

We say shy hellos and he walks me out to my car and then kisses me, just like that! Like on a whim, we kiss. I say, "Goodnight Mike" and we laugh and I get in the car. Two months later I walk to Whole Foods for dinner. And there's Mike, buying a Naked juice. We smile and say, "Huh, grocery stores." "Yeah, grocery stores." And then we walk up to the check out and all I can think is, "I wonder if he'll do it again."

Mike says, "Did you park in the parking lot?" "No. No, I walked," I say. "Oh," he says, "I'll walk you out." And I've got like electric spiders jumping up and down my spine cause I just don't know if he's gonna do it again and we walk outside, AND HE DOES IT. We have this great kiss and then I say goodbye and skip off with some brown rice sushi swinging back and forth like a trampy little West Hollywood Red Riding Hood.

I have no idea what this story even means, but it's one of those things you don't have an urge to figure out, you just get to marvel about how passionate kisses can happen anywhere. Sometimes all you have to do is go to the supermarket. I love that.

The other reason it's great is that I don't think Mike and I were supposed to do anything except have a few random smooches in well-lit parking lots. I walked away both times feeling very complete with the experience. But maybe that was just because I had secured dinner. Who knows.

Thanks for finally answering the Diana question. That's always the best part, the meeting, the beginning. That's how I feel. (Of course that's how I feel, I am the certified serial monogamist.)

Are you going out with Bernice again? I am not calling Richard (even though he left another message saying "how pretty I look" in the photo he found).

Are you going to drink green beer somewhere tonight?

Honey, this is all kiss and tell, so saddle up and ride.

– A.

P.S. OH my gosh – I totally forgot, I met a guy at Whole Foods who asked me to see his artwork. Is this a date?

March 18
To: Amy
From: Mark
Subject: Etchings

A –

I thought it was only in comedies from the 1950s that men invite women up to see their etchings. I dunno why I'm being so skeptical today, but your Whole Foods guy gave me a Whole Body shiver.

To answer your question – any time a guy invites a girl to do something alone with him, it's a date. Meaning: and complications may ensue...

You're right. Beginnings are the best.

You never forget your first left nipple. I guess that's the big problem with online dating. Not a day will go by for the rest of your lives that people won't ask, "So how did you guys meet?" And the answer is as exciting as brown rice (apologies to your sushi).

What is it about Mike that limits him to a little va-voom at Von's? Not that there's anything wrong with that. (When I was a kid I used to love that movie Same Time Next Year where this couple saw each other just once each year – actually, someone told me Bill Gates has this arrangement – once a year he goes to an island with his high-school sweetheart for a single weekend – and no one, not even Melinda, asks any questions. Rumor mill? Perhaps. But I still love it.)

No green beer for me last night. I have an aversion to Irish pubs, and to bands of drunken white boys in general. Something about that gang-rape scene in Leaving Las Vegas always struck me as too true. I'm like Jesse Jackson in reverse. I see a bunch of drunk white frat boys coming, and I cross the street.

I'll have you know you were wrong about Bernice not lasting two weeks, thank you very much. In fact, she didn't last two days.

I went to pick her up at her place last night. Turned out to be her mom and stepdad's place in Thousand Oaks. She's 30, lives at home, and when I arrived she was ironing her stepfather's trousers while he sat in front of the computer in his boxers and brown socks, playing solitaire and smoking Swisher Sweets. Bernice's mother was "upstairs" I was told. Something about seeing her there, doing his laundry...

I took her out for a drink, about 8 blocks away, then drove her back home. Didn't even plant a good night kiss. I didn't want her to be too confused when I never called again.

In a few days I'm meeting #2 – Katya. Details to follow.

– M.

March 20
To: Mark
From: Amy
Subject: Mikey's Marketplace

M,

Okay then, speak for your gender and give me the guy's perspective – why hasn't Whole Foods art guy called? Sometimes I think guys just ask for your phone number to see if they can get you to give it to them. The way women buy Dolce and Gabbana if it's two sizes too small and 70 percent off. They know they'll never wear it, they just do it because it's there.

Last night I went to Molly Malone's with Shelley (gay Shelley). We always have fun, plus she's the only girl I know who drinks beer, so she's extra good for St. Paddy's Day. We were at the bar and this guy stood between us and said "Well, well, looks like I'm in a Hot Girl Sandwich." Which was funny because my friend is gay and has absolutely no interest. So really, he was in an Open-Faced Hot Girl Sandwich.

I never know what's a date anymore. I used to always assume that if a man was talking to me, he wanted to sleep with me. But that just came to feel so jaded, so I'm trying to keep an open mind.

That's what I like about you Mark, you're a real guy and man enough to know that when you ask a woman to do something, it is an unmitigated romantic gesture (except when you suggest e-mail correspondence). Seriously, I hate pussyfooting. That was the great Mike paradox, he never did ask me out.

I think Supermarket Mike is really a stressed out Hollywood guy even though he looks kind of geeky. I think he's sad and eating a lot of Xanax. Just a hunch. He's a successful sci-fi producer. The weird thing was when we would see each other at the market – oh God, I'm going to regret writing this down – there was some sort of unspoken loneliness, and it acted as a magnet.

It was like, 'Hi lonely person." "Hi lonely person." "Wanna kiss and then hide from emotional experience?" "Sounds good. Paper or plastic?"

And the innocent spontaneity of it all was hot. But he's not alpha enough to just ask me out like a normal dude, and I'm not going to muscle my way into a date. So the mystery market kisses will have to suffice.

Creep out on Bernice. Where are you taking Katya, and what has attracted you to her? (Besides her uber sexy name.)

I'm depressed and going to the gym. At least I can watch the gay boys stairmastering. Something beautiful about being the only woman surrounded by men in tiny white t-shirts with handlebar mustaches, a sea of sweaty, swarthy Schneiders.

Maybe we will watch rodeo TV together.

Me

March 22
To: Amy
From: Mark
Subject: On the road again

Dear Amy,

Ah, the old ask-for-your-number-then-never-call chestnut. Guys totally do that. Get a number for the sake of getting a number.

We don't do it for bragging rights (well, sometimes). Most of the time, it's for the endorphin rush of momentary omnipotence – not much different than runner's high – a feeling that anything is possible, all doors are open, the world is our aphrodisiac oyster.

In a guy's mind it's no different than when a woman flirts just for the rush of getting a man to gander and smile at her. An invitation is implicitly extended by her, but it's a bridge to nowhere. A long walk on a short pier. The moral of the story: do NOT take it personally.

What you SHOULD take personally is that you're a stunner: smart, articulate, stylish, strong. Of the ocean of men out there, only a trickle can rise to the occasion of a woman like you.

That said, with 5 billion peeps on the planet, that still leaves a lot of options. So don't despair, not even for a minute. Pickings may seem slim, but they're not. Just sucks that you've got to wade through the gauntlet of pussyfooters and numbskulls to get there.

As for me, I'm now on Day 2 of the longest first date I've ever had. Katya and I are in Santa Barbara. With a dog. In a hotel. I'm using the hotel lobby computer while she showers. (Katya, not the dog.)

We played with alpacas today. I must sound insane. But I'm not. I'm in love. (Is there a difference?) I promise you a full debrief. And an invitation to the wedding, of course. But I'm scurrying back to the room now. I want to be there when she emerges from the shower, misted in a swirl of steam. Tonight is her birthday and I booked the best restaurant.

The luckiest boy in the world,
Mark

March 23
To: Mark
From: Amy
Subject: First Dates Gone Wild

WHAT THE – how did you wind up on a first date in Santa Barbara?

As for me: Goody Goody! Artso Fartso finally called. His actual name is Lance and he paints for fun but he's really a camera operator guy. He apologized for taking a few days to call (mother was in town) and asked me to dinner.

I suggested something shorter – I prefer to do coffee first – unlike my dear friend Mark who does CLUB MED VACATIONS first.

Thank you for the sweetest pep talk. What's an alpaca?

As for your 48-hour tryst, don't tell me about having great sex, tell me about what you ate for dinner. At least I can re-enact that. Or, you know, go to Bristol Farms and pick up a little container of it.

I hate what you said about guys getting off on collecting phone numbers like lint. What do you think the solution is? Leaving it up to the universe is hard.

My friend from work, Allison, wants me to go to a stripper exercise class with her. I find it offensive.

She asked why and I said, "Because there are so many other ways to work out without glamorizing hungry little girls with lost daddy complexes. We could go to a fireman workout," I suggested. "Or run the wooden stairs up the cliffs above the beach in Santa Monica, like Rocky."

She just looked confused.

– A.

March 24
To: Amy
From: Mark
Subject: Haldol, take me away!

Oh, Amy...

Spoke too soon, I'm an idiot.

Guys on the rebound should come with warning labels. Garment handling tags. Either all is right in the world and we're newly in love, or we're all lonely and bleak as a stolen Munch painting, screaming away in a thief's unlit garret.

I totally fucked up. Katya turned out to be a raging psychopath (and I mean this literally). I can't even write about it now. I need a few days.

FYI, the Santa Monica stairs are under repair, crushed by the weight of too many bouncing Balboas. As for guys who play phone games, just turn the tables. When they ask for your number, don't give it, ask for theirs instead. Then their belt remains notchless, they're at your beck, and you control the waiting game.

I'm sorry. Love's not really a game, but I'm too miserable to give good advice. Like the Magic 8 Ball says, "Ask me later."

m.

April 2
To: Mark
From: Amy
Subject: Katya got ya

Hmmmm. Okay, no judgment here, no lectures, but just a thought: maybe you will rethink your first date policy? As in, stay in the same zip code for a few hours, find out if she's employed and on meds? And then call it a night. I'm telling you, Sparky, you've got a thing for the dark and damaged ones.

As for asking men for their number, there is part of me that's such a dopey fifties girl. I've done that table-turny thing before, and it just doesn't feel right. "Hi, it's Amy, I was calling to see if you wanted to think of something neat to do with me tonight. I like sloe gin fizzes, walks in front of shop windows and anything else that you would see in a Frank Capra movie." Ehhhh. No can do.

I met Lance last Tuesday at 3 p.m. for coffee. Sort of. He suggested the Coffee Bean and Tea Leaf on Beverly. I looked all cute and sat there with the rich teenagers and waited. For a while I did the math based on each ensemble (median outfit cost – Seven jeans, Abercrombie t-shirt, down vest and Nikes, three hundred and fifty dollars – obviously sans accessories).

At three eighteen I started to get pissed. At three thirty I was fuming and I checked my phone (I always turn off my phone when meeting an actual living breathing person). Lance left a message: He hoped I hadn't stood him up and then I realized, two more Coffee Beans live on Beverly. I called him back and he met me at my bean.

He pulled up in his truck with a mountain bike on top. Sexy. I learned a little bit about him (from SoCal, college in San Luis Obispo, art school, ambitious, cute in army pants, seems smart) and told him I had to go (I had to work).

He asked when we could have dinner and I told him I was busy at night, but maybe another coffee. I don't mean to play hardball, I just want to chat more, without wine and candlelight. I am not getting a clear gut reaction so I will proceed with caution. He's cute. I hope he doesn't blow it and tell me he's a married Scientologist or something.

xoxo
A.

April 3
To: Amy
From: Mark
Subject: Sucker for Romansch

Dear Amy,

I can learn a lot from you, your take-it-slow with Lance. (You mentioned his bicycle – he's not that Lance, right? If so, so much for your love of guys with balls. Sorry. Bad joke.)

Do you cost out your dates' ensembles, too? I guess it's different for a coffee date – army pants seem ok for the Tea Leaf.

So you don't feel anything in your gut. Do you usually? Or when you do, and you go for it, is that usually an important sign? I can't tell anymore. I'm still kind of freaked, and feel lost without my bearings more than ever. My gut seems to be hurting more than helping.

If you hear me out about the sort of first impression Katya made, maybe you won't think me so manically impulsive for flipping so fast.

Katya. Half-Hungarian, half-Serbian. A former dancer and a current model. She quit dancing because she tired of the "mawkish sentimentalism." She accuses American choreographers of caring too much how the audience and the dancers "feeeel" (pronouncing this word with disdain). " Whatever happened to pure form?" she asked.

As a model, she gets pretty offbeat gigs. She is a regular at Trekker conventions, so perhaps she knows your pal Mike. She doesn't wear pointed ears, she (this is top secret) shows up in the guise of a fan.

Seems that as trekkoids age, they become aware of their lack of social standing. So seeing a few hot chicks at the conventions boosts their morale.

"Hey, we can't really be losers if those babes are into it!" She knows nothing about sci-fi, has no interest. She just shows up, paws through some trading cards, and leaves four hours later, pocketing $2000.

I was dog-sitting, so Stella was over – a hulky Retriever who tends to the stand-offish. But in Katya's touch she melted like tallow. To me, a great sign.

(I have long held a theory that people use pets to show a potential mate how they are in bed. Alone with the dog or cat you might just pat it on the head. But in the presence of the paramour, you stroke or play rough-and-tumble to express your physical style, even if it's subconscious.)

I prepared a five-course meal, but Katya cleared the table, insisting we picnic on the floor. Over dinner, she spoke somewhat heavily of the brother she lost in Serbia, and another still missing. When I served her tea and offered her sugar, she snorted, "Americans, putting sugar in everything." Something about the strength of her convictions mixed with the softness of her curves just wowed me.

Then she had me close my eyes. She placed her lips by my ear and whispered words in fluent Romansch. Whatever they were, she cast a spell.

Around 2 am, we were lying in bed and for no good reason I asked her when her birthday was. "Tomorrow," she said, bored. "WHAT!?" I exclaimed. "I see no reason to make a fuss on the anniversary of leaping from my mother's womb. More sentimentalism."

I know she sounds horrid, but I was fascinated. I insisted we do something to celebrate. As she drifted to sleep she said she'd always wanted to see an alpaca.

Was this a joke? A challenge? I lay awake much of the night, unable to calm my skin, unable to take my eyes off this exquisite beauty lying an inch away, her hand on my chest. In the morning—

Shit. Sorry. My client just got here. Have to finish this later.

Gotta go,
M.

April 4
To: Mark
From: Amy
Subject: Let the Katya out of the Bag

I'm obsessed with Katya. Please go on. Please!

April 4
To: Amy
From: Mark
Subject: Cont'd

As you wish...

I couldn't sleep. Surfed the web and found an alpaca farm about an hour north. Figured all farmers get up early, so called around 7 am and asked if we three could come visit (Stella still being my charge). The ranch-lady had this, "anyone who loves alpacas is alright by me" attitude. Katya appeared, wrapped in a sheet, even more beautiful in the morning sun. She'd overheard.

Shit, I cringed, is she going to kill me coz I made a big deal about her birthday? She ruffled up my hair and asked if we could stop by her place to pick up a few things before we hit the road, asked where we were spending the night.

She didn't invite me in. While waiting in the truck, I called a few places 'til I found one in Santa Barbara that allowed dogs. The ride up was a dizzying array of her gypsy tales. I noticed that apart from her two missing brothers, she never mentioned family. I sort of brought it up, but she changed the subject.

At the ranch, Stella strutted her stuff for two tall dark and handsome Anatolian Shepherds while Katya and I met the alpacas. Almost a hundred – chocolates and ivories, ebonies and rust. Katya stomped fearlessly through the ankle-high shit and embraced them around the neck with unbridled strength and affection. I offered to buy her a sweater or a scarf – after all it was her birthday – but she shrugged, uninterested.

At the hotel she showered (that's when I wrote you) and we dined on popcorn shrimp, cornbread, jambalaya, red peas and rice at a famous N'Orleans transplant.

This is where I should have ended the story. A kind God would have sent the lightning then and there, so I could've died a very happy man.

Back in our room, Stella slept through our riotous love-making. Near the end, I was on top and holding her hands and she shuddered and came, and I smiled, happy as could be, and looking her in the eyes said, "Happy Birthday." I thought it was cute.

She almost broke my fingers as she slammed me to the side, punched me in the neck and shrieked, "Why the fuck would you say that!? What the fuck is wrong with you!? Who the fuck do you think you are!?" Stella barked.

I replayed everything in my mind and came up blank.

The bathroom door slammed and she didn't emerge for an hour. Then she sat on the bed, switched on the TV and watched four back-to-back episodes of Wings. And laughed at all of the jokes. It was 4 am. I tried to speak, and she spit at me. "I don't know who put you up to this, but I am going to find out," she said.

I slept a couple hours on the floor, paid the bill, we packed up and left. In the long, awkward ride back, she told me she had been cursed at birth by her grandmother, who suspected her grandfather had strayed. She was cursed to forever be unable to distinguish real life from her nightmares. She said the doctors in America had thought her crazy but she knew they were trying to get her pregnant with their pills, so she'd flushed them.

A glutton for punishment, I asked her, "Katya, what exactly did I do that upset you?"

She turned and stared, dry ice in her eyes and intoned, "You know what you did..." And those were literally the last words she spoke. Another hour we drove in silence. Arriving at her place she petted Stella, kissed her on the mouth, and slammed the door shut.

Am I drawn to crazies? Are they attracted to me? Are these questions one and the same?

Going back to what I said before – I can learn a lot from your slow-hand with Lance and the rest. From here on out, I want to take it slow, and when possible vet these candidates with you before I stick my neck out again. (Only to have it punched.)

It's late. Sweet dreams.

Shaken, and stirred,
Mark

April 7
To: Mark
From: Amy
Subject: Amy plus Lance

I get it. She was exotic and hot, you were heart-broken. You would have been better off with a foreign film (usually equally quirky and sexy and confusing).

Note to Mark: make a date a date and don't run away with feelings. Literally. Or alpacas. (Why won't you tell me what those are, mister flowery-descriptive guy?) You are still drawn to crazies. Then again, you're doing this online so you are drawn to pictures of crazies.

Sex on the first date is also grounds for crazies to be crazies. You're opening up the most intimate part of a woman, you bet some wacky shit comes with that. We've all got it, and it usually slips out post-orgasm. That's why it's good to wait, because if they've already seen your rational happy fun side when you wig out into, "Sometimes I just feel so lost and vulnerable," it's a little more palatable.

Answer me this – what did her fingernails look like?

Lance and I met at the Bean and he violated none of my fashion rules (no sweatband on wrist, exceptionally baggy pants, or more jewelry than me). I SO WANT THIS GUY TO KISS ME.

We talked about plays and movies and music (good taste in each area) and he did that staring, you know, where he can't stop looking at you so you just look at your shoes and giggle every few minutes. It was so much fun.

He was on location in Fiji last month so he had good stories about a drum circle and some ritual where they passed around a coconut filled with restorative liquid and the actress (a soap star named Karen) insisted upon pouring hers into an Evian bottle instead of the communal coconut. Then he walked me to my car and kissed me on the forehead!!! THE FREAKIN FOREHEAD! LIKE IT'S MY COSMIC THIRD EYE THAT NEEDS HIS LIPS!! Okay I liked it and though it was sweet. I'm dying to get his cooties. He told me he wanted to cook dinner for me this weekend. I told him that would be fun. This is bad. Am I being too available? I kind of like him.

Mmm, at least you had some jambalaya.

Oh and Mark, I don't want to be a big jerk, but don't call it lovemaking when you met five hours ago, call it what it is: transitory pleasure balling.

xoxo

A.

April 9
To: Amy
From: Mark
Subject: Holding Pattern

Dear Amy,

> alpaca, *noun.* A domesticated South American hoofed mammal, having long, soft, silky fleece, related to the llama and believed to be a variety of the guanaco.

Her fingernails were recently manicured, a paler shade of Pepto Bismol.

The forehead kiss is not only a bad sign, it's freakin' bizarre. What is he, your priest? Here's my question – when you really want a guy to kiss you, how do you (non-verbally) communicate this to him?

By the way, that drink in the coconut shell? The shell is a tanoa, and the drink is yanquona, made from the pepper tree, a mild barbiturate. I know this because as a boy I won a game show, grand prize being a trip to Fiji to star in a documentary. There I had to drink gallons of the stuff; they only drink it for special occasions, but their idea of a special occasion is akin to that of a used car dealership (bi-annual Lincoln's Birthday sale, Arbor Day in Greece sale, etc.) Getting a 12-year-old stoned is a grand prize indeed...

What does your gut say about Lance now? Are you totally averse to taking the initiative, physically, and planting a kiss (lower than forehead, but high enough to be respectable)? I want to know EXACTLY what he cooks for you – spare no details, please.

Must dash. Got another client coming and my place is a mess.

April 15
To: Mark
From: Amy
Subject: Lance pulls me into his cave

Pepto pink, eh? Fingernails AND toes?

A woman's manicure-pedicure color choice is the modern-day Rorschach test. If a woman gets baby pink ballet slipper on her fingers and fire engine drippy wet cherry red on her toes then she is definitely renting a condo in the virgin/whore complex. It's 'let me show you my pretty little hands I'm off to a Charity League luncheon and then BLAMMMO! I take off my Ann Taylor loafers and I am your very very bad little girl.' I will know I am balanced the day I ask Trang for either Chanel Red (or Shell Pink Mist) on both fingers and toes, but until then...

That whole nonverbal communication thing is a problem. I am vibe dyslexic, guys I don't want to kiss me have no qualms about trying to kiss me and guys I want to kiss, well, this one moved into my t-zone.

I always think I'm sending out a vibe. My friend Shelley says that I'm not, but not to worry because I can't control it. When I am ready it will be on the radar and returned. Shelley's a very evolved lesbian and thinks all this worrying about kissing and dates is ludicrous. Easy for her to say, every relationship she gets into lasts at least ten years. You're a boy, what are the 'non-verbally communicating' signs? Besides a miniskirt and a tongue in your ear.

My 'vibe' must have been right because Lance and I did lots of kissing (and I did not take initiative). You know me by now Mark, I'm all gruff and full of nonsense but I want the boy to pull me into his cave. I have walked into caves before and it's just not right. I have waited in caves for ages and it's more fun to get pulled in. I am no longer a cave stander. This week.

He invited me over to his house and he made chicken marsala with a fennel and parmesan salad and a not-pretentious but not cheap bottle of Chianti. Isn't that delightful. Should I be concerned that his house is decorated well and very clean? He showed me his bedroom, oh my God, total love fest bed. High off the ground with super high thread count linens (I touched). We made out on his red couch for hours and my lips are still tired in the best way.

I don't want to go to work. I want to kiss and hear more of his stories. Isn't it weird how when you're getting to know people you find yourself telling them intimate details you hadn't planned on? I told him about the way my mother gardens in a giant sun bonnet with her creepy dishwater-colored lowrider underwear hanging off her butt. He thought it was funny. I also told him about our little e-mail correspondence and he thinks it's a good idea, charting our emotional waters together. M., I really had a good time with him. My gut is positive. I don't know exactly what I like about him. He just seems "together." Does that make sense? (Plus he's handsome in a Leif Garrett surf guy way and seems to like me.)

Your impudent love don,
A.

P.S. What was that about a client? I thought you were an art consultant. Do you keep the art at home?

April 17
To: Amy
From: Mark
Subject: Signals, or how to greenlight a prospect

Dear Love Don,

Or I should say Love Don Rickles, the way you ride my ass...

Yes, I am an art consultant on weekdays. But on weekends and some evenings I have a roster of private clients for self-defense classes – most of them women, but I have a strict no-dating policy and I've never even come close to violating that. To me, it would be really wrong to take advantage of a situation where we're stirring up someone's deepest fears amid a lot of bear hugs, grappling and yes, even simulated sexual assault scenarios. It's intense stuff, but I feel like it's one of the greatest gifts I can offer someone: the knowledge necessary to feel safe and secure. Does that sound hokey? Probably, but I actually mean it.

Back to the art world, I met someone yesterday at the Getty Center. I'd been sent there to woo away one of their famed art restorers, Bob. Bob turned out to be short for Bobbie.

(And no, her hair was not short – it was shoulder-length, kind of a gun-metal bluish black.) We were looking at a Tamara DeLempicka, and she switched off the lights so she could show me some overpainting with a black-light wand. Her teeth were glowing a dazzling white. (I imagine mine were, too.) No, I didn't kiss her. I'm going slow, remember? But I asked her to dinner: tomorrow. She knows her stuff, is articulate and focused, serious but with an easy smile. And we already have a lot in common.

I'm thrilled that Lance is jousting his way into your cave. He's sounding better and better, and since he did leave the forehead for moister pastures, I'm not sure you really need my advice.

But since you asked, any sort of physical familiarity of a non-sexual nature is a great maneuver. If he's wearing a chain or choker or eyebrow piercing for that matter, lean in close and finger it admiringly, then retreat. Touch his arm as you emphasize a story detail, or in response to some tale of his, then leave your hand there for a second too long. Take a drink from his glass, or a bite from his plate.

And then there are the two I'm-interested hugs (you already know the lean-away and the back-pat to show no interest): gently stroke your thumb in a circle on his shoulder to show affection; or press your pubic bone against him hard if you're good to go then and there. But these are all second-tier. Top tier, there's only one sure-fire way:

Remember when you said he was staring too long, and so your gaze dropped to your shoes? That's where you slipped. Don't drop your gaze. Stare right back. Don't speak. Just breathe. Lock eyes, and don't move a muscle. You're in each other's kinosphere, and animal nature is straightforward – from this position you can only do two things: kiss or kill. (The possibility of the latter is why all first dates should be in public places.)

Don't worry about Lance's neatness. Maybe he's Bi. Maybe he's got OCD. But most likely, he simply has self-respect. And that tends to imply a lot of respect for others. So consider this a good thing.

Your pal,
Mark

Art consultant/Warrior

April 20
To: Mark
From: Amy
Subject: What about Bob

Mark, those are some great ideas, but if he's wearing an eyebrow ring, a choker or a chain I should get myself off the Backstreet Boys tour bus immediately. I need ideas that don't require accessories.

I always touch when telling stories, often gets me in trouble. Richard despised this habit, said I was "throwing out chum to sharks." I thought I was just me, animated and easily excited.

The long drawn out stare, so Mexican soap opera-ey, lock eyes and don't move a muscle? I don't want to look like the Tin Man. I think I should save that stuff for when it really feels important enough to not move a muscle, or maybe I move a muscle and he says, "Hold it." Yeah. If romance is a dance I want to be in Martha Graham's company, not the Joffrey.

Speaking of ballerinas, is it bad that I almost bought a dreamy pink ballerina-inspired sparkly formal dress yesterday? So lovely it needs nothing but shoes. It is a self-sustaining dress, it is the Prius of dresses. I have nowhere to wear it. It would be wishful purchasing. Ever do that? What do guys wishful purchase?

A self defense teacher – jesus Mark, do you have any idea how hot that is? Strong, burly and using it to help women feel safe and self-sufficient. Captain Intellectual Bad Ass, I salute you.

Bob sounds foxy and maybe not damaged by pogroms. Take her somewhere nice and don't forget to mention that your hobby is helping women not get raped. Give me the details. And note the manicure.

I am starting to suspect that Lance has more books on his bookshelf than he has read. This is forgivable but it makes me wonder. Did he just get the cool guy manual? He has a bunch of Bukowski and I asked him if he liked the story about the shrinking man and he said he didn't remember that one. I let it go.

Ten minutes later he admitted he hadn't read any of the stories in the book. Yet. He bought the book because he "likes the cover."

Perhaps he just made me chicken marsala because... he likes my cover? And if so, is that bad? Isn't that how humans work? And if so, why do I find it so distasteful and frightening?

A.

April 20
To: Amy
From: Mark
Subject: The Curse of the Art World

A,

First, let me handily dispatch all Bob questions: a) I didn't realize Bob was gay, and b) she didn't realize I wasn't. End of story.

Second, you rock. Still laughing about Martha Graham. (And I wonder why Bob thought I was gay...)

Third, is it bad you almost bought that pink confection? Not at all. Providing your name is Björk.

You should never judge a book by its cover, but when faced with stack after stack, it's an excellent way to decide which invites further inspection. (That or word of mouth.) You may find it frightening, but it's a fact of life. We pick up a book if we like its cover. Then we flip through, get a taste of the style and content, and then we keep reading or we put it back down.

I used this principle to weed through the pile of online responses. I've selected five. Tomorrow, a trifecta:

- Morning coffee with Lynne, a Korean cosmetologist
- Afternoon coffee with Hannah, some celebrity's personal assistant
- Happy hour drinks with Kate, an industrial designer

The day after, two more:

- Afternoon coffee with Josie, a writer (movies, I think, not sure)
- After eight drinks with Rebecca, a Welsh Jew preschool teacher

What Mel Brooks does with jokes, I'll try with dating: fire a shotgun shell in hopes that some of the buckshot's bound to hit something. Or maybe I'm just banking on the Law of Averages.

Can I confess something, Amy? I miss being in love. I know that's a bad place to be. But I can't help it.

Multi-tasking,
Mark

P.S. There's a company called Books by the Yard that sells... books by the yard, for people who want people to think that they read. You might want to look around Lance's place for a receipt. Anyway, at least he collects books and not midget porn. And even if he is trying to impress women with his books – that may not speak well of his education or erudition, but it speaks volumes about the kind of woman he's trying to attract. I still like Lance.

April 22
To: Mark
From: Amy
Subject: Smiles Everyone Smiles

Maybe books are Lance's wishful purchase. I bought the dress today. Why won't you tell me if and what you wishful purchase? And Katya – did she have Pepto pink on fingers AND toes? Dammit Mark, don't give me the opportunity to give the "men don't listen" rant.

Sometimes I can be a bit of a medium (psychic or after the holidays when my jeans are tight). I have a good feeling about Lynne and Josie and an okay feeling about Kate. Wow, the sheer volume must make you feel like the Sultan of Brunei. I wonder if the ladies have such a full schedule or if dudes are a scarce online commodity. Ask them will you, I'm curious.

You're not going to like what I have to say. You miss being in love – peeshaw. Fall in love with the world and then you will become interesting enough for a cool girl to fall in love with you.

Oh never mind, chase all you want, at least I get to hear all the gory details.

Lance and I went to the movies last night and he gets peanut M&M's and popcorn and dumps them together. He's a food mixer like me! (I confessed to him that cottage cheese smooshed around with Kashi and jam is my favorite food.)

Afterwards he came over to my house and asked me all sorts of questions about the pictures of my dad, my mom, my brother and Susan that I have in the kitchen. Lance had a rough growing up, young unmarried mom, critical stepfather. He seems to be in touch with how he feels. I like that. He's very close with his mom and swears that I will love her. Hellllllloooo? Mom talk on the fourth date?

I opened my mailbox today and there was a postcard in it. A picture of Fiji and on the back he wrote, "Just thinking about the way your smile lights up my world like a Fijian sunset."

I know it's nerdy, but I love it. Got a little Jell-O kneed in fact. I am not going to judge him for being a trite poet. I am going to continue to enjoy myself. So there.

Tell me about your date-a-thon. All that smiling and listening, did you do the Miss America trick and put Vaseline on your teeth?

Interesting that you're using the social lubricant with the preschool teacher.

Dorky and giddy (but more than usual),
A.

April 23
To: Amy
From: Mark
Subject: Reviews

Dear Amy,

Cottage cheese with Kashi and jam? My jaw hangs open. Wait, better close it quick. Some of that might get in there.

I haven't yet earned my Listening Badge? You're a fierce task-mistress! (And I, apparently, am not interesting enough!!?)

I didn't mention Katya's toes because, well, I hadn't noticed them. I try to take in everything, but I'm just not a big foot or shoe person. I know you all love your shoes (and pedicures) and put so much into it, but I think I'm like a lot of guys in that I can't really appreciate the difference between Payless and Blahniks. And the message sent by fire-red nails doesn't quite strike home. And when you asked, "What do guys wishful purchase?" I wasn't sure what you meant.

Like, what's something frivolous I get giddy and stupid about buying? The latest gadget, I suppose. No wonder the Energizer Bunny keeps on going – I probably buy a new pack of AA batteries a week. Started when I was ten with Mattel Electronic Football, and it never ends...

I still like Lance, so I am really happy for you, Amy. Saying you'd love his mom, or vice versa, is a genuine, embracing thing to say – like he really wants to invite you into his world. Not the same as picking out china patterns. (Which based on the thread-count of his linens, he'd probably select handily. Then again, he may have a decorator who picks out his books and sheets, so we'll see...) A postcard? A poem? All I can say is: Lance and Amy, sitting in a tree...

I don't feel at all like a Sultan. Like Twain says, men don't need harems and I agree. Couldn't do it. For me, there are two ways to handle the online scene. Either you spend a lot of time exchanging e-mails, then talking on the phone to really vet someone before you actually meet in the flesh – OR, you meet immediately, something quick (no protracted dinner-date) to see if there's any chemistry. I'm trying the latter. Saves a lot of time. And I don't feel like I'm the one holding the reins – I'm being dissected and grilled, too. That said, here's the farm report:

Lynne: arrived late, just had big fight with mom, cursed about her all through coffee (which she gulped), bitter, angry. Complaining excessively about anything on a first date is a major turn-off. So, nope.

Hannah: immediately made it clear that as she didn't know me, she could not reveal the identity of her employer. Then proceeded to use the words, "My employer" to begin the majority of her sentences. Haughty. Pure Hollywood. A kind of Attitude she herself hadn't earned. Situating oneself on someone's coat-tails is not, in my mind, a great talent. She also answered her cell phone three times. And had to make a call to change the time of an eyelash tint appointment for Her Employer. Pass.

Kate: Wow. I was instantly smitten. Great curly locks, sizzling green eyes, and a smart pin-striped suit which managed to be uber-professional while also affording some serious cleavage. Arrived from work with a brushed aluminum attaché in hand, which for some reason really aroused me. I had a million questions for her – and her expertise was dazzling.

I had no idea how much research and development goes into designing plastic coffee cup lids. I'll never look at them the same way again. Where the bumps go, the doming, the sip-mechanism. Did you know there are over 75 different styles? (She's responsible for six.) Smitten, I tell you. After about 20 minutes she asked, and I quote, "So how much money does an art consultant make?" I was taken aback by the question. And she frowned when she heard the answer. The date lasted only five minutes longer. I asked for her number (we'd arranged the date via e-mail) and she bluntly replied, "Sorry, but no thanks." Ouch, Amy. Ouch.

Josie: kind of a mess, said she hadn't slept in a couple days, recently single, chain-smoked American Spirits. Goes to Narcotics Anonymous. She was interesting, and very funny. I hadn't laughed so much on a date in a long time. But I have to tell you – I felt invisible. I wondered if her lines were rehearsed. She didn't seem to see me at all, didn't ask me anything. It was uncomfortable, and I couldn't relate at all to the whole Recovery thing. So, well, that was Josie.

Rebecca: FINALLY! I didn't save the best for last to be dramatic – just happened that way. Who ever knew there were Welsh Jews? We met at Deep in Hollywood, where she knew the bouncer. Three burlesque dancers pantomimed in post-apocalyptic ensembles in a large Lucite cage above the bar. Rebecca's deep brown eyes were sweet and sparkling, and when her hand graced mine, her hands were cool but her touch soothing. I held her hands to warm them up and we shared a very quick, innocent kiss. This was in the first ten minutes, just a little gesture to reassure each other we were on the same page. Then we talked and talked 'til 3 am.

She works with learning disabled kids by day, and by night, man can she dance. When I hugged her good night, she kind of curled up in my arms – we were standing by her car, but somehow the geometry was just like we were reclined on a quilt by a fire. Felt so natural, so right.

Her stories are endearing (like when she buried treasure behind her school and gave her kids a map, or how she still plays Hopscotch, every day, as her favorite spirit-picker-upper). On Friday we're having dinner at the Buffalo Club.

Back-on-the-horsedly,
Mark

P.S. I did ask 4 of the 5 about the male:female ratio on these sites, and it turns out men (straight, unmarried, employed) are a very rare commodity.

April 25
To: Mark
From: Amy
Subject: Miss Rebecca

Rebecca sounds awesome. Teachers are so appealing and noble, plus she's funky and has good health insurance coverage. You're the one who said you're looking for Miss Right. Babies cost money – the woman has full benefits and dance moves. Give her a whirl.

Yes, get the Kashi out of your ears and listen: wishful purchasing is when we buy something that we don't have a real need for, but we still hope to have a need for – be it fancy cookbooks, metallic-green eye shadow or wedding gowns.

I can't believe you slept with a woman and didn't take note of her feet. I am speechless.

And now convinced your Sensitive New Age Guy routine is a thin veil concealing the Grunting Quarterback with a kielbasa and sweatpants. (But we also like that guy, so don't be afraid to let him out.)

So, Buffalo Club? Pretty fancy. I hope she's a light eater. If I were a guy, I'd be in trouble – I'd calculate every hundred dollar date as a negative drop in my Road-Trip-with-Susan-to-Dollywood Fund.

Let me know how that goes.

Nice date place, Buffalo Club. A fancy architect took me to dinner there once. He was quite charming until he announced that I was to be his muse, "at least for the next six months or so." I appreciate honesty but my God, expendability factor coming right up with your tenderloin?

Men are driving me crazy. I went to work at the restaurant and my manager said, "Amy, what's that in your hair?" and I touched it, it's this brilliant hair product that sometimes gets a little crispy/flaky. I said, "Oh, it's just a hair product I use." Then he said, "I thought maybe Lance gave you the money shot last night. But like, in your hair."

You guys can be such tards.

Lance wants me to meet his mom. It feels a little premature for a family holiday. We haven't even done it.

A.

April 28
To: Amy
From: Mark
Subject: Men are from... sperm 'n' eggs, just like women

Hey Oscar –

Don't get all grouchy with the "you guys are all..." routine. I swear to God we don't have a newsletter, or regular meetings in basements where we smell our own farts.

Yes, your manager is a dolt. Yeah, the guy who pointed to the expiration date on your carton before you'd even had hors d'oeuvres is a narcissistic loser.

And no, Lance isn't perfect – and I agree, meeting mom before your bodies have been properly introduced is premature. (Are you sure he's not religious?) But he seems to be keen on you, and willing to do the work. And anyway, if I recall, you like us a little rough around the edges – a touch of scruff. (And I never claimed to be a new age guy. Goddess strike me down if ever I do.)

Bottom line: we're not enemies. And this isn't war. It's supposed to be the opposite.

I'm sorry, I'm probably talking way too much and overstepping all kinds of lines. I'm in a really lousy mood.

Last night was the Buffalo Club. I agree with everything you said about Rebecca. But here's what happened:

This great Devo cover band was playing. On a second date, conversations get more relaxed, more into the minutiae. Which is when it came up that she hates cardamom, and coriander, and cilantro, and cumin (are you detecting a pattern? I wouldn't even ask her about celeriac or cloves).

But wait, it gets worse – she HATES dogs. Who hates dogs? "But PUPPIES?" I asked.

Yes. Rebecca hates puppies. I was already signaling the waiter when she also let it slip that her favorite movie of all time is Pearl Harbor. Please shoot me. Hard. She's great in so many ways, but long-term, which is what I want (ideally), I couldn't cotton to a life without dogs (not to mention the spices of life).

That's not all. I was getting ready for a presentation, looking in my computer for some scanned images of a Sam Francis painting, and there, accidentally filed among them, was a snapshot of Diana, New Year's Eve, a few years back. She was wrapped in a tight shimmering silver dress, sitting on my lap. We looked so happy.

I want to call her. The buttons on my phone are scarred with hesitation marks. I'm not going to. But I want to.

–M.

P.S. Almost forgot – my wishful purchase: Once, in Istanbul, I bought this long white cotton dress – nothing fancy, it was the picture of simplicity. I didn't have a girlfriend at the time. But I had this dream that one day I'd find the right wearer. When Diana and I started dating, I gave her the dress but it didn't fit. I'd say I'm still waiting, but I can't remember where I put it.

April 28
To: Mark
From: Amy
Subject: Good Marks

That was sad, that 'hesitation marks' thing about calling her. Still, no matter what, don't do it. You want the truth? (This will seem mean and insensitive but I'm giving it to you for your own good, I'm saving you from yourself.) If you call you will just seem pathetic.

If you have to, write her a letter and put it in a drawer and never actually mail it. She broke up with you. Break up means, I don't wanna any more. This relationship was way too intense and deep to have a 'seen any good movies, how's your brother' conversation at this point. Be still. Go people-watching at a mall if you need a pastime, but don't dial. Remember what you said when Richard called me? Listen to yourself, Intellectual Bad Ass.

Me and Lance got seriously intimate.

A.

April 29
To: Amy
From: Mark
Subject: The Island of Beautiful Women

Dear Tease,

Seriously intimate? Do tell. I need a vicarious romp. I'm still in the dumps.

When Diana first told me she needed to be on her own for a while, she was still in love with me (she said) and told me her fantasy was that she could send me to The Island of Beautiful Women which also had all my favorite foods and TV shows. I'd hang out there to pass the time while she was doing her own thing. This would assuage her guilt, and if/when she returned, I wouldn't have had to suffer.

A week later (it took us about a week of serious summits to finally make our peace, aka have the realness of this breakup sink in to my skull), she repeated the same wish, but this time it had changed.

She said her fantasy was that I would slip into a coma, so she could go off and do her own thing and if/when she returned, I wouldn't have had to suffer.

How I went from the Island of Beautiful Women to a Coma is beyond me. Even in the realm of fantasy, I got screwed.

And speaking of screwed... you're not the only one who wants gory details. You guys are more than k-i-s-s-i-n-g? Spare nothing. Spill.

– M.

April 30
To: Mark
From: Amy
Subject: Sweating

Okay, you asked for it:

We were having dinner at my favorite Italian place on Beverly when he popped the question, "Amy do you go to the gym?"

"Why?" I replied, while I casually dropped my breadstick.

"I thought you did. You're in really good shape."

I relaxed and was just picking up my breadstick, when he said, "Tomorrow you should go to the gym with me. It would be so much fun!"

'FUN'? What's 'fun' about seeing me all clumsy and grunting and sweating in a ragged jogging bra with no make-up?

I could hardly sleep when I got home, I just saw myself huffing and puffing surrounded by perfect female specimens who made their living as Julia Roberts' body doubles, my old sneakers and unhip Capezio gay man Fosse-friendly spandex, declaring me new to the hetero gym.

Mark – it WAS great! We wound up running next to each other on neighboring treadmills and playing a game we made up, "Deformed Celebrity Bingo."

We'll see somebody and then have to describe them in reference to a celebrity, like, "Don Knotts on Vicodin" or "Jewish Jessica Simpson." We go back and forth until we hit the right combo and then it's a bingo. I laughed so hard I almost fell off my hamster wheel.

More Nautilus than Anaïs Nin: I am sorry if this is not the vicarious romp you needed.

I understand Diana's need to wave a magic wand over your pain, though. I think most of us feel that way when things end. Unless there's adultery and lies. And then we just wish that the other person gets audited and ends up requiring a whole series of root canal work.

A.

P.S. I'm meeting the parents this Sunday.

P.P.S. I'm so crazy about Lance I don't want to have sex with him. What if he's bad in bed or weird or something? I like him so much the way I see him now.

May 1
To: Amy
From: Mark
Subject: The treadmill

Dear Amy,

Did he give you a deformed celebrity moniker? What's his?

So it sounds like we've both been running in place, only yours was much more fun, since you had company on the treadmill next to you. Between that and your breadstick curls, you're on the road to Action Star.

If bad/weird sex were really a deal-breaker for you, don't you think you'd have instituted a policy by now, where an early test drive is mandatory? You know, before things progress to inventing your own language and meeting the 'rents? Since you don't have this policy, my guess is that you're of the hopeful variety; assuming a guy's got something to work with, even if his first missile launch is a dud, you can still school him. Which can be fun. All guys are hot for teacher.

(I'm comparing you here to another friend of mine who's kind of the opposite. She doesn't bang on the first date, but she's a total size queen, so she's sure to end every first date that shows promise with a long enough kiss so she can push in, let her thigh or fingers do the walking, and survey the parcel. If it's not up to snuff, a second date is instantly out.)

Neither your way nor her way is the "right" way, in my opinion. But each way reveals where priorities lie. I happen to really like yours.

Are you more curious about his mom or his dad? If they're amazing or horrid, will it change the way you see him? Be honest!

Me, I've got nothing. Been taking smoke breaks down in the office courtyard with a really cool gal – Beverley. Early 50s. I think she used to be an actress. There's a kinda vibe.

Over and out,
Harrison Ford on Nitrous

May 3
To: Mark
From: Amy
Subject: Mom Curious

No dingy, you don't name yourselves (bonding happens when you mock others not each other). Though when we see someone interesting, like a drooling baby or an old woman blinking a lot he smiles and says, "That's you in five minutes." I laugh every time.

Early test drive? Eck. I'd have the germs of a New York subway if I took that approach. This is the deal. I have this friend Sam, Sam is great in every way, athletic, Harvard graduate, handsome. My mother begs me to date this guy right, BEGS ME. (We are from the same hometown and have kept in contact.)

So we go out, we have fun, he kisses me at the end and WHAMMMO, pointy freakin tongue, darting at my palate like a sardine. I kid you not, the kiss was so bad I could never see Sam again because I feared the tongue taco.

I cringe here in my apartment alone just thinking about it.

What if Lance is one of those minute men, what if he's all wrapped up in his own experience, what if he's got a weird weenie or is double-jointed? AHHHH! These are important things.

The truth, I'm super curious about his mom. Dad is a step, so I guess some conditioning issues will be revealed, but really, it's mom. If they are terrible will it change the way I feel about him? Hmmm. The way he's described his mother, she sounds so sweet and hip I'm already in awe of her, but if she was a barking trailer troll I would still be crazy about him.

I have no desire for him to meet my parents. If/when he meets my mother (she will be wearing an oversized Christmas sweatshirt even if it's June, pants that she has hemmed five inches above her ankle with her home-bleached hair helmet) she will force him to eat oatmeal cookies and look at her vacation pictures of France (where I'm quite sure a law has been passed forbidding her return after she scolded someone for bringing her an 'aperitif' – "That's a drink you know, I thought it was an appetizer.") He could get scared away.

I'm more like my father. The man who lives on hot dogs, paperback spy thrillers and afternoon naps. Again. He could get scared away.

Early 50's eh? Good luck with Mrs. Robinson. Courtyard, smoking, ex-actresses. Very dramatic. It's just gay boys and protein powder in my neighborhood.

Tata,
A.

May 4
To: Amy
From: Mark
Subject: Bad Kissers

Dear Amy,

Ok. I have more dirt on Beverley. But that episode has been pre-empted by your tale of taco tongue. I hereby give myself permission to vent. Amy, sit back and grab an air-sickness bag. I am now going to regale you with Tales of Bad Kissers.

1. The Corkscrew

At the Formosa, met a bright writer who was shackled to a show on the WB. Not only did she have a stiff, pointy tongue, but she swirled it around concentrically, never stopping, swabbing like a Q-tip. Having my teeth scraped by a hygienist is more erotic.

2. The Plunger

Popular misconception – only men shove their fat tongues down throats. Hardly. Liz, a civil engineer, was – what? – clearing out my drainage system? I actually gagged. Like being force-fed a banana slug. (If you've never seen a banana slug, look it up – the similarity is uncanny.)

3. The Python

You know the way a snake sticks out its tongue, darting in and out? Dallas (the only city-named girl I ever went out with) made these hesitant little forays. It tickled, but not in a good way. At least when I got home there was no need for me to floss.

4. The Garbo (aka The Corpse)

Annalise, a German social worker, simply reclined, kept her eyes open in a dead stare, and slightly parted her lips. Her body went limp. No response, none at all. Almost had to hold a mirror to her mouth to see if she was breathing. And this wasn't about her lack of interest. She's the one who'd pulled me down beside her. We had one more date. And she Garboed me again.

5. The Skull

If you think you've heard it all, I saved the best for last. Australian anthropologist (I am embarrassed I've forgotten her name). Great blonde curls, sparkly blue eyes, tons of chemistry, fascinating stories of aboriginal spiritual centers. And then we kissed. She opened her mouth AS WIDE AS IT COULD POSSIBLY GO, and then held it there. I'm not joking. Which left me only two choices. Kiss normally, and stick most of my face inside her mouth. Or open my own mouth as wide as it goes so we'd line up. Game, I tried the latter. And we just locked like that (lockjaw is more like it), frozen. Our teeth clacked. I remember I was deeply aware of our skulls – it felt skeletal, and very wrong.

And now I climb up on my soapbox, Amy, to pronounce the following: good kissing is a dance. You adapt to your partner. If you have a shtick (i.e. if some asshole like me can give your style a stupid label), you are automatically a bad-kisser.

Good kissing is shtick-free, it's different with everyone you kiss. Always a dance and a titration – finding a balance, a meeting point – which is what coming together should always be about.

END OF RANT

Thanks for listening.

Signing off from the Crypt,
Vincent Price

May 5
To: Mark
From: Amy
Subject: Embrace your inner El Guapo

Get off your soapbox and get a margarita. Lance and I are going to El Coyote to celebrate the gringo favorite, Cinco De Mayo.

The deal is, he is a great kisser, that's why my fear is so behemoth.

I went out with a guy in New York, lovely, I was crazy about him, EXCELLENT DANCING/KISSING and then he was the ever popular jackhammer in bed.

How do you 'adapt' to that? Become concrete?

May 7
To: Amy
From: Mark
Subject: Dinner and a (teen) Movie

Happy Cinco de Amyo,

Everyone says, "Food at El Coyote sucks but the margaritas are great." I totally disagree. I think the margaritas suck, too.

So, yesterday was meet-the-folks day... I'm all ears. Did mom live up to her hype?

Beverley's a booker for a modeling agency right above my office. We never planned it, but always end up taking breaks at the same time. She had one big role – co-starring in a sexy teen comedy in the 70s. I was five. Then she vanished. Into a bag of coke. Several decades blurred. Now she's 54. As in Studio.

I've dated a couple other women around the same age, and I'm not being defensive, but none of them had a maternal bone in their bodies. So I don't think I'm looking for a mommy. Beverley does have a sixteen-year-old she's trying to keep out of modeling. But now that I've seen them together – Beverley's the sister-pal kind of mom. They share clothes, giggle, swap stories.

Beverley invited me home for dinner. Really nice (except the food – tuna casserole and lettuce tossed with red wine vinegar, semi-frozen pound cake for dessert, right out of the tin). Nothing happened. But there's something there.

I'm still checking my online personal thing. But no one interesting has written. I might 86 my passive thing and actually write someone – there's one profile up there I keep coming back to, willing her to write me. Time for me to act.

I don't know what to do about Bev. Can't get a read on what this is about. Any suggestions?

Olé,
Mark

May 8
To: Mark
From: Amy
Subject: Hot Mamas

Oh my God. You are disgusting. You actually ATE the red wine with lettuce and frozen pound cake combo platter? That is like supreme aging model food. Any second, you're going to prance down a runway and start whining about your rock star boyfriend.

You really don't know what's going on? Well, are you attracted to her? Does she make your blood boil? Why did nothing happen? I bet it just didn't feel normal to go at it after all that acid and protein was sloshing around in your tummy. Why don't you just take her out? Another older woman, eh? Pattern pattern and it's not Pucci.

I understand why older women are sexy though. They are mysterious and not as insecure as the twentysomethings. I look at myself at 21 and then at ahem, my later twenties and there's a world of difference. I've stopped wasting my time with endless self-loathing and superficial minutiae.

But I have to go because I have a green tea colonic/monkey placenta facial/paraffin elbow session scheduled in fifteen minutes.

Honestly, I don't think the older woman thing is that confusing, what IS confusing is just silly semantics that have nothing to do with affairs but more to do with life. Like, do you want to have kids? If so, a 54-year-old mama is not the mama.

Speaking of mamas, met Lance's. I'm in love with her. Andrea is wonderful, showed me baby pictures of Lance and had me try on her new Prada sweater. (No. I am not acting like I touch Prada sweaters all the time, but I had to be sort of natural.) Stepdad is nice in a Herman Munster-ish way.

'Andy' and I yammered like lip-glossed magpies. She said, "Lance has told me a lot about you. He thinks you're fantastic."

I blushed. We've only been dating for three weeks. Of course he thinks I'm fantastic. Everybody's fantastic in the first three weeks. He hasn't even been through a PMS cycle with me, or a bad meeting at work when you're humiliated by your ignorant upper-managerial community college dropout power-hungry boss, or a holiday with my mother where she clears your plate while you're bringing your salad fork to your mouth because "it's time for cake."

That being said, she was a smidge too gregarious and then I got nervous. It went like this...

Lance's mom: Amy, why don't you come to Palm Springs with us next weekend?

(Subtext, you have nice teeth, maybe Lance could hunt your eggs.)

Me: Uhhhhhhh...

(Subtext, do I get my own bathroom?)

Lance: MOM!

(Subtext, I'm the DUDE. LET ME BE THE DUDE. I'm 29 please stop planning my parties!)

Me: If Lance still likes me, that would be great.

(Subtext, if we're sexually compatible and our room is soundproof, okey doke.)

Go write to that girl you're so curious about.

A.

May 9
To: Amy
From: Mark
Subject: Seeing (former) Stars

Dear Amy,

Palm Springs, huh? Andrea sounds great. Too bad she's not single. Joking. But speaking of which – no, it's not a pattern. There are no patterns, near as I can tell.

No, the problem with Bev, I figured out, isn't her age. One of the hottest dates of my life was years ago – met a 52-year-old Portuguese widow in a restaurant bar – we got as far as my car, completely overheated (us, not the car) but never made it out of the parking lot.

It's that she is lacking the security that normally comes with experience. Like I said, she missed out on decades of her life, so she's still an insecure 20-something actress in her head. But she's stuck inside a 50-year-old body stuck inside the piranha pond that is Los Angeles – where she's used to being asked out by men in their 70s and (her last date) 80s. Which breaks her heart. She told me she and a bunch of her friends want to move to France – she says it's their Mecca – the only place where older women are swooned over, and not treated as invisible. (But another friend of mine warns against this; she's sworn off Frenchmen, saying they're "all croissant, and no baguette.")

The only type I have is this: the confident type. So I don't think things with Bev are going to go any further. But she did invite me over on Saturday for a swim, when Juliana (her daughter) is at a friend's...

I don't think it's too soon for you to go away for a weekend with Lance, do you? I mean, with the folks is a bit much, but maybe that's a nice buffer. Has he been pressuring you at all about the physical stuff? God, I'm envious of your honeymoon phase. I bet he still compliments you all the time.

Gotta run,
M.

May 9
To: Amy
From: Mark
Subject: Monstrous Balls

Ok. I did it. I wrote to her. Savoy. That's her name. Runs her own ad agency. Ivy League pedigree x2. Speaks French, Italian, Mandarin. Runs marathons. House in Bel Air. And... she is the unfuckingbelievable separated-at-birth identical twin of Halle Berry. I am totally ready to take her to Palm Springs with my parents. And we haven't even met. (Or spoken, or corresponded.) This is too good to be true, right?

– M.

May 10
To: Mark
From: Amy
Subject: Strange Fruit and Cheese

Go on a date with Savoy. (Katya, Savoy, such saucy names.) Perhaps your dream girl is a Susie or a Jane and you keep passing her by for the Katya's and the Savoy's. But as you wish, my paragon of single man-dom. Powder your shorts and off you go.

You know, you give me the criteria on your ladies, but I'm still not sure what you're really after (sure, sure you said confidence, but it's not just confidence or else you'd date a crossing guard). And Ivy League, Shmivey League. Doesn't she just have to make you smile? (And get a baguette.)

As for the long-gone Beverley, wow. What a bummer for Bev. I thought I got to look forward to aging and the wisdom it brings. Wisdom being a deep sense of security, a conditioner to unbrainwash my tired head that gets so tangled up it can't trust itself, and children to drive me to doctor appointments.

Weird, my mom is on a constant rant about moving to France, too. She's also Bev's age. I think they have different intentions.

Mmmm, as for the Frenchmen being all croissant and no baguette. A professional cheese maker once told me (don't ask) in order to make cheese, "you repeat an ancient formula as faithfully as possible, then you wait for something extraordinary to happen – for a visitation that is never guaranteed."

I have a heart made of cheese, I've grown my own mold to seal the flavor in, ripe and bursting like a camembert or mont d'or. I've been waiting for the baguette, but my condition had always been a breeding ground for jerks.

Until now. Lance and I were cooking and drinking wine in his kitchen and he's chopping peppers and I'm swaying around to Springsteen's Nebraska album (he has a record player, how dreamy is that) when he looks up and says, "Is it weird that I think I love you?"

And I say, "Maybe you just love me to this soundtrack," and he says, "No. I don't think that's it." We start making out in the kitchen and wind up having mind-blowing sex. I am in a bliss bubble. There is nothing else to say.

Happy happy joy joy,
Me

May 11
To: Amy
From: Mark
Subject: There's a reason bliss rhymes with kiss

Darling,

You have (temporarily) extinguished the cynic in me. What you wrote made me so happy for you, I'm just going to smile and not make any silly comments (I won't even sneak them in parentheses, by saying what it is I'm not going to say).

Man, I'm just on vicarious cloud nine (it comes with floating binoculars). My own dates seem so stupid in comparison. But then again, looking back to where this all started, I said it myself. I don't know if I'm looking for anything right now, today. As I said, this is medicinal dating. I'm trying to forget. While remembering what it is I really want – not necessarily today, but some day.

I can distill it all down to Nat King Cole: "Just to love, and be loved in return." And you're right, the details don't matter, the pedigree. What matters is that you wag your tail like a dog when you're on your way to see her or she's on her way over, and when you're together you don't want to part.

And then this feeling lasts, not for three weeks, or even three years. But a lifetime. Not a lifetime of roses and heart-shaped boxes of chocolates. But I believe that once a day, every day, forever, your eyes should glisten and so should hers.

Thanks for floating me up to this cloud, Amy. Oh, and hey – Savoy wrote me back. Just a short note, but she sounds interested.

Fondly,
Mark

P.S. What do you think, should I go to Bev's on Saturday or not? I'm, er, concerned about getting into a grey area.

May 11
To: Mark
From: Amy
Subject: To Bev or Not To Bev

Now Beverley reappears? Hmmm. Saturday night with Bev... Intention, my man, it's all about intention.

Why don't you just hang out with some dudes and play darts or something? I think you'd be better off. Wait, maybe you're not the kind of guy who plays darts in bars. You might be more of a bookstore and cognac at home alone kind of guy. I think Bev is out, unless it's your civic duty to be the young swashbuckler who rescues her self-esteem from the hands of father time.

This whole intention thing might be something to think about. I mean, medicinal dating? Is it really fair to the women you're meeting?

Go out with Savoy if in your gut you are open to a new friend, and leave it at that.

As for me, I have become a sex zombie. I don't eat, I don't sleep, I just roll around with Lance and get myself to work. I feel like someone rubbed oxycontin on my sacrum. Of course, the second I walked in for my 5 o'clock shift the bartender Marla says, "Uhhh ohhh. You've got the glow." I played dumb for about a second. "What glow?" I said. "Well honey, I don't need to explain 'the glow,' same way I don't need to explain watermelon." Marla is from Tennessee and prone to colorful language. Dr. Phil with a martini shaker.

Radiant and rated R,
A.

P.S. Lance got me a present for our one-ish month anniversary. He's giving it to me on Friday.

P.P.S. I bought the sugarplum fairy ballerina sparkle dress yesterday. I am positive that Lance and I will be somewhere that requires sparkles on Dec 31st, and I'm going to be prepared.

May 14
To: Amy
From: Mark
Subject: Bald men and olives

Dr. Phil with a martini shaker! Is Marla single yet? Aroooo!

To answer your very fair question – my conscience is clear as far as leading women on. The choice I made when I first signed up was a commitment to be totally honest in my profile, and on my dates. No games.

No, I don't make an announcement at the outset, "Just so you know, I'm emotionally unavailable," like a public health declaration that I have herpes or something. But, almost invariably, dates ask if I've been married, or why I'm single, etc. And I'm always upfront – I'm recently single, just now getting my sea legs back, etc. After that, it's their choice how to proceed.

So... I took your advice, and on Saturday, instead of taking the plunge with Bev, I went out for drinks with Savoy. Took her to the Little Door, where they have maybe the most extensive wine list in town. I just had it in my head that this date called for a vintage champagne. Fuck I'm pathetic and transparent when I'm trying to impress.

So Savoy arrives, and I recognize her at once. In fact, more heads than mine turn. She is indeed the spitting image of Halle Berry. Shimmering in a green and gold ensemble, hair neat and close.

By now I've had about half a dozen online dates which ended fairly abruptly because the women looked absolutely nothing like their photos (I haven't even wasted your time to recount them), so my relief was visible.

And we drank, and we chatted, and she was everything she claimed to be in her profile. Smart, sharp, refined, and...

We had absolutely nothing in common.

We took turns serving volleys – about travel, favorite books, family, pets, restaurants, traffic routes – but nothing.

On paper, Mrs. Right. In person we had no spark. I guess I'd never really been out with a corporate type before. And she had next to nothing to say to the likes of me.

Even a few glasses of champagne didn't loosen us up. And so, $100 later, we parted. (To answer your earlier question, I guess I do calculate.) And that was that. Being the crème de la crème doesn't matter, if you can't churn each other into butter.

And you? Have you come up for air? Can you even walk? My curiosity needs to be Lanced.

You're totally averse to the online dating thing, aren't you? I know – you tried to warn me. I'm thinking of quitting. Starting to feel like a big waste. Things always look so good in catalogs. But when the postman rings and you dig through the Styrofoam peanuts...

You're right. I should buy a dartboard.

Pffft,
Mark

P.S. Are you going to get a gift for him?

May 15
To: Mark
From: Amy
Subject: Darts, Butts

I didn't suggest you get a dartboard, I suggested some pals and a bar that had a dartboard. You are going to drive yourself insane with the girlfriend search, work, and lady combat class. I feel like you need a little male bonding right now. See what the other wolves are up to. (What do you do to just hang out and relax? Was I right about the bookstore and solo cognac or the bar with buddies?)

So Savoy was not so savory. Too bad. But it confirms my hunch that the internet is an impossible way to meet a mate or even just a date. Everybody looks great on paper, but that's not how it happens. Magic, it's magic and it's not data. I say cut your losses (100 bucks on the first evening, hmm, you are so all or nothing, and women can smell neediness).

Start walking around your neighborhood with a mischievous look in your eye and just live your life.

A.

P.S. Not getting Lance a gift. I like the old 'give without expecting to receive' idea. In life and in uhm, other places.

P.P.S. Susan and I were discussing embarrassing moments in bed and she claims that she makes all of her boyfriends "trim." I think that's weird.

May 22
To: Amy
From: Mark
Subject: AWOL

Hey Stranger,

Sorry to read and run. I got in a week of guy time. Flew to Seattle to hang with an architect pal from college. We talked about doing some fishing, but that's the closest we got to serious man-and-man action. More later – am jousting a week's worth of bills.

Susan's rule is more than fair. She should hang a sign over her bed: "Want Trim? Trim."

So... what did Lance get you Friday night!? Bigger than a breadbox?

Answers:

To relax: I cook elaborate meals (even for myself) while listening to vile talk radio. Or sometimes I hang upside down.

Relaxing with friends: I prefer casual dinner parties in someone's home – or a walk-n-chat down the Venice boardwalk or around the canals. No piña coladas. No getting caught in the rain.

Back to ketchup,
M.

P.S. Kiss me. I canceled my online membership today.

May 22
To: Amy
From: Mark
Subject: In Seattle

On Capitol Hill, ran into a girl I had a crush on in grad school – she was a townie and way too young. But we became fast friends for a coupla years. She still looks great – Angelina Jolie meets Pippi Longstocking – but with her penchant for dating felons and IV drug users, and with my absolute terror of any disease, it was easy to stay platonic. We sat in a park and drank a bottle of Maker's Mark – come to think of it, she's practically a guy friend – thinks like a guy. Half-blotto she sits on my lap and says, "Mark, you move like a young guy, you act and talk like a young guy, but those lines on your forehead give away your age."

If she's the guy, I'm the girl. I got back last night and already made an appointment in Beverly Hills for Botox. I know I'm gonna get shit for this, so play nice.

Vainly yours,
Maker's Mark

May 28
To: Mark
From: Amy
Subject: Girls Make Love Even When They Say Fuck

Really? You think it's fair to ask a guy to trim? Ick. So effeminate. But then, I'm talking to a man who is going to inject a 4-H project into his face.

Do guys actually walk-n-chat? I thought only Beverly Hills wives did that, but then, I thought only Beverly Hills wives got Botox. Is your face that bad? And when did it become bad to have a face that 'gives away your age'? Isn't that what it's there for, a big fleshy symbol that says, Hi, I'm not a toddler, or Hi, I'm allowed to drink whiskey.

Don't be a sucker man, embrace your Robert Redford. Or don't, embrace Dallas Raines, your TV weatherman. It's all up to you.

The thing about these procedures though is, you can't make them a secret. If you do this and then you have sex and your partner wonders why your brow doesn't scrunch when you come and she asks, you have to say, shamelessly, "Baby, I'm a Botox man."

Congrats on leaving the packs of lies peddled online in the name of poontang.

Emotionally connected sex is the most fun thing ever. I'm remembering Ted sex and it was so comparatively vacant. I think that if a woman is honest, she will admit that when she sleeps with a man there is at least part of her that is in love with him. It is very rare to move with simply a physical M.O. That being said, boys and girls are different, see area that the bathing suit covers and brain. I am in love.

Lance gave me the anniversary present. It's a gift certificate to a tragically hip salon for a haircut/style. At first I was a little offended, I mean if the guy thinks my hair stinks and hair is sooooo important to him then forget it. Then I remembered telling him how I needed a haircut and that my psychic hairdresser Ron just moved to the Bay Area. All Lance did was listen and I was about to chew him out.

The hairdresser, Cheryl, is a stylist he met while working on that goofy WB show last summer (you know, the one with the attractive teens and the community that is so hard for them to amalgamate into).

They are still friends and she's really excited to meet me. Hooray for hairdos! I'm scheduling my appointment for the Friday before we leave for the weekend away with the parents in the desert. I will be superchicstreamlined Amy. Right now I think there are four rubber bands and a bicycle in my tresses.

Still Annoyingly Jubilant,
A.

May 28
To: Amy
From: Mark
Subject: Wax Candles, Not Faces

Dear Amy,

You said it! You're in love! This is spectacular. Listen, I know we have our e-rangement, but I do want to invite you and Lance to my birthday party this coming Friday, on June 1st.

My birthday was actually yesterday, but everyone I know was out of town or busy, so I rescheduled. But if I'm getting the dates right, I think you're going to be in Palm Springs with Lance, the parents and the ghost of Sonny Bono. Still, if you can come that'll be great. A totally unswank affair on the beach near my house – tiki torches, volleyball, beach blanket bingo at night.

Sure we guys walk-n-chat (we call it "hanging"). Some of us can even chew gum at the same time.

I don't think trimming is for gurly men. No more so than deodorant, shampoo, cologne, a few afternoons at the gym, a little dab of hair gel... Women want to look their best. So the secret's out – even manly men do, too. I like it for myself, but it's also a sign of respect for the woman and all of her hard work.

That said, there's a limit. I found mine. I went to the plastic surgeon Bev recommended (had her boobs done there on her 50th). I sat in the chair and he told me there were some risks with the forehead. The skin could actually droop, so that the brow hangs down over the eyes. Unlikely, but possible.

I may be a combat trainer, but I don't want to look like a Neanderthal.

"If I leave right now, do I still have to pay?"

"Yes."

"I don't suppose I could just get a haircut?" He was not amused.

I high-tailed it out of there. Another $100 well-spent. With Savoy, it was worth it – I learned to see past the curriculum vitae. And this time, I learned a shaving brush and a bottle of cologne are enough for me. I've earned my furrows. And I'm not going to kowtow to this nonsense ever again. Call it temporary insanity.

Please let me know if you guys'll be in town and I'll send a proper invite.

Cheers,
B-day Boy

P.S. Planning anything radical with your hair?

P.P.S. Do you know the Meat Loaf song – "I would do anything for love... but I won't do that"? I never knew what the That was, but for some reason I always imagined it involved pubic trimming.

May 31
To: Mark
From: Amy
Subject: Mark Leaves the Womb

I think that your whole 'look their best' thing must be defined. If best means a trim, okay, but where does it end and where does common sense come into play?

It's so creepy to me, all the girls I work with are hairless. We're all such visual sheep. What we need are fully-pubed porn stars and then this madness would dissipate a bit.

What do you want for your birthday, Sparky? Pretend you're blowing out the candles, what do you wish for?

I think it's great that you're throwing yourself a bash, people aren't mind readers and you deserve a beach blanket bingo. I do worry that someone will sing Kumbaya at the end of the night. As your friend I'm warning you, if a guy shows up with a case of Corona and a guitar, just take the guitar away.

We will be in the desert, surrounded by butter-colored Cadillacs and golf. I am still trying to find a bathing suit that's vacation-with-the-family-cute-but-not-Shirley-Temple-cute.

Lance is a bit of a fashionista. He said that he thinks it's hot when girls wear miniskirts and tennis shoes. If I did that I would look like Popeye the cheerleader. I think he was dropping a hint. I can ignore it right?

I told Marla about the haircut and how I was initially offended and almost blew up at Lance and she said, "Darlin', it's all about the Pause."

The pause?

"Yeah, before you order another tequila or yell at someone or buy sweaters in July, you just make yourself get still, focus on your breath and do the Pause. If you still need the shot, or to scream at your man or to buy the sweater, then by all means. But usually the Pause will contact your gut which will contact your truth, tequila makes you hurl, the man loves you and nobody needs more than one sweater in Southern California."

I'm getting my haircut in the morning and then we leave. And no, it's just a nice, fresh cut, nothing extreme. Cheryl's salon is in West Hollywood. It is called 'Blow.' No punchline needed.

Make all your friends bring foxy single chicks to your party.

Maybe I'll send my best friend Susan. She's got double D breasts, blue eyes and a cupid's bow mouth, so that could be my present to you, just some major visual stimulation. Let me know if the birthday invite is transferable.

A.

June 2
To: Amy
From: Mark
Subject: My Present Came Without a Beau

Dear Amy,

It's the thought that counts, so thanks. Susan would've been quite the party favor.

By now you're riding through the desert on a Lance, with new mane. So this'll be waiting for you upon your return. (Unless you're a dork like me, who checked his e-mail in Santa Barbara, what seems like years ago.)

By the way, there actually ARE big bushy porn mags. A thickety subculture all its own. We could play a game where we name any noun, and I'll bet somewhere in the world someone's got a fetish for it (e.g. grapefruit, fuzzy slippers, Simchat Torah...).

Yeah, you can ignore Lance's tennis fantasy. I confess I've had the same one before (complete with puffy balls on the back of the socks). But the fact that not one girlfriend has ever dressed like that never caused me actual disappointment. Just let it hang in the air like a soap bubble until it pops.

So the party... was a great success. I was nervous at first. A year ago, Diana threw me my first surprise party. Very hard to sneak around behind my back. I was impressed. I don't think I've ever felt so loved.

At last night's party, 25 showed, about 80% couples, most married. But guess what? It was totally cool. I completely forgot all about my cares, ran and swam, drank and danced.

Then around 9 pm, I noticed a guy and two girls walking past, smartly dressed. One of the girls kept looking over. At 10, they passed in the other direction. At 10:15, the one who looked came back on her own, carrying her heels in her hand.

They'd dined nearby, a double date, except Addie's guy (that's her name) never showed. A blind date, some DJ, blew her off. Asshole.

She said she could use a good time, and this looked fun, could she join in. "The more the merrier," I said.

Amy, she was incredible. She instantly merged with my friends. Tossed back some beers, served a mean volleyball, chatted easily with all my buddies, affable, laughing. I was wowed by her social graces.

About midnight, a Hasselhoffish Beach Patrol cop drove up in his modified Pathfinder and put the kibosh on our party. No fire allowed on the beach, not even tiki torches. He was about to write me a $250 citation when Addie stepped in. Seems she's a park ranger (at Will Rogers, in the Palisades) and this gave her some kind of pull. Don't know what she said, but Hasselhoff laughed and drove away.

The party broke up around 1 am, and I asked her for her number. "I don't like phones. Just meet me here, a week from today, 8 pm sharp." And she was off.

Welcome back, Amy. Maybe I'll soon be joining you in Happyville.

Love,
Mark

P.S. When's your birthday?

June 6
To: Mark
From: Amy
Subject: Hack

I've been hacked. And I am no longer a resident in Happyville. I am now a card-carrying citizen of vain superficial fool land.

See, I had the big Hair Appointment at Blow on Friday. Cheryl shows up 45 minutes late. She is a chubby over-made-up rat-faced lady who squints her eyes at me and says, "So you're Lance's new girlfriend."

The queen Steven in the stall next door gives me the once-over.

Cheryl says, "Amy girl, you need a major trim and we might think about shaking those natural streaks out with a rinse. Girl, do you brush your hair with an eggbeater?"

I laugh at her stupid joke (and ignore my biggest pet peeve, white chicks who call each other 'girl') because I'm so excited to get a haircut I just nod. "Go ahead," I say. She goes outside to conference and smoke with Steven.

As Cheryl rambles on about how she met Lance on set and they used to eat lunch together every day, it hits me, "Oh shit. This woman has a crush on him." Meanwhile she is hacking my hair off at the earlobes. Mark, I am a victim of beauty terrorism. I was uglified under the guise of an anniversary present.

I left the salon (I tipped her for God's sake) and cried all the way down Santa Monica Blvd, an hour late to meet Lance and his family. I walked into Blow with hair hanging past my shoulders, now here I was, a more severe Louise Brooks.

I pulled Lance into his bedroom, "LOOK! Look at this! That Cheryl chick was in love with you and she did this to make me look stupid."

"Honey, it's not stupid," he goes. "It's different. And functional."

FUNCTIONAL??

I sobbed deeper and louder than before. I HATE FUNCTIONAL!

FUNCTIONAL is Formica and cotton dresses with big pockets in the front. FUNCTIONAL is make-up purchased at a pharmacy.

FUNCTIONAL should never be on my HEAD.

I miss my hair and am looking for espionage equipment online. I want a KGB cigarette case so that I can offer Cheryl a smoke and blow her ass to bits.

I'm glad you met Addie. I really am. That's sexy, the meeting thing. She's a take-action-save-the-bullshit gal.

My birthday is November 18th. You can get me hair.

– A.

P.S. I'll tell you about the weekend later. Lance gave me a miniskirt. I looked in the mirror and thought that I was a Soviet tennis player.

June 8
To: Amy
From: Mark
Subject: Anticipation

Dear Amy,

Girl, I am so sorry. If you'd like, for an early birthday present I could teach you a couple of moves to quickly disarm a scissors-wielding maniac. Or, you could show up with a tennis racket, say you're Amy's brother Boris, and then tan her hide.

I'm going on about this to bide my time, and take a break from pacing. Tonight's the night.

Do you think Addie will show?

I'm bringing along a shaker of martinis, and a little jar of olives in my pocket (in case she's wondering if I'm happy to see her).

Nervous,
Nelly

P.S. You have great face bones. Girls with great face bones can get away with short shitty hair. And, like the ability to love and be loved, hair does grow back even after the worst massacre...

June 8
To: Mark
From: Amy
Subject: Strange Hairs in the Night

I know, but still, all weekend I missed my hair. Lance's mom said it was "very classic" and then I started crying and told her what happened. I forgot how bonding beauty catastrophes can be.

I am going to embrace the new 'do the same way I embraced the surrogate family last weekend. New and different at first, ultimately easy to manage. I had so much fun. His family is so different than mine. Maybe it's because he's an only child or they're rich or something, but they don't yell, his mom is super hip and (gasp) sexy, and they eat dinner at nine o'clock. My father is snoring in his La-Z-Boy with an apple core on his t-shirt at nine o'clock. I feel so provincial.

I can't wait to hear about the Addie adventure. Tell me tell me tell me. Did you guys really meet in the dark on the beach?

Your follicley challenged friend,
A.

P.S. That was a nice thing to say, about my having "great bones." I do drink milk. Thank you for the sentiment.

June 8
To: Amy
From: Mark
Subject: Make mine a double...

Oh, Amy.

She didn't show. I waited an hour and a half, then walked home, drinking warm martini straight from the shaker.

Figures. And no way for either of us to call. Bad planning.

Oh well.

– M.

June 9
To: Amy
From: Mark
Subject: Sitting on the Dock of eBay

Ok, so it's a sand dune on the beach. A little slope above my drop point with Addie. Laptop on my lap. A fear of sudden sandstorms, as it's out of warranty. Maybe something came up, and she had no way to call, and is going to have the same thought and show tonight, Saturday night. Better late than never. It's almost 8.

--

It's 9. This is kind of cool, being lit only by my laptop screen. No moon tonight. Typing's hard, but a good distraction. If I wait here long enough, she's bound to show, and your hair is bound to grow back.

--

10. I feel like Big Ben. Not really. Feeling decidedly unbig.

--

It's 11. I got some work done on my taxes. And got a big wet snout in my ear from a passing mastiff. And that is all...

--

Home, James, to send this to you, and send myself to bed without dessert.

– M.

June 12
To: Mark
From: Amy
Subject: M.I. Addie

Dear Mark,

You were doing your taxes in June? That is so hot.

Seriously honey, I am sorry about your getting stood up. I think that's probably the worst feeling. I always feel like serial killers are the ones who had birthday parties and no one came. I mean, it just feels so devastating.

With Addie, truthfully, anything could have happened. You can't take it personally. What if she's some flaky chick who lost her bus pass? What did you 'feel' with this person you knew for a few hours? Isn't it a good sign? There are women out there who make you feel things. (Savoy, party of two for one hundred dollars' worth of ten-cent tertiary conversation and snore.)

I am dreading the parent meet. Not because my parents are bad, simply because they have nothing in common. If Andrea starts talking about going to Pilates, my mother is going to chime in about how she too has traveled to Greece. It's fine. Really. Oh God.

Lance Romance (that's what you have to call the guy if he draws you candle-lit baths with rose petals) is shooting a short in Temecula this weekend so I am staying at his place. It will be fun, I can stretch out (two bedroom house) and snoop. I already saw a picture of his ex. He had it by the kitchen sink the first time I came over for dinner. Is that bad? She's gorgeous and he doesn't want to talk about why they broke up. I hate that. I think it's a neon sign blinking "No Closure."

xoxo

a.

June 14
To: Amy
From: Mark
Subject: Hope Springs Infernal

Dear Amy,

So what if the ex is gorgeous and his mother is sexy and cool? This simply translates to: you now belong to a select club.

I've liked this guy from the get-go, and that he's still treating you like an Empress (which you are) confirms my suspicions. That said, at this stage in the game I think he should talk openly about any and everything. Why they broke up is not irrelevant. Not at all.

Get him comfy. Unthreatened. Not on the defensive. Not one good conversation has ever occurred between a man and a woman when one of them is in fight-or-flight mode. If you're not both feeling warm and snug, there's zero chance of a decent tête-à-tête. (I'm so fucking anal about those accents, have you noticed?)

Then ask. Just don't let him feel like it's a quiz show, that if he gives the wrong answer or doesn't phrase it in the form of a question he's going to plummet through a trapdoor.

Parents, shmarents. I'm just impressed your mom's been to Greece.

Tomorrow night is a week from last Friday. I am going to go to the beach, at 8, and wait only one hour. And I promise you and myself that this is the last time. (Maybe she meant the following Friday...?)

I guess I have a kind of peace. She's made the best first impression of anyone in my life. I really felt in awe of her ease. That's it. Like she'd figured out some secret to life. There's this scene at the end of a Kurosawa movie where a city guy goes to the country and meets a very old man lifting water from a well. The city guy watches and says, "Life's hard." The old man looks up and smiles, "No. Life is easy." Addie is the old man. I'm happy just to have met her.

Fingers crossed,
Mark

P.S. Last year's taxes. I got an extension. And I am not a serial killer. I am always kind to animals.

June 16
To: Amy
From: Mark
Subject: Subtract Addie

June 16
To: Mark
From: Amy
Subject: Lance Romance

I'm sorry about Addie. Going to meet her was cool. You were telling the universe that you are present, ready to show up. Somehow, it will pay you back.

She must have really wowed you to bring to mind a Kurosawa movie. Do you think it's possible that you're a major romantic and mythologizing a little bit? Just a thought. We all tend to do that, especially when feeling extra vulnerable.

I asked Lance about Meredith (the ex) on the phone, all sweet and cuddly like you said and he blew up, "Amy, Meredith's crazy. Please. Do you want to talk about YOUR crazy exes?" and then I'm stumped, because I really don't want to. I mean, telling him about Richard, Captain Vaginismus, no thank you.

I do think 'crazy' is a bullshit blanket excuse. I put her picture in the closet. It was on the kitchen sink next to a sponge and a plant and I got tired of Meredith looking at me while I did the dishes.

Now all I do is think about it. That and the fact that she has the body fat of a 12-year-old Romanian gymnast. Did I mention that she's in a black bikini?

Lance comes home tomorrow night. Today I went to the farmer's market and got the purple basil he likes, then I wrote love notes and stuck them all over the house (in the pantry on the jar of olives I taped "Olive you Lance," I am such a dope).

He keeps talking about our babies and our future vacation compound in Mexico. Last Thursday we were sitting on the couch, his eyes got all heavy and he said, "You're the one."

And I said, "In the room," and he shook his head all serious, "No, you are the one."

This is some big talk. It is scaring me. Future? "The one"? Co-creating babies? I still don't even know what I want to be when I grow up.

I've got fishbowls of dirty thoughts in my head. Funny how when you are having wonderful sex and it goes away for a few days you feel so famished. I'm ditching everything on Monday so he can play afternoon Atari on my lady motor.

Love,
A.

P.S. Did I tell you how Lance loves to make eggs with basil and cinnamon coffee for breakfast?

P.P.S. Did I tell you how Lance washes my back and reads me Neruda poems in the bath?

P.P.P.S. Did I tell you how Lance blows his nose with satin hankies, hand-sewn by blind Tibetan monks? (Okay, I may be gushing. I know it's gross, but it's where I'm at.)

June 19
To: Amy
From: Mark
Subject: Olive your attention to detail

Dear LoveSlave,

So, missy, WHO'S the hopeless romantic? It's like the heart-shaped box of chockies calling the rose petals on the bed saccharine. Yeah, you're disgusting. But like all of life's guilty pleasures – Howard Stern, taking a big dump, McDonald's French fries – a little lovey-dovey talk can be most enjoyable.

So I'm far more thrilled for you than I am nauseated. (And yeah, a little envious; Diana used to leave me notes like that, whenever she went out of town on business. It'd take me a week to find them all.)

But Lance has his first demerit. There are two possibilities with Meredith. A) She is crazy. B) Lance is the kind of guy who, when things go south and he's not getting all his needs met, or he's just getting restless in a relationship, he skedaddles and blames everything on the girl.

I'll give him the benefit of the doubt for now and say it's A. But either way – you guys have been exclusive for a while, so that picture by the sponge is insulting, rude. You shouldn't have had to stow it. That was his job, weeks ago. Give him a little hell. He deserves it.

– M.

June 23
To: Amy
From: Mark
Subject: Best Man

Dear Amy,

Haven't heard from you in a few days. That must be some game of Atari. Are his thumbs sore yet? Can you even walk? Drop me a note when you come up for air.

Can I be in the wedding party? I'd settle for lowly usher. Or you could set up a computer with Wi-Fi, and I could attend the nuptials Max Headroom style.

Me, I've got nothing to report. At least I'm getting a ton of work done.

Love,
Mark

June 25
To: Amy
From: Mark
Subject: Mysteries of the Universe

Dear Guru of Love,

Since I have squat going on and you're now officially AWOL, I thought I'd take this time to educate myself. So here are some questions I've always wondered about. You don't have to answer them all, but any elucidation would be hugely appreciated.

- Do women really care what kind of car a guy drives?
- If on your first date you've got something in your teeth, should the guy say something?
- How much does height matter? Too small, do you throw them back?
- If after the first date we're not interested, and it seemed fairly obvious (but tacit) at the end of the date, do we really have to call? Even if nothing happened?
- They say it takes half the length of the time you dated to get over an ex. For me, it's been about six months. Am I really supposed to wait another year and a half? Seems a harsh sentence.

- Why are women so drawn to musicians? Why not, for instance, elevator repairmen?
- How often are you supposed to change your sheets?
- Do you care if a guy's shirts are ironed?
- Am I a horrible person if I can't really imagine raising another man's kids?
- Would you rather get an amazing home-cooked meal, or an elegant dinner out?
- Would you rather get an original hand-written poem, a bouquet of your favorite flowers, or a gift certificate for Barney's?
- If, when you're not looking, your girlfriend/sister/mother hits on us (of course we rebuff), do you want us to tell you? Or would you rather not know?
- If you're having a nice first date, and you go for a walk, and the guy puts his arm around your shoulder, and you sling yours around his waist, and you happen to feel the unmistakable crumple of a condom in his back pocket, are you offended?
- Is there any possible acceptable answer besides "Of course not, dear" to the question, "Does this dress make me look fat?"
- If a guy you're seriously involved with wants to know how many partners you've had, should we ask or stifle our curiosity? If you ask, should we decline to answer, answer, or lie?

Inquisitively,
Mark

June 27
To: Amy
From: Mark
Subject: You don't know what you've got 'til it's gone

Ok, now I'm worried. WHERE ARE YOU!? I'm assuming the best – that Lance whisked you off to Bali or something. But it's been ten days. I'm trying not to feel forsaken. But mainly, I'm worried a little now. Just a funny feeling in my gut. Shit. Now I really wish I had your phone number. Even more than I wish I had Addie's.

Not 'til today did I fully realize how much I've come to rely on you and your perspective. I can't ask Dean the things I ask you. (I mean I can, but what's the point. Might as well ask my own id.)

Please do drop me a line – just so I know you're alright. Please?

Yours,
Mark

June 28
To: Mark
From: Amy
Subject: Shock Treatment

Dear M.,

I'm in bed and I smell like beer. Sorry about the delay, but I've been hiding out. Lance came home Sunday night, and so I put on the brown slip dress that he likes (I hate dresses, he loves dresses) sat on his custom-made velvet couch and waited. He walked in the door and said, "Honey you look lovely, let's have a glass of wine."

He then poured me a super big gulp style glass tumbler of cab and said, "Sit down."

I already was.

He gave me an achy smile, "This is probably the biggest mistake I'll make in my entire life, but I am not ready to be this responsible and I can't be in this relationship anymore."

Feral, in slow-motion shock I said, "Well if that's all you had to say, then why did you pour me so much wine?" and stood up.

He then tried to body block the door to "explain everything" to me. I wanted to claw his eyes out, so getting to my car was quite the obstacle course.

What is there to explain? I was thinking, there is not one reason you can offer that will make your decision palatable, the only thing I want to hear out of your mouth is that you're wild about me, the way you were wild about me a week ago. Anything else you have to say is irrational nonsense. He stood there banging on my car window when I drove off. I was careful not to run him over, I don't need a lawsuit on top of a broken heart. Jesus.

I drove to Susan's apartment and cried on her couch until 6 am. I also drank beer while she deleted all of his erotic text messages and phone numbers from my cell.

Oh sure. I'll be fine. I just need to stop crying. I went to work and my manager asked me if I had hay fever, asthma, or hereditary dark circles.

I hope Lance gets hangnails and has lots of non-injury car accidents.

I hope you are well. I do. Thanks for listening/writing. Those are some good questions, I'll answer soon. Right now I have to go to the store for Kleenex and Kashi.

Looks like it's back to square one. God, I am square one.

– A.

P.S. If I would've gone to a gypsy on Sunday and she'd told me that Lance was going to dump me that evening, I would have laughed at her.

June 29
To: Amy
From: Mark
Subject: Speechless in Seattle

Amy, I don't know what to say, I don't have the words. I'm over a thousand miles away right now, in Seattle again, but I want to fly back and be a shoulder, a real one. I'd even wear the purple taffeta bridesmaid dress, the one that's already tear-stained. I am so sorry.

I'm not going to offer to kick his ass (I can't even type his name anymore, he doesn't deserve even that), because I figure if that's what you wanted you would've asked me by now.

But I totally understand your reaction. Of course he's got no possible valid reason. (What, "I've been enlisted by the C.I.A. and they're sending me to Jupiter and I might never come back"???) But still. I know it's a girl word, but I have to use it: closure. How can you get over this without – oh, nevermind, I don't want to give any advice. I just want to be there, be a shoulder.

I'll be home on Monday. Please let me know if there's anything I can do.

Much love,
Mark

P.S. I am totally floored.

July 1
To: Mark
From: Amy
Subject: Cold

I will CSI the whole thing in a week or two, but today I just need to lick my wounds. And frozen yogurt. I could sell pints of "Fuck That Guy French Vanilla." Tell me what you were doing in Seattle.

July 1
To: Amy
From: Mark
Subject: Cowardly Lyin'

I'll tell you about Seattle if you answer some of my questions from June 25th. (If you don't still have that e-mail let me know and I'll resend.) I'm just kidding. It's not about a tit for tat. I was trying to think of something to take your mind off the s.o.b.

– M.

July 2
To: Mark
From: Amy
Subject: All the Answers

Okay, so you ask whether or not women really care what kind of car a guy drives?

You want the truth? You can't handle the truth.

This is the deal, I've dated Porsches, Range Rovers, a beat-up 1979 Toyota truck with camper shell covered in dings, the carless, Volvos, a fellow who had a private plane and a town car with driver, a '59 Impala, and mother fucking minivans.

The man I loved the most, the man who broke my heart? Camper shell covered in dings. It's irrelevant.

First date, if I have something in my teeth do you say something? You say nothing, you lovingly reach across the table and nonchalantly flick it out for me like one monkey picking the nits off another. Margaret Mead me.

Do women care about height? See cars.

Waiting half the length of the relationship to date again? Every heart is different, that's between you and you. I'm an emotional hemophiliac and not the one to ask.

Women are drawn to musicians for the same reason that children are drawn to fireworks. As a child you see the big displays at the local park (see MTV/arena concerts), you fall in love with them, with the idea of them and the way the whole world can't help but be attracted to them and look at them, the colors and the charisma.

Then you turn twelve and you take your allowance to buy them at the Boy Scout-sponsored stand (you go to the record store and spend all your cash on righteous rebelling rock 'n' roll boys with things to say and tight pants). By fourteen you look forward to the Fourth of July like crazy and it comes (you go to your first local rock show). Soon you can't stop blowing stuff up (kissing musicians) until one day you're not careful and you lose three fingers with a roman candle (they break your heart when you see them with another girl). You realize the rest of the year is as fun as that one holiday and you begin to be attracted to other guys. But you never stop loving the summer.

Elevator repairmen have no good press.

Change your sheets once a week, more often if you sweat a lot or have frequent nocturnal emissions.

Shirts can be unironed, but they must be unstained. And they can't be unbuttoned more than three inches.

I don't want to raise another man's kids either, and that makes us both horrible people.

Is this a date or are we in a relationship? In boyfriend/girlfriend land I like home dinners, but if you cook and don't pay attention to me then I'm going to feel neglected and hungry (you guys always spend like four hours chopping garlic). Supper at home with hump breaks between courses is a brilliant thing. Also, I look weird eating salad with my hands in restaurants.

I'm such a sucker for flowers. I hate the idea of a gift certificate, whaddya gonna do? Leave it on the nightstand? Holy impersonal whore bait, Batman! Stick the poem on the flowers and we all win.

If my friend/mother/sister hits on you? Do not tell me about those bimbos, unless you plan on doing something about it. Then just leave.

If I heard your condom crumple I would laugh my ass off and say, "Gee (insert date name), got anything else in there that we're NOT going to use tonight? Bath tub speed? Riding crop? Gift certificate for the Olive Garden?"

When your girlfriend asks if she looks fat in this dress, with enthusiasm say, "You look perfect and that is a damned lucky dress." Or you tell the truth. Depends on how you feel about oral sex.

Oh get present already, but if you must ask how many men have lifted our petals, ask away. Then take that answer and play the lotto with it because that's all it's good for. Girls never tell the truth. Why, because you don't really want to know.

I think we tell very, very close to the truth, but we all skip a couple, maybe more than a couple. You're not going to have any more love for us when we tell you about that hilarious one nighter at Janie's wedding in Oxnard.

You can waste hours wondering how we learned that nifty ball tickle trick but at the end of the day we are all God's creatures and God just made us this way (trampy or not, intuitive or not). Wanting to know qualifies as annoying and points to low self-esteem. Can you not trust that we are happy with the present penis (i.e. yours)?

Good lord. I remember making out with my ninth grade boyfriend and rubbing my leg up his and him pulling back and saying, "Wow, how did you know how to do something so sexy?" He was a moron (and a Catholic). I was embarrassed, because it just seemed normal, not a plotted-out intellectual decision to be "sexy."

I stopped seeing him after that. He is now a policeman in my hometown and last month he pulled my brother over for speeding but did not give him a ticket, so let's take this moment to salute my intuitive innocent and beautiful teen sensuality.

I hope she doesn't, but if she does ask how many women you've slept with, and if you can't be nice (have an answer under 20) then be vague. If you have slept with 34 women, every time we get in the sack I will think of Mrs. Slaughter's second grade classroom because I know there were 34 kids in there, so while you're kissing my neck I'm looking through the front row at Ted Webster eating paste and smelling like pee.

For both of us, simply smile and say "Enough."

July 2
To: Amy
From: Mark
Subject: Q&A/T&A

Dear Amy,

Just got in two hours ago.

Wow. You answered them all! I didn't expect that. But since you made good on your tit, here is my tat:

Seattle – this time was for work, saw Angelina/Pippi again. And I was going to tell you that story, but something else has happened. And I now have a much bigger tat to tell.

Listen, since the day we met not only have I been 100% honest with you, but I have also refrained from ever censoring myself. Until now. But instead of presuming, I'll just ask. You're not in any mood to hear good news, are you? I don't feel like I should tell you my news for another week or two. Seems wrong. But let me know, ok?

Love,
Mark

July 5
To: Mark
From: Amy
Subject: West Hollywood's Second House of Blues

Oh boy, I can hear it now, you've fallen in love with Pippi/Angelina and are moving to Seattle to live in a mildewed apartment on top of a bookstore where you will have no internet connection but will wear lots of flannel and be peaceful and introspective and make your own mulch. Go ahead. Leave. I can take it. And then, if you could, make me chew glass.

Tell me the good news. Please. I want to hear something besides SCHWOOOP (that's the ripping sound of picture postcards with shitty poems written on the back).

Keep it uncensored, I need one honest guy in my life.

I'm going to work. My friends/co-workers keep hugging me. Even the manager gives me a little 'poor baby' smile.

Like my dad used to say when I'd hurt myself as a kid, "It's a long way from your heart."

Oh. Wait.

Happy fucking Independence Day,
A.

P.S. If you know anyone who wants to buy a sparkly ballerina dress, let me know.

P.P.S. Shelley came over yesterday. She brought more beer.

July 5
To: Amy
From: Mark
Subject: Of all the gin joints...

Dear Amy,

No, I'm not leaving you for Pippi. I'm sure your friends and co-workers are reminding you daily that you deserver better, and you do, and it will come. But I want to give you more than platitudes, even if they are all true. For now, I'll give you what you asked for. You want good news? You got it.

Every lover knows: there is good pain. And there is bad pain. But there is no pain like Au Bon Pain.

As a former baker, I'd never be caught dead in the place. (And don't even get me started on bread-machines.) But when your red-eye is delayed and it's the only joint open in Sea-Tac airport, you're a captive audience. How bad could a pre-fab wrap be?

In fact, it could be manna. If when you reach the register you happen to see, sipping a jumbo cup of Mountain Dew, none other than... Addie.

Even under the flickering blues of the fluorescent tubes, she was more lovely than I'd remembered.

Flashback: Friday, June 8th. 8 pm. Mark waits for an hour and a half. Walks home swilling and sulking. Flashback: Friday, June 8th, 10:15 pm. Addie arrives, certain she'd said, "I'll meet you here in one week, same place, same time." That time being 10:15. She waits for an hour, writes me a note in the sand with her finger, then leaves.

Punctuality is a point of pride to her. She's certain that's what she said. I don't know where I got 8 pm.

But who cares. I found Addie. And she me. We both nearly exploded. We hung on each other's words until my flight was announced. She walked me to my gate.

I asked her again for her number. She wrote it down. I looked, but it was only two digits. "It's my flight number. I get in on Sunday. THIS Sunday." And so there are no more near misses, she made clear it was Burbank airport, not LAX. She wrote BUR on the napkin.

Bur. I'd never been less cold in my life. (But Addie, she was en route to Fairbanks to visit her father, a transplant from Iceland. Mom ran off years ago with a tree surgeon. Bur.)

And then we hugged. Even after they announced final boarding, I didn't want it to end. Neither of us would let go. But we did.

When I got home I wanted to shout from my windows, but my crazy Italian neighbors have already been threatening to call the cops for noise violations.

And so. Sunday. A second chance. How about that.

Giddily,
Mark

July 7
To: Mark
From: Amy
Subject: Me Monster

This Addie is punchy. It's cute, but I will remind you of my first date theory. If this defines your relationship with her you're going to need a Thomas guide and a bloodhound at all times.

What's with all the tracking? Is she a woman with such bad credit that she can't get a phone line? A slave to serendipity is still a slave.

Sorry. I'm in a rotten mood. I dreamt that I was sleeping next to Lance in his parents' house and I was so warm and safe and happy, really happy, with those feelings taking up all my physical real estate. Then I woke up, in bed alone, spooning the throw pillow from the couch. WHEN DOES THIS STOP????

I want a romantic lobotomy. I want my secrets back, I want my old haircut back, and I want what I did to him on his birthday with chocolate mousse back. This relationship has turned me into a sentimental monster. Start with one part vulnerability, two parts lust and then subtract the object of your affection.

I must get out of this apartment and that is what movies are for. Two hours where you don't have a past. (Oh Jesus, I'm getting too dramatic for myself. Call the thespian police, we've gotta live one.)

Drama Nerd 1A,

– A.

July 10
To: Amy
From: Mark
Subject: Cut and Paste

Dear Amy,

This is going to be strong medicine of the tough love variety. But here goes.

This e-mail is brought to you courtesy of a very cool and wise upstart I happen to know. Her name's Amy. So open up and get ready to swallow.

>Listen to yourself Intellectual Bad Ass.

>Guys who can't be clear about the last gig usually screw up the next one.

>Sad is okay... feelings aren't good or bad, they just are.

>I think partners show up at certain times to teach us certain things and I am
>a lifelong student.

I have always had a profound admiration for people who go to movies by themselves. I never do that. (I did once, in Austria, but I was just trying to find a warm and dry place to take a nap. Doesn't count.) It's not always a sign of loneliness. Sometimes it's a sign of character.

And splurge. Get Sno Caps (they're non-pareil!) and Chuckles. And save the purple one for last.

Love,
Mark

P.S. I'm saving Addie stories for when you're in the mood.

July 11
To: Mark
From: Amy
Subject: S.O.S.

Hmmm, that girl 'Amy' is wise, cool, and HYSTERICAL – LANCE'S MOTHER JUST CALLED AND INVITED ME TO LUNCH?!!?

Oh cripes, that just can't be right, sobbing on Andrea's shoulder over whitefish salad upstairs at Barney's. I told her I'd think about it. She sent me a card saying she loves me and is sorry. It had a sad looking pug dog on the front.

Tell me all about Addie, but not if she leaves you for no reason and then her dad calls and asks you out for a burger.

Did you do the Burbank shuttle shuffle? I often think I am going to get into heaven based solely on the number of times I've picked people up from the airport.

– A.

July 12
To: Amy
From: Mark
Subject: All About Addie

I'm with you. BUR is the bomb. Pickups there are such a pleasure, I'm laughing all the way to the Burbank. Where I followed the signs to Arrivals...

Addie. Addie the Golden Girl, the Cover Girl, the Girl Next Door, the Girl on the Moon.

Waiting at baggage claim I joked, "So, Addie. Short for Addison? As in DeWitt?" (My alternate was "Short for Addison? Is your mom from Isconsin?") I'd assumed it was short for Adelaide.

Her eyes lit up. "How did you know?! It was my parents' favorite movie!"

No brighter light has ever dazzled the eye than Addison Petursdottir. Addie. But more of Addie later, all about Addie, in fact.

An unkind person might call her pear-shaped. I'd punch him in the snout and shout, "That's a COMICE pear, you sack of crap!" Sweet, succulent, blushing.

Her pewter eyes squint beneath a two-story Mona Lisa forehead, framed by lumbar-length strands of caraway hair. Her mouth turns downward, wide like a trout's, puffy like she'd been swimming in salt water. Her hands twitch quickly, seemingly unconnected to the rest of her body. When she's really excited, she spins around. She wears size 10 1/2 Timberlands and bites her nails. She is beautiful.

Unpretentious, full of spunk. Her favorite food is hot dogs; the best, she swears, come from Reykjavik, made from lamb, "but they taste the exact same!"

She wears first-rate second-hand clothes. She brought me a slab of dog salmon, smoked by her aunt in the Aleutian islands, wrapped in foil and a newspaper ad for block heaters.

Addie, 33, is, as you know, a park ranger, and hates the phone. She doesn't have a computer. Likes pencils better than pens. But gets over 400 channels on her TV, which she adores as a thing of beauty.

A raspy voice like one of the guys, even though she doesn't smoke. High-waisted, she has strong stocky legs – from a childhood of semi-professional ice skating. In fact, she spent two years on the Care Bears Tour – she was the pale yellow one, but I forget which one that is. Career cut short by a bad bout of IBS. These days, she plays on a semi-pro (i.e. amateur) women's hockey team.

I said this would be All About Addie. Had your fill?

As for lunch with Andrea, politely bow out. One of the best things about dating is the world of great new people you meet. But she's his mother. George Washington warned about entangling alliances. And he's the father of our country for chrissakes.

You frankly did not know Lance long enough for you and Andrea to have your own bond. And do NOT let her do her son's dirty work. He's probably the asshole he is BECAUSE she's been cleaning up after him well past his teens.

M.

P.S. I haven't kissed her yet.

July 13
To: Mark
From: Amy
Subject: Momma apologized for days like this

I couldn't bow out of lunch, I dated Lance for four months and talked to his mom on the phone at least once a week. Also, I was sad and lonely and needing something Lance-esque. So now of course I'm miserable.

She said that she was shocked and wanted to apologize for Lance's behavior. That was embarrassing. I really didn't want her to do that.

Then it slipped. She said, "I can't believe he just moved in with her when he got home from shooting that project."

"Her" being Karen, the B soap star he was working with in Temecula (and Fiji). Apparently he moved in with her the day after he dumped me.

She has a tree house in Beachwood Canyon so they are now playing Hollywood Swiss Family Robinson.

I think Andrea was monogramming towels for me. She likes me because Lance has gone through a series of snotty mysterious divas and inevitably she sees me as more accessible and totally unaware of the peril.

I thought about all the things I know about Lance. He's had a girlfriend since he was ten, like for the last twenty years he's been in a relationship.

I think that's sissy. You've got to have some time alone. How else do you get any perspective? What I am saying is, he was talking about children and vacation homes two weeks into it. He's one of those people in love with love, the idea of it. Like maybe I didn't even matter, I just came around the corner after sink picture girl.

I am still full of anger and hate (and I have to get some articles of clothing from Dickhead) but I am being set up by a friend at work. Just for fun.

I'm still so confused. Lance did everything right. He even passed the Belinda Himmel test.

Sorry I'm making sculptures out of the lint in my bellybutton. Addie sounds like a hearty interesting gal. A Care Bear skater eh? I know I'm grumpy, but watch out for people who 'hate the phone,' that's usually code for, "I have lots of places I like to go where I don't want you to call me."

That was Jeremy's routine. Addie reminds me of him. He was great, but I just couldn't compete with the majesty of the mountains or the ranch, both of which deliberately had no ringy dingy.

– A.

July 13
To: Amy
From: Mark
Subject: Boil that Lance

Dear Amy,

You went? Damn, I wish you hadn't. At least now you know the stuff he's made of. In the beginning, he didn't call for a week coz he was off with his mom, and now his mom calls coz he's off playing Tarzan. Except he's not king of anything.

I feel like an idiot for having rooted for him. I didn't ask you enough questions. I'm mad at myself for not pushing harder to find out what he did with his exes. His history. His patterns.

> I am still so confused. Lance did everything right.

This is no mystery. The simple truth is that even the biggest asshole still has his moments. That's how they get their foot in the door. I'll bet even Hermann Goering brought his wife flowers once or twice, maybe even wrote a sweet note on the side of a canister of Zyklon-B. Isolated gestures mean nothing. All that matters are patterns.

Doorbell. Addie's here. Sorry to write and run. You totally rock and I hate seeing you hurt, and I just don't know any better way to say it than that.

Love,
Mark

P.S. What is the Belinda Himmel test?

July 13
To: Mark
From: Amy
Subject: Pass or Fail

Belinda Himmel is a dear friend of mine who does exercise videos for a living. She is the strange physical hybrid who graces the kinds of video covers that make women shell out $15.99 in the hope that they will wake up with legs like balsa wood chopsticks and giant natural tits, i.e. Belinda Himmel.

Men look at Himmel and turn into sand.

When things get serious, you do the friend meeting, and so begins the Belinda Himmel test. Lance passed with flying colors; he was polite and cordial and did not study the way she brought her hummused cracker to her lips like an ornithologist discovering a glittering rare hummingbird. Nor did he ignore her physical assets.

Me: Belinda's pretty hot huh?

Him: Yeah. But in a boring way.

Then he kisses me with the power of Pamplona bulls.

Enjoy the evening with Addie,
A.

July 13
To: Amy
From: Mark
Subject: And then there's Maude

With Addie, I would definitely pass the Belinda Himmel test. No question.

Reminds me of the Bea Arthur test. I know this very dear painter, Andy, and on his bedroom wall hangs a photo of Bea Arthur. When he brings a man home and the man asks, "Oh, is this your mother?" Andy thinks, "Ok. Sex." But if the visitor cocks a glance and inquires, "So Bea Arthur, huh?" then Andy thinks, "Ahh... this could be love..."

July 14
To: Amy
From: Mark
Subject: Mary had a little dinner

Dear Amy,

Addie came over last night. First time. Me, I like to bring a gift when I visit. Bottle of wine. Maybe an African violet. Addie shows up with an entire leg of lamb. In Icelandic tradition, it was cured with dung smoke.

"Had this thing in my freezer forever. You said you cook. So here you go."

She told me she's useless in the kitchen, and asked if she could dance while I cook. I told her to knock herself out, and she requested hip-hop. I asked her to fill the bathtub with hot water to rapid-thaw the leg while I ran out to my truck to grab my iPod. "I told you, I don't cook," she protested. I was pretty much speechless.

"Oh, hey!" she shouted. "You've got an Xbox! I'm on it!"

Me, I'm mincing a half-dozen onions and squinting through streams of tears when the music starts blasting. She's started Grand Theft Auto: Vice City, carjacked a lowrider, parked it in an alleyway, and tuned the radio to the hip-hop station.

She's not playing the game. Just using it for tunes. Next thing you know, she's all over the kitchen, shaking here, shimmying there, thrusting pretty much everywhere. And not bad, not bad at all.

The leg wouldn't fit on the grill (stupid Mark) – so I hacked off a foot with a cleaver and made a lamb tagine with preserved lemons and olives while I set the better part of the leg to marinate. And Addie, she was marinating in the most prodigious production of perspiration I have ever seen in my life. I swear to God she got the floor wet. I nearly slipped.

By the time I got the grill going, she took off her top. She was wearing a seriously padded bra that took her from barely B to full C.

"Disappointed?" she asked. You know, Amy, I've been asked that exact question twice before. Both times I lied and said no.

Thing is, I'm not a breast guy, could care less the size, long as they look nice. But with Addie, I was honest, and told her, "Kinda, but only coz you don't seem like the false advertising type. Everything else about you is so real. How would you like it if you found out I've been wearing padding?"

All this, and we still hadn't kissed.

She must have read my mind. "Hey, you," she said, "did you ever skip first base?" Next thing you know, I'm kissing her breasts and she's grabbing my ass.

The kitchen timer goes off and I tear myself away, my cheeks glazed with her sweat. No force on earth could let me ruin a meal, so I turned off the fire, rushed back, and planted one on her lips.

"So much for patience," she said with a smile. And I guess she was right. After all I did just give a hot bath to a leg of lamb coz I didn't feel like waiting. And then I thought of you, and your admonitions to slow it down. And I did.

We dined. A peck goodnight. And she drove home. We're going for a hike on Sunday.

Fondly,
Little Beau Peep

July 15
To: Mark
From: Amy
Subject: Fire Starters

Good for you Sparky – way to save the first date meat.

Second date, hiking? I wonder if she will keep her shirt on. Just curious, is that a sexy activity, hiking? I can't get past the brown uninspired footwear. Not that you're supposed to fly her to Paris or anything, I'm just wondering what's attractive about walking at an incline. It just seems so 'pal-sy wal-sy' or later in the relationship to me.

Did you have fun with her? Did she light you up?

I've been thinking about men a lot, and why I seem to go from sparks to full-blown Fourth of July pyrotechnics on the White House lawn in five seconds flat. I fall goo goo gaga gangbusters and then either –

1. Roll over a few months later and wonder, what happened to the sexy mysterious guy with all the dreams and plans? Who is this snoring co-dependent wildebeest who will spend all day reading the newspaper cursing the fates and Wal-Mart for his lack of opportunities?

2. Roll over a few months later and wonder who left this puddle of pomade on my pillow and said things like, 'rock star phase' or 'I love cowboy life more than city life,' or 'I just can't be this responsible yet.' Citing anything except the truth, and that is, that I am not their dream girl. WHICH IS OKAY (despite the initial sting) and is in fact WAY BETTER than the aforementioned platter of lukewarm bullshit.

Went out on the setup. The man talked about his breakfast of egg white omelettes for twenty minutes like protein was a new religion. Then he told me about his fitness regime for another twenty minutes. Then I bench-pressed the table away from myself and told him to give me his number and we'd be in touch. It was a bummer. He was trying so hard to convince me of his long term hotness. I felt like I was having a margarita with a telemarketer.

But I love summer. It makes me feel so sexy I want to lounge around like a Tennessee Williams character all ginned up in a ragged slip. Instead I will put on some white pants and a tube top and go to a civilized party at a screenwriter's house in Venice.

Still Healing,
Amy

July 18
To: Amy
From: Mark
Subject: Hot Fun in the Summertime

The summer sun has sweat and straps slip.
And a sundress can undress what I like best.

I am now officially a poet. And Addie is amusing the hell out of me.

She showed me every inch of Will Rogers. Named all the birds and the bees and the trees. At the Ranger station she lifted a tarp to reveal a mini-fridge stocked with nothing but Guinness, and she drank 'til her pores smelled of the stuff.

We rolled in the grass and kissed a little. Then picked the bark from each other's hair.

She's indomitable. I'm exhausted. Maybe I need an egg white omelette.

Jesus, Amy, your stories are making me glad I'm a straight guy so that I don't have to date one. I wish I could say you've just had a run of bad luck, but sadly, I think you're on to something. I've been guilty of that, too. So afraid of confrontation that I'll say anything to stop the water-works. How do women keep it up? Why do we lose our edge?

Maybe what it comes down to is that a perfect pairing is truly rare. And everything else is just biding time. Coz with Diana, never once did I grow bored. And I find it almost impossible to imagine that ANYONE could ever be bored with Addie. But all the others? The fireworks petered out all too soon.

How was the Venice party? You were right around the corner!

Cheers,
Mark

July 20
To: Mark
From: Amy
Subject: Snakes and Muppets

The Venice party was interesting. I was feeling slithery yet perky so I put on a snakeskin skirt and an orange t-shirt and gold heels. It was very Garden of Eden/CalTrans worker. I went with my neighbor Johnny Z. Johnny Z. is a local legend, professional power ballad singer, yoga enthusiast and gaaaaaaay.

I was standing rudderless when I caught the strains of a Lucinda Williams song, the one where she asks that "her lover don't cause no pain, just play her John Coltrane."

"I love this song," I said, and then a man with dark hair flopping over his eyes and cheekbones that could cut glass confirmed, "It is a very sexy song. She's crazy. I was at a bar in Nashville and the bartender almost tossed her out cause she was so mean."

Then Johnny Z. came over and opened his mouth wide like a Bette Davis Muppet and cried out, "Bill, did you meet Amy? This one's smart AND single."

I met Bill. We talked about how relationships are really destructive if you're trying to focus on your career, personal development, that sort of thing. We were in complete accord about what a waste of time and an incredible, life-sucking construct they are.

Then he walked me to my car and asked for my number.

That was Sunday night. He left a message later, recounting our fine conversation and the fact that neither of us is in any shape to be dating, but asking if we could have a drink, "It would be fun, confirm or deny." He has a terribly sexy growly voice.

Yeah. I didn't grow bored with Jeremy either, but that's because he had like a fireman schedule with me, a weekend at my station then a week off on the ranch.

You sound pretty excited about Addie. Those nature chicks can be very seductive. Has she given you a phone number yet?

And you say you're afraid of confrontation? Wake up, everybody is.

Now don't argue with me. A fight like 'chocolate is better than vanilla' is pillow-fight fun, but when it's about feelings, real feelings, oh God, I just want to jump ship. Maybe that's more obvious than I think. Maybe that's why Lance left. Maybe he could tell I'm a scared baby.

Maybe some day I will stop cramming my brain full of these theories. Hmmm, Dark Bill. Dark growly-voice Bill.

My mother keeps mailing me clippings of engagement announcements for girls I went to high school with. I thought she would stop when I mailed her that Polaroid of me dry humping the furniture but no such luck.

July 20
To: Amy
From: Mark
Subject: Zamboni & Zinfandel

Dear Amy,

I have an idea regarding your mother. Why don't you start sending her obituaries of people she went to high school with?

"Dating is stupid, relationships are pointless, can I have your number?" Nice, Bill. I admire a guy who's not afraid to completely contradict himself in the space of a minute.

Please don't ever stop coming up with theories. I knew a brilliant mathematician in college. One of the finest logical minds. And a devout churchgoer. One day I got the balls to ask her why she goes to church. "God appreciates our attempts to understand."

God or no God, I appreciate your attempts to understand. So don't stop. Please.

I still don't have Addie's number. But I kinda like it like that. With her it's always fresh. And I'm not sure that someone who watches four hours of TV a day counts as a "nature girl." She's one of those paradox people. The kind I like.

Well, last night I got to see Addie in action.

Full pads, ice spray, slap shots and very little body checking. I confess I sat up front, hoping to see her flatten some soul against the Plexiglas. No such luck. I brought some B&B in a hipflask, but left it in my pocket. It was a plaid and Wranglers crowd, and I felt like a dandy out of soda water.

Her team won. She slapped the penultimate goal. After a quick change, the stands filled with players and their peeps. Cheap wine-from-a-box began to flow.

For the first time since my birthday party I got to see Addie work her magic. Affably flitting from teammate to someone's grandma to a niece to a brother-in-law and a couple of his buds. Charming everyone's pants off and letting them do the same, listening, laughing at their jokes, she sat on some guy's lap (I lowered my gaze to my Styrofoam cup). At one point she had the grandma belting out the Canadian national anthem.

She drove me home and I told her she amazes me and she said that she liked the fact that I was there watching. Don't know if she meant the game, or afterwards.

Tonight we're going out for drinks at the Good Luck Bar.

Wish me luck,
Mark

July 22
To: Mark
From: Amy
Subject: Mail Friend

Hey –

You're dating a park ranger who drinks Guinness, plays ice hockey (are there female ice hockey pick-up games?) and knows the difference between a pine tree and a whatever kinda tree isn't? She is a nature girl and I hope you are wearing condoms because S.B.T.D.s (sleeping bag transmitted diseases) are no fun and easily preventable. A little latex between the polar fleece and you're good to go.

Did you send her a homing pigeon with a sticky-note stapled to its ankle "Good Luck Bar 8:00"? For the record, I am saying that the no phone thing is shady.

We probably drove right past each other on Sunday night. I met Bill at the bar in Silver Lake that used to be a firehouse. I forgot to mention, Bill is in his forties. I have never, ahem, well, I'll just say I have never dated that deeply out of my age range.

He had scotch (see, forties) and I had a vanilla stoli with a scoop of bubble gum ice cream and a booster seat. Okay, okay, so the age difference is not going to work for me. The truth is, I didn't notice it when I met him, he felt very thirties. He is, in fact, quite close to my father's age. Gross. Not his fault, but gross.

We talked for a while, he's divorced and a music supervisor (which is why he was in Nashville observing drunk and angry country music stars). Nice Jewish boy/man/father. Lovely smile. I was sitting at the table, secretly congratulating myself for even having the 'nads to go on a date when I realized I was actually having fun.

We talked about work, Bill said, "Here is the secret, never do anything you don't want to do." Well then, my career as cottage cheese and Kashi eating kissing bandit, shoe shopper, gourmet grocery store meanderer should be secure and hopefully comes with a dental plan.

Usually after spending twenty minutes with a person I can tell if I want to kiss them or not. I was not sure about Bill so I was charting the exit.

"Well, big day tomorrow, I gotta run." He walked me out to my car on the street.

Then he says, "You seem like a woman who has a lot of male friends." I laughed and said I did.

"Well. I don't want to be your friend." Then he politely kissed me on the cheek and walked away.

That was the sneakiest, hottest move ever. The old peck on the cheek turnaround. Damn.

Are you wearing a Go Climb A Rock t-shirt?

– A.

July 28
To: Amy
From: Mark
Subject: Mark Gets (Good) Lucky

Dear Amy,

First a peck on the forehead makes you smile, and now it's one on the cheek. You're funny. But I think it's sweet.

Are you still adamant against the age thing? I put no stock in the stuff. I've met youngies who are OldSouls, and oldies who act like infants. If she's legal and not on HRT, my mind is open.

Music biz men tend to deserve their slimeball rep, but there are always exceptions. But I don't buy the no friend line; I've never felt fondly about anyone I didn't also want to be friends with. Anyway... Last Friday...

Good Luck Bar. Addie in action again. Must've been Fleet Week or something. A dozen sailors. She ended up wearing one's cap and another one's jacket. She dove on me in the backroom and kissed me – she'd had a few Guinnesses. First time I'd smooched someone in uniform...

Back at her place, we... watched TV. A re-run of Elimidate. We shouted back at the screen. She had TiVoed a Mexican soap opera. Doesn't speak Spanish. But she's addicted to the syrupy drama. She sat on my lap and we made up dialogue. We fell asleep on the couch.

I woke up to the sound of running water and there was a towel over my head. The bathroom door was open, steam spilling out. Still half-asleep, I had to pee and wasn't sure what to do. Figured what the hell, so I did. After I flushed, her hand comes out of the shower and pulls me in. Clothes soaked, she helped me peel them off. I woke up fast. We soaped each other up without saying a word and just glided along each other's bodies like ducks on a pond. When we couldn't stand it anymore, we ran to her room, dove on the bed, and went at it.

A lot of times, girls have flirted with me by mentioning how flexible they are. And I've been with my share of dancers, yoga instructors and a couple of circus performers (no, Amy, not freaks, performers) and yeah sure, they were super flexible. Addie is not. To say the least. But this dumpling has something they all lacked: fun, zest, sheer unadulterated joy. Gurgles of pleasure.

We returned to finish our shower (still had soap in our ears, cream rinse in hair). After I had coffee and she hot chocolate stuffed with marshmallows, we returned for seconds. And yes, Amy, well-latexed thank you very much. See earlier e-mail about morbid fear of pernicious cooties.

I gotta say, and I could be wrong, but I get the sense there's something about Addie you don't like. Am I wrong? I think if you met her you'd love her. She dances to a different bassoonist.

Tonight I'm taking her to a monthly dinner party I have with my friends.

xox,
Mark the Mudpuddle
1122 Loverboy Lane

P.S. Waiting is fun (and sane). You were right.

P.P.S. You don't staple sticky-notes. That's why they're sticky. Plus, PETA doesn't like it when you puncture pigeons.

July 30
To: Mark
From: Amy
Subject: The Thin Music Man

What I don't like about Addie, you still find quirky and charming, so it doesn't matter. As I said, she has many qualities that remind me of Jeremy my ex.

They are the most buoyant original lovable people and because they refuse even the convention of the telephone, they have this weird control. You are always waiting for them. Until the day you decide you want someone who you can actually contact, that you deserve to have needs.

Until that day comes, it's adorable, quirky and hipster beatnik. And that's fun too. I hope the dinner party goes smoothly. I think she's going to flirt with your friends (you've mentioned her flirting with strangers quite a bit). How are you with that?

Okay, my turn. Went to the movies with Bill. He gives me his Cliff Notes, "I'm forty five, I've been married, I'm not rich, I can't deal with materialistic women." I laugh, "You've been in LA too long." He's funny, honest and terribly angular.

The thing about the 'I don't want to be your friend' line is, I was about to pull a 'Hey, nice to meet you, new friend Bill' because I was so undecided. Usually undecided is a no.

With seven words he nailed me to the wall like an extra-credit butterfly in his high school biology project. He was clear about what he was interested in, he wants to be the guy and he wants me to be the girl.

I know it sounds immature, but the truth is, the alpha stuff is sexy. If you're not friends you're not going to want to waste fifteen minutes sipping your cocktail. Friendship is the mandatory baseline.

The point is, I was discounting him for superficial reasons (he isn't the 'boyfriend' I see when I close my eyes, not that I actually SEE one, but I feel one, and he's younger and heavier). Then he stuck his intention out onto Rowena Boulevard and he was instantly brave and attractive.

Kinda lonely,
A.

August 3
To: Amy
From: Mark
Subject: Things You Can Skin

Dear Amy,

Bill needs to step up his game if you're still feeling lonely. Has he called yet, with plans for a next time? A good alpha should've by now. I don't want you to be lonely. I want you to meet a great guy. Did you ever see Strangers on a Train where two strangers kill for each other? We should've worked out a love version of that deal. But for now, I'm more than happy with Addie, quirks and all.

So once a month for about four years now, seven other guys and myself, along with our better halves, meet in a home (it rotates) to prepare an elaborate meal for the ladies.

We do all the work, including cleaning, and their job is to sit, converse, eat, and afterwards vote for the best dish of the night. Sweet deal, eh? Diana and I were founding members. Everyone adored her. Hasn't been the same since. I've skipped a few and brought a couple nugatory dates who felt left out.

Everyone is married except for Dean and I. This time Dean hosted at his panoramic bachelor pad/spaceship high in the Hollywood Hills. Dean's flavor of the minute was a 20-year-old Russian roustabout who stared at the floor and wouldn't deign to push the food around her plate, let alone eat it. The wives tried to include her, and she graced them with monosyllables. At first I thought they'd resent her youth and flawless figure, but in the end they were just bored with her, and a bit sad.

Everyone remembered Addie from my birthday party and were delighted to see her still in the picture. The girls were all fast friends. Addie tried on Emily's shoes, made an appointment to get a Feng Shui consultation with Tara, and promised to take Leslie on a guided tour of Will Rogers.

The food stunned, as usual. The theme was Things You Can Skin. There were stuffed grape leaves, a dessert featuring peeled grapes and pudding skins, there was rabbit stewed in fennel, potato skins with crème fraîche and caviar.

And me, not one to ever be outdone, I home-smoked in alder, then grilled, two whole rattlesnakes and a dozen alligator tails, lovingly smothered in what I call my fire sauce – a lethal red with too many ingredients to list (but including smoked Hungarian chilies and ground cantharides flies from Morocco). My "prank" was a side that looked like cooling sour cream, but was actually laced with a pound of fresh-grated horseradish.

And I learned something new about girls. My dish was a gauntlet I thought only the men would pick up. But everyone (except the Russian) gave it a go. The rabbit, on the other hand, delicate and subtle, was easily the best dish of the night, but went untouched by any girl except Addie.

I'd predicted that the Ick Factor would be the determinant. Turns out girls don't mind eating ugly. The real factor was the Cute Factor. Since bunnies are cute, they are not to be eaten. Women still surprise me. I am indeed a lifelong student.

The grape leaves won, and I was good and said nothing.

And I take it back. I won. I got to go home with Addie for our own shedding of skins.

Her birthday is Sunday.

Mark

August 5
To: Mark
From: Amy
Subject: Tricks Are for Kiddie Pools

I blew it. I invited Bill over to play in my kiddie pool today (I get a new kiddie pool every summer), had a coupe of gin rickeys and blammo, I'm playing footsie, we're making out in my apartment, all my pent-up Tennessee Williams trampiness explodes.

Mark, he's just soo skinny. Tell me if this is bad, we were doing it and I was closing my eyes trying to pretend it wasn't him, that it was some phantom detachable penis.

The fun was over and then I told him I had plans with Susan so I had to go. Nice Saturday afternoon.

He called in the car on the way home and left a message saying "what a beautiful experience" he just had. I lay on my bed and tried to assuage my middle-class puritanical guilt. It's fine, I'm an adult. So what if I wanted to make Lolita look like a club-footed beekeeper.

Could this be a medicinal booty call? (No, I'm not going to hell; just think of all those people I've driven to the airport.)

I am now keeping condoms in the first aid kit. Sex is more like an accident these days.

Repressed, Re-dressed,
Amy

P.S. It's cool that Addie fit in so easily with your pals. She is making you happy, no? She give you phone number? How does she pick up her dry cleaning?

P.P.S. Those dinners sound amazing, sans the bunny burrito. If it's been a pet I don't want it on my fork. I would just resent all the years I spent changing hutch newspapers and be unable to enjoy my meal.

August 6
To: Amy
From: Mark
Subject: Too Many Bulls

It's way too late in this kiss and tell for you to go all guilty on me. I believe you once called it "transitory pleasure balling."

Or maybe that's the big vat they have at Chuck E. Cheese and Ikea...

So how skinny is he? Did his ribs puncture your pool? How was the kissing?

Don't blame yourself for not being attracted to Bill. You may as well blame a dog for chasing a cat. You like him in one way but not another. Imagine if I said, "That is the most beautiful sunset I have ever seen, but I am so sad because I cannot eat it like an omelette," or "That mountain is stunning, but I cannot make love to it." If you have romantic thoughts about someone physically incompatible, it is no different than embracing a dead man, a stone, or a sea.

I think you're trying too hard to like him, to like SOMEONE. This is dangerous. You witness a prince through the glasses of roses and wishful thinking, only to wake up in bed with a toad.

Yes, Addie has a phone – no cell, but one at home – a push-button even! No answering machine. No voice mail. No call waiting. Isn't it funny how that makes her a barbarian? As you can guess she does not take anything to the dry cleaners, so there's nothing to pick up. But if she did, it would be in her M&M brown 1978 VW Dasher Diesel.

Like me, she threw herself a birthday party. Rented out most of Saddle Ranch on Sunset Blvd. for brunch. Not surprised how many friends she has (about 65 showed). A little surprised at the guy:girl ratio. You couldn't swing your dick without – well you get the picture.

The centerpiece was the mechanical bull. Addie's tightly clamped thighs brought back a dozen (nine, actually) fond memories. A few guys went next, thinking they'd outdo her, but fell flat in a minute or two. Then it was my turn. I'd never done it before, but I figured I was a horseshoe-in, as I've been riding since I was a tyke. Out to impress, I left my hands off the pommel. And in five seconds flat, I swung to the right like a rotary dial and landed on my head. Setting the party record for worst rider.

And I was already in a shitty mood. Addie introduced me to a few of her best friends as part of a group. "K.C., this is Tom, this is Alan, this is Mark, this is Avery." What!? No this is my boyfriend? No crown, no throne, no scepter?

So I pouted like a 20-year-old Russian girl through most of the party. At one point she came over, straddled my lap and kissed me on the mouth. That lasted fifteen seconds or so.

Grumble grumble,
M.

August 10
To: Mark
From: Amy
Subject: $10,000 Dating Pyramid

You can't be in a shitty mood if you clarify what's going on between you two (okay, you can still be in a shitty mood but at least you'll know what the mood is about).

What is going on? Dating? The weird pyramid of hanging out, seeing, dating, boyfriend/girlfriend twenty-first century courting model that we're all trying to figure out.

My people-reader still says Addie's shady. I know you don't like that, but it's how I feel.

From shady, we will move on to dark. Dark Bill, as I like to call him, and I have been spending a good amount of time together. Even not having sex. He thinks we are a great match. He claims that because of his having been married and in relationships with creative career-minded women, he knows how to deal with us.

"You all need your space." I think this might just be the best thing ever. He's very funny and quite the punster. (I'm a sucker for puns.) The thing that won't go away is the man's thrift. And my not being attracted to him.

I spent the night there, and this morning he goes out for coffee and snacks, I wait for him in bed feeling lazy and sexy like a Hilton sister. He comes back and gives me a croissant. I am trying to be bon vivant cool, as if I always start my Friday mornings with pastry when the truth is unless they are made of complete protein spelt flour I dodge croissants (strange things that define 'cool' for each of us). I notice that the bag has a big black mark on it.

"What's that?" I ask. "I didn't want you to know how much it was," he said. Mark, I think he was serious.

Bill hasn't gone to work since I've met him. He says he's "working on a project" at home. I don't ask him anymore, but he is still angry about getting financially drained from his divorce.

It's not that I care about money so much, it just seems like he puts all of his energy into being mad at his past. I sound like I don't like him, I do like him. I do. I feel very feminine around him.

That and he has no interest in changing me. I like that. Lance was always giving me his L'Uomo Vogue style tips and I was starting to feel unattractive. (How could he not understand that this season's Gucci sandals were not in my budget?)

I feel like I could wear a paper sack around Bill and he would find me attractive.

And smart and funny. Lance was a little threatened by those things. He would get snitty when we'd go to a party and his friends would laugh at my meaningless stories.

Bill's pushing me to go to dinner at his friend's house. I don't even know where I am on the pyramid.

The friends are married and have kids, because that's what people in their late forties do.

August 12
To: Mark
From: Amy
Subject: Bill's in my Grill

Went to dinner at the home of Bill's friends, the Harpers. Social black hole. It feels like just yesterday I was vomiting on the steps of the Viper Room looking for one of my four fake i.d.'s, and now I'm saying, "God this salmon is so great, what did you use for a marinade?"

Bill started talking in we's, right there by the outdoor grill. Instead of "I didn't like The Last Samurai," it was now "We didn't like The Last Samurai."

I didn't even see The Last Samurai.

He's depressed all the time. All he does is blame the music business for destroying innocent artists. I've started calling him 'Eeyore' in my head. Like, "Going to the Thai place with the C on the window with Eeyore tonight." Sigh.

August 14
To: Mark
From: Amy
Subject: My Bad

Mark, did I offend you with my Addie judgments? I am sorry. Seriously, is the art consultant biz especially heavy in August?

August 16
To: Mark
From: Amy
Subject: Don't Pet Me

I bet you took Addie on some wacky Guinness-fueled vacation. I had to write anyway. Please deal with this situation immediately...

So Bill had to go see some blues guitarist in New Mexico. I missed him a bunch. The night that he came home he had to go to a friend's birthday party.

Still feeling the social black hole of dinner at the Harpers' home I declined the invitation but invited him over after the party. Fooling around immediately, kissing his fingers, nibbling the soft part between thumb and index I tasted a taste I'd recognize anywhere.

"Oh my God," I said, my hand sandwich making me sick. "Did you do coke tonight?"

"Oh God," is all he says.

"You did coke tonight. Are you retarded? Why would you do that when you know you're coming over here?"

"I just did a bump."

"That's lame. You're lame." This is my opinion of coke – WOW WHAT A GREAT DRUG – something that gets you to grind your teeth into mini-marshmallows and tell whoever is geographically closest that they are the greatest friend you've ever had and can we go buy another pack of cigarettes.

"Honey it was stupid. I'm sorry. I don't do drugs all the time."

"Whatever. I can't believe I just tasted it on you. I feel like a German Shepherd."

"Next time I come over I'll bring you a 'don't pet me I'm working' vest."

And you know the moral of this story, it's all about the first encounter. The night that we both claimed relationship incompetence, I was wearing safety orange.

I think that I'm giving myself a time out now.

August 16
To: Mark
From: Amy
Subject: HELP SPARKY

Hey, I really need your help here. Is this or is this not a red flag?

He has apologized three times to my machine.

August 18
To: Mark
From: Amy
Subject: No More Silent Treatment

Okay. If you're mad, just say it. I know you hate conflict, but Mark, we're close now, you can't just vanish.

Maybe your computer blew up in the summer heat.

I broke up with Bill. He's been calling every day, talking in circles, "You weren't my girlfriend, you could be whatever you wanted to be, of course I wanted you to be my girlfriend, and it's okay for one person to love more than the other. I know I love you more than you like me..."

It's making me sick. I hate not being able to reciprocate. And I feel sad that I don't know what happened over the last month with Eeyore and I don't know where you are. Am I just making every mistake? I really am sorry if I said something to hurt your feelings.

What am I talking about? You're not mad at me, you just took Addie away for her birthday. You love to do that. You're probably at a peacock farm in the Santa Inez Valley.

Dude, where's my e-pal?

Always,
Amy

P.S. I know that I'm getting closer to actually being able to do this whole deep relationship thing. At least Bill and I were brain compatible. (He actually read the books on his shelf.)

P.P.S. You know why it was so easy for him to give me 'space.' He wasn't working and he didn't want me to see. Note to self, next one will be brain compatible and employed.

August 19
To: Amy
From: Mark
Subject: Mea culpa

Dear dear Amy,

I am SOOOOOOOOOOOOOOOO sorry I vanished! Fact is, I have no good excuse. Computer's fine, didn't leave the country, things with Addie are great, and I was not and am not mad at you AT ALL. In fact, I realized when I got your e-mails that I can't even imagine ever being mad at you. (I vaguely remember a scene in which Pinocchio chucked a shoe at Jiminy Cricket, but he wasn't really trying to hurt him, he was just expressing himself and I think Jiminy understood that, and anyway, I might be remembering it wrong.)

No, I've just had shitty time management skills. And I'm really sorry. But I won't let it happen again. I promise. And yes, this is a man making you a promise. We made one on Valentine's Day, and I didn't forget, and I'm not going anywhere.

And I'm sorry I wasn't there for the Overdue Bill Breakup. But you did the right thing – isn't it obvious? Bill came along too soon on the heels of (I still can't type his name, the coward), and wasn't special enough to warrant pre-empting your program of mourning. And I don't think he scratched out the price of the pastries – I think the black mark meant they were day old and thus on sale. Jesus, I complained about the Frenchmen who offer up croissants; at least theirs aren't from the bargain bin.

Jumping to the we's was way too fast – no, that's not what I want to say – especially me, of all people. Time is time, subjective and personal. What I mean to say is that jumping to the we's was an unearned quantum leap. Unless it got lost in the cyber-ether, I'm missing the e-mail where the two of you make each other fabulously happy and enrich each other like King Arthur flour.

A friend of mine recently wrote me a deceptively simple sentence: "A healthy relationship is supposed to make you feel happy, stimulated, connected and secure the majority of the time." I know. Obvious, right? But I think I'm going to put it on a sticky-note (or three – one by the phone, one by the computer, and one on a pack of condoms).

Well, post-divorce bitterness, a few lines of coke, and sunken cheeks just don't cut it.

I'd like to think if I'd been around more I would have said, "What do you mean he HAD to visit a blues guitarist. Who HAS to visit a blues guitarist? Sounds like a codeword for his ex. Dump him now." But I missed my cue.

And yes, of course of course a horse is a horse I have a hundred and seven Addie stories to tell you, but I really wanted to at least TRY to make up for my absence. I won't leave again. And if I ever have to take a sabbatical, I'll be professional about it and give you two weeks' notice.

More in a minute.

Much love,
Mark

August 19
To: Amy
From: Mark
Subject: A Roller Coaster That Only Goes Up

Dear Amy,

Wheeeeeee! Life with Addie is like an All-Rides pass at the world's best amusement park. So fasten your seatbelt...

In the past two weeks, we've played miniature golf (she carved our initials in felt behind Paul Bunyan), went to the grocery store and switched all of the lemons to the lime bin and all of the limes to the lemon bin (this was her idea), went bowling (she sweet-talked the guy behind the counter to give her a can of shoe deodorizing spray which she now proudly displays in a shrine of favorite objects on her mantel), had a day o' bbq in which we cruised around to five different rib shacks in four different area codes, had sex in a treehouse (a first for me), had sex in the backroom of a 99-cent store (a first for anyone, I believe), sang karaoke at Amagi (me: Straighten Up and Fly Right; she: L.A. Woman in an unbelievable baritone), got side-by-side massages ($20 each) in K-town, rented wave-runners, rented mopeds, had a radish-eating contest at Zankou Chicken, painted each other's bodies with Cray-Pas pastels, tried to have sex at Griffith Observatory but got chased away, played hide-and-seek in Target, and somehow, somehow, I also managed to get all my work done.

So, Amy, I'm asking permission, has it been long enough? Am I allowed to announce that I'm officially I.L.?

Cotton Candy and a Waffle Cone,
Mouseketeer Mark

P.S. Shady? How can someone with the sunniest disposition be shady? She meets every criterion I have – ok, so a few times I didn't feel secure – but that's more about my petty jealousy than anything else. When I got home I always reminded myself that it was her gregariousness and unrivaled ease with all kinds of people that first attracted me to her, so how could I be mad if she's a little flirty...

P.P.S. Our three-month anniversary is coming up September 1st. I decided to count from the night we met, because – well, because it feels right. So I need help from you. Help me think of the perfect gift – not too over the top, but something really nice – not jokey.

August 20
To: Mark
From: Amy
Subject: Addiementaly in Love

The promise on Valentine's Day. What was it again? To expose ourselves emotionally and physically to virtual strangers and call it sport? Oh yeah kids, great idea. You know who I have exposed the most of myself to? You. And all I can remember about you is that you were a guy at a table in a tux who, when I said, "Welcome to the singles table, loner," looked me in the eye and said, "Who ya callin loner, free bird?"

Get Addie an unpadded bra. Maybe a simple necklace, necklaces are good, they say, "I like you, you're pretty, wear this thing next to your face and above your breasts and think of me." I am a sucker for a locket. But that's a pretty obvious symbol. Richard once gave me a locket with his picture in it. I took his photo out when I left him in Paris and felt appropriately dramatic tossing it into the Seine.

That was me, as a 21-year-old drama queen. I'm still wearing an empty locket.

A.

P.S. I am happy that you are in love.

August 21
To: Amy
From: Mark
Subject: Strangers in the night...

Dear Free Bird,

So a necklace... ok, but tell me more – gold? silver? short? long? She never wears jewelry or even make-up, but I actually think she'd like to have something really nice. Something light years beyond a gag gift or a can of shoe deodorizer. So tell me more. Specifics.

Well last night was a new one for me. We're sitting on her couch watching Celebrity Justice and The Little Rascals (Addie likes to flip back and forth; it's a new condition called ADHDTV) when she switches off the tube and tells me to put my shoes on. Um, ok.

She takes me out onto her front deck and without saying anything, she takes my hand and walks me over to her bedroom window and pantomimes. She points to a little nook inside the frame of the screen and makes a poking gesture. She repeats this twice. Um, ok.

Then she dashes back inside the house and slams the door quickly behind her. I hear her double-bolt the door. Right. Ok. So there I am. A crescent moon and the best L.A. can offer by way of stars – four or five pale luminaries up in an over-washed night sky. The piercing cry of crickets in the distance. Or maybe it's a car alarm.

All the lights switch off inside. I THINK I see where this is going... I poke my finger into the nook and... the screen pops at once out of its frame into my hands. It's too dark to see inside, but I silently rest the screen on the deck and hoist myself through the window.

Inside, I see that Addie is "asleep" in her bed, under the covers. Um, ok.

So I undress and I climb in bed. Addie bolts upright, snatching the sheets around her. "Who are you!!!?"

"Just your friendly neighborhood cat burglar," I purr.

She breaks character for a second, "Shh. Don't say anything."

Um, ok. Trying to hide my trepidation (this is the nightmare where you're on stage in the school play and you don't know your lines), I lift up her nightshirt, grab her firmly by the hips and start kissing my way down.

She breaks character again, "No, not like that!"

Right. I forgot. So I climb aboard in my best impression of a grunting dockworker and get right to it. (I was relieved she didn't criticize my lack of verisimilitude when I paused to grab a condom from her night-table drawer.) Amy, pardon my French, but she'd never been wetter. When she came it was like holding on to an avalanche.

Alright, so it wasn't exactly my cup of XXX tea. But I realized then and there – some of my friends have now been married just long enough that they're beginning to complain about the absence of spice, which they quickly wave away saying it's not that big a deal. Maybe I'm a fool, but it's impossible to conceive that Addie and I will ever be wanting for spice and variety. She is a living, breathing passion play. Even if she is a bit out there.

Stealthily,
The Cat Burglar

August 23
To: Mark
From: Amy
Subject: Peccadilloes

Three months and we're into the rape fantasies. Shit, by this time next year you'll have anal beads by the front door.

Honestly, whatever. Girls have so much brain sex. If in Addie's head she likes to be swept away by an anonymous prowler and you don't mind wearing a face mask and you give the neighbors a flyer clarifying your sexual role-playing so that a SWAT team doesn't shoot you in the back, then it's fine.

The most important thing is to not make fun of the request. Bill kept begging me to tell him what I liked in the sack (which is NOT TALKING in the sack), finally I gave him a little cue card, he made fun of me, and I hated him.

I am through whining about Bill or anyone else. For me, males are like vitamins: supplements to be taken when needed. Right now I am quite healthy.

Susan and I are going to the Beverly Hills Hotel to have Camparis and watch the old rich people. No more 'poor me' bullshit, just sunshine and sparkly red drinks.

xoxo
A.

P.S. Okay. The necklace for Addie – you might want to book a personal shopping appointment with me, but if not here are the facts: You wanna play it safe, any piece of Peretti from Tiffany's. Think silver an inch below the collar bone. That being said, it's a little too traditional for our lady of the foot deodorant shrine. I would stake out some of the high-end vintage stores or go for a sweet natural gem.

There's a place on the east side where all the pieces correspond to healing properties of the rock. Maybe they have a pendant in "Rape Me Rose Quartz." (That was an extreme example of what not to say to Addie. I was just testing you.)

August 26
To: Amy
From: Mark
Subject: Small wonders

Dear Amy,

I thought vitamins are meant to be taken daily, as PREVENTATIVE medicine. Antibiotics and Ambien are what you take when needed. So I'm not sure about the men=vitamins theory. But in your current state of mind, maybe men=Flintstones chewable vitamins so you can really bite down and crunch them to a fine pink Rubble.

Thank you for putting my mind at ease about my first "she came in through the bathroom window" experience. If I had spoken to you first (which would've been impossible), I might have allowed myself to actually enjoy it. But as it felt so... so... I dunno... razor's edgy to me, I felt more like a performer than a participant. There's always next time. But for now, I have a totally different tale to tell.

Friday night Addie slept over and we both slept in. Around noon we stepped out onto the beach, took a right and walked north. Made our way to the Santa Monica Pier. A young girl was lost, and Addie took her hand and calmed her down, gently petting her hair until the sniffles stopped. She even coaxed a smile. It wasn't long before mom appeared, confused at first, but then grateful.

A ten-year-old boy was sitting on a bench, kicking the ground, pissed that he was being punished for throwing a cup of ice off the Ferris wheel.

Addie sat next to him and said "Whassup?" He ignored her at first, even scooted farther away. But by the time I'd blinked, Addie and her pal had invented a game where they tried to spy the person who had the most pockets on his or her clothes.

"That one's got SEVEN! Look he's got one on his sneakers!"

Amy, I actually cried. I'd never seen her with kids before. If I had ovaries I'd swear I could feel them hum.

Less than a week 'til our anniversary. God, I want to get her something great. I've never met anyone like her. We're completely different in almost every way. But it's getting hard to imagine life without her.

Pinch me,
Mark

P.S. Thank you for the jewelry suggestions. I'm gonna start looking tomorrow.

August 27
To: Mark
From: Amy
Subject: Who's your Daddy

Mark, are you getting your period?

I'm kidding sweetie, it's quite touching the way Addie was with the kids. I think you learn everything you need to know when you see people interact with children. Jeremy talked to them like peers, perhaps because they were.

Oh God, I still think he was the one and I blew it. (Did I just say "the one"?) Welcome to West Hollywood Fairy Tale Theater. Sometimes I feel like I've been a million different women and yet I've always had the same cuticles, the same wrists, and the same flaws.

In 1980 I had a crush on my neighbor Tiger Doyle. I told my mother I liked Tiger and I wanted to invite him over for my favorite things, macaroni and cheese and Mr. Potato Heads.

I searched everywhere for my yellow pinafore and my Mr. Potato Head, then I cut yellow sour grass from the backyard and put it in a Dixie cup. I was so taken with the theme, it was 'yellow for Tiger' and it was a smashing success. He loved macaroni, making Mr. Potato Heads, and yellow (I don't think he gave a shit about the ruffly pinafore).

We held hands and played games and he pushed me on his skateboard and I think it was the happiest I ever was.

Why am I telling you this? Because maybe I have not evolved, maybe I just want to wear a ruffly pinafore and have the theme be 'happy yellow.' Maybe I don't want to be an adult with a heart and consequences and sex and addictions and almost in-law mothers and men who disappear or cling or talk about protein or hypnotize me with their bodies. Maybe I just want some weeds in a cup and a box of noodles.

Where the hell is Tiger Doyle?

– A.

August 28
To: Amy
From: Mark
Subject: First Loves

Dear Mrs. Potato Head,

Maybe it's not about hunting for Tigers. But it is about searching for that creamy happy yellow. If you haven't yet guessed from my Addie tales, she and I are definitely a couple of happy summer campers.

But puppy love is a thousand times more precious when you're a couple of old dogs. When my mom and her new husband hold hands and twinkle it's about the sweetest sight in the world. That they had first met almost fifty years ago in high school is even more of a thump-thump moment. I think Addie is my Tiger. And I know that yours is out there, too.

M.

August 29
To: Amy
From: Mark
Subject: Mission Accomplished

A. –

Ok, I got the goods.

I picked up Dean at the ER (his MG was in the shop). I haven't told you much about Dean. He's not sick – it's where he works – an ER doctor with the best grosser-than-gross stories in town. He's my age but rumor has it he can go nine times a night. (Please tell me this is overkill so I can feel better about myself!)

He went with me to pick up the necklace. From the top secret HQ of Chrome Hearts in West Hollywood, tucked away in an enclave near John Varvatos. Way too cool to have a normal sign, a roaring outdoor fireplace near the front door lit the way.

Addie's sweaty sunburned neck will soon be graced by a rope of chunky tarnished silver, subtle as a bicycle chain, but if you closely examine the rugged links you'll see that each is hewn to a barely perceptible heart.

You'd figure with Dean's quadruple-digit conquests he'd have nothing to do with commitment and romance, but that's the great thing about him. A total romantic, a softie at core.

But SUCH a romantic he's set his standards sky high, so he finds fault, no matter how trifling, after the first or second date.

Most people would be shocked, but I've known him long enough not to be – Dean is a deep believer in monogamy (for his friends, anyway). He LOOKS like the President of the He-Man Woman-Haters Club, but he's a far cry from it. Sure, he's not perfect. (Me and Addie once double-dated with him and a lanky Costa Rican gal whom he introduced as Carmen, the librarian. Addie had some questions that had always been bugging her about the Dewey Decimal System, but I smiled, knowing that "librarian" is Dean's codeword for call girl...)

Yeah, yeah, I know. But he's still my friend. And consider it a sign of my friendship and affection for YOU that I've never once suggested setting you up with him, ok?

He's met Addie four times now, and right before he climbed out of my truck to pick up his MG, he turned to me with wide-open eyes and intoned, "Mark. I really like Addie. Please. Please, don't mess this one up." And he was gone.

Amy, I don't want to mess this one up.

– M.

August 30
To: Mark
From: Amy
Subject: Lovey Trinkets

I know this sounds bonkers but I can't stop thinking about Tiger Doyle. And do you know what this means? This means I'm ready to date someone in my peer group!!!!! I can't believe how exciting this information is to me. I'm ready to stop dating cowboys and musicians and old dudes and I AM READY FOR A PEER!!

Why are you mean and hiding Dean?

Is he in my peer group? How can someone look like the president of the He-Man Woman-Haters Club?

I'm sure Addie will love the necklace. (Chrome Hearts is a little too Cher for me, just so you know, in case I fall in love with a peer soon and he makes you go shopping with him because you know all of my trivia. Size sheet to follow.)

You did good Sparky.

September 1
To: Amy
From: Mark
Subject:

its 1005 im at Deans using his compuetr. went to her place at 9 and th tv was loud.music channel yo mtv raps or something like that. thought of the time she dance to grand thetf auto. knocked but it was too loud so i stuck my finger in the nook, neclace in hand, and climbed in the bedroomm window.

She was fucking this guy Tom from her birthday party.

I cant say for sure i was climbing out as fast as I could but I think she didnt even look fazed

theres a tarnished heart necklace lying somewhere on euclid avenue if anyone wants it

on my third double of markers mark and think iom going to be sick now. Seriousl

September 2
To: Mark
From: Amy
Subject: The Morning After

Mark, the time is now. What do you want and deserve in a relationship?

Stop with the "a relationship should make you feel happy and secure and blah blah blah." At the end of the day, the world is going to give you what you tell it you deserve.

Now aside from my being so seemingly heartless and cruel, I will tell you I am sorry. I am sorry you fell in love with someone without asking the not-romantic questions, like "ARE YOU SEEING OTHER PEOPLE," and then informing her that you wanted to be the only one.

Do you or do you not deserve to be the only one? Is that important to you?

I'm sorry that you're sad. And I am sorry you did not keep the receipt and the necklace so that we could return it and buy you a Chrome Hearts dog tag or something.

You and I both need to clarify what we want and deserve in a relationship (who knows if we'll get it, but we have an obligation to ourselves to clarify it). Honey, you are a good friend and a good man. Everything is going to be alright always. Now clarify. Just to me.

September 2
To: Amy
From: Mark
Subject: death

What do I deserve? That's easy. Better than this. Far better. I didn't ask the not romantic questions coz I thought some things go without saying when you're seeing someone almost every day. So that's it? I go for "tacit understanding" and now this is the punishment? I deserve better.

It's been 21 hours. She hasn't even called. I figured she'd have shown up with flowers by now. WHAT THE HELL?!

September 3
To: Amy
From: Mark
Subject: Alien

So I called and she didn't answer, of course. So I went by her house but she wasn't there. And no I didn't go anywhere NEAR that nook to look inside. I found her at Will Rogers. Talk about fucking dramatic – she was holding a machete when I arrived (clearing brush for trail maintenance).

"Hey."

That's what she said when she saw me. Like nothing had happened.

"Hey"? "Hey"?!!

You will not be surprised when I tell you that what followed was a whole lot of yelling. But you might be surprised when I tell you that the person doing all the yelling was Addie.

"Who do you think you are that you own me?!" was one line I remember. "How DARE you judge me!"

Seems I was the one who made the mistake. I'm the one with the bourgeois values. (And, she did have a valid point, I'm the one who never once had a normal conversation with her about what our deal was, about our "status label." On that one, she had me. Not that I admitted it to her...)

The closest she came to an apology was, "Well I'm sorry you feel that way."

Okay, I lied – I did plenty of the yelling. And I guess that didn't help. When all was said and done, SHE dumped ME. In no uncertain terms.

"I've never seen this side of you, Mark. I had no idea you were so possessive. And it's not attractive. It's downright ugly." As she was talking I already knew that from here on out the smell of Guinness would always make me puke.

At one point, I won a place in the Smithsonian of the Pathetic by asking her to forgive me. I can't even remember how that apology arose. My train of thought had long since hit a cow, an oil tanker, a glacier, and the abyss that is my gut.

"Mark, I don't want to see you again, now that you've shown your true colors. I was having a really good time with you, but I'm never going to be able to forget this."

Moral of the story: opposites attract, but so what? That kind of attraction is the stuff of clouds. What lasts requires rocks in your pocket and feet on the ground.

[Note to self: next time, before buying an anniversary present, check to make sure you're actually a couple.]

I've started grinding my teeth at night. That's just what I fucking need.

Happy happy joy joy,
Mark

September 4
To: Mark
From: Amy
Subject: Wish List

The fact that you want 'better' is obvious. It's good, but you've got to get specific.

Here, I'll start. I want someone:

- not closer to my father's age than mine
- who wants a sexually monogamous relationship and can say it and live it (this applies to me too)
- who has a job he is passionate about, or is working TOWARDS that job but is employed in the meantime (this applies to me too)
- who respects himself and his body, but not in a creepy obsessive four hair products and self-tanners gay kind of way (this applies to me too)
- who does not have to get piss drunk to say 'I love you' (this applies to me too)

- who lives under a tank of gas away, and
- who makes my underpants turn into pudding when I look at him

Okay, that's me. You're up.

(Did you notice that what I have here is a whole new way of looking at my life? I know that it's time for me to stop obsessing over nonsense, to start being really passionate about my job, and stop needing two cocktails to talk about my feelings. Naturally, that means that these problems have little to do with the guys and more to do with me, don't they. Shit.)

September 5
To: Amy
From: Mark
Subject: Diana

Today I'm pissed at Diana. If it weren't for her none of this would have happened. Why did she have to pick up and leave like that? Out of nowhere, after all that time, with no signs, no room for appeal?

I know that Addie's just being Addie. She can't help it. But Diana's the one who turned on me, who strayed out of character. She was supposed to be sane and solid. This is all her fault.

My mother says health is the most important thing. I think peace of mind is more important.

When you let a lover into your life, you entrust your peace of mind to each other. You now have the power to destroy it.

I am going to be very wary before ever again giving some woman the keys to my peaceable kingdom. Addie sabotaged the works. My insides are churning. I am useless.

September 6
To: Amy
From: Mark
Subject: You

Ok, so today I'm pissed at you. Yeah you said she was shady, but you made it seem like it was all about her not having a stupid cell phone so how was I supposed to take that seriously? I mean, really. You're the one with the big theory about how first dates foretell everything and on our first "date" she was all over everyone and faithful to none. The only time she paid full attention to me is when she had an audience of one. Someone who makes up her own rules is a whole lotta fun until you realize that this means: she can make up her own rules. It all makes sense now but I was IN IT, whereas you had the luxury of an outsider's eye.

AMY! I know we've got a pretty laissez-faire thing going on with some friendly advice here and there, but tell me – if I were about to walk off a cliff would you sit back and watch and then write about it later? I don't understand why you didn't push me harder, kneel on my neck, and read me the riot act sooner.

I'm sorry. I'm just really pissed.

September 7
To: Mark
From: Amy
Subject: Sex Goggles

Ahhh, the five stages of grief. Go ahead, spew all you want, I'll be here when you're done and ready to take responsibility for your lovestruck blindness.

Mark, you know as well as I do that if I had said, "Addie's an attention junkie slutbag and you need to stop wasting your time," it wouldn't have done you any good. Besides, you went hiking, you had sex in the back of a 99-cent store, and you learned that you must be clear about who is seeing/trusting/loving/faithful to whom.

We call that "edumacation," my man.

But two people's emotions have to fly in the same general air-traffic patterns. You were crazy about Addie, but she was crazy about the whole world. Now you know. And you won't do this again. Repeat after me, "I won't ignore my gut feelings when the woman I'm dating lap dances a fleet of sailors."

Susan is setting me up on a date with her neighbor tonight. Alex. She said that when she talks to Alex, she feels like she's talking to me. We're meeting Susan and four other people from her building at Ye Rustic Inn. I like that place. They play a lot of Springsteen on the juke.

xoxo
A.

P.S. Hey – you have NOT gotten out of the clarifying what you want in a partner assignment.

September 8
To: Amy
From: Mark
Subject: non compos mentis

Dear Amy,

Ok, first, I'm really sorry about the last few e-mails, especially for blaming you. It's been rough.

Dean offered to take me back to Kaua'i on his dime, but I can't get away from work for awhile. I canceled all my appts these last few days and have some serious catching up to do.

My plan, in this order: Shave. Shower. Shower again. Eat something that doesn't end in -zza. Drink a lot of water. A lot. Open all of my windows and both of my skylights and cook some onions in sweet butter to make my place smell like a home again. Open my mail and put it into piles. And then sit down with yet another tall glass of water and answer your question about what it is I am looking for.

I think somewhere around the second shower I will again be in shape to be a decent listener, and able to go back and re-read the last few e-mails you sent which, obviously, I totally ignored as they did not begin with Sto and end with Lichnya.

Much love,
Mark

September 10
To: Mark
From: Amy
Subject: Arrggggg

Okay, I know you're kinda metro, but it didn't take this much time for a shower. Now once and for all, what do you want in a partner? Then we get to establish if you can give it back, and how you can do it. Baby steps.

As for the girl who has told the universe what she wants (hi, that's me) – I met Susan, Alex and their international singles gang at the Rustic on Saturday. Alex was quite gallant, and had a little back-east sexy conservative dirty professor character from an Updike novel flavor (V-neck sweater, button-up oxford, khakis). He stood up, all six feet four of him, got me a drink and the rest is a blur (and I only had one drink).

Alex and I are a little similar. Okay, we are a lot similar. We talked for three hours in that geeky way where you focus on each other so much that the group you came with just gives up on you, and you don't care because you are having the best time with this new person, they get your references (and in this case, they're tall and handsome, and – oh man was it exciting).

Then he walked me out to my car and kissed me. That's right, an official slobbery delicious full-mouthed kiss! He asked for my number, I gave it to him, it was all so simple and casual and honest and I was on cloud nine.

And then he told me that he's moving to Cleveland in two weeks.

WAAAAAAA!

He called and left a message today, but now I don't know what to do. I'm very attracted to him, but two weeks? It just seems so futile. I cannot believe Susan didn't tell me that he was moving.

She says it's worth burning out (i.e. sticking around even though there are problems. You have to 'burn it out' so that when you finally do separate, you can both be really sure that you did the right thing).

Did I not clarify in my mandate for man dates that he must live within a distance that is less than one tank of fuel from here?

September 10
To: Amy
From: Mark
Subject: What if it's a very, very big tank?

I'm kinda metro? Look, I know how to safely dive from a moving car at 60 mph, and fend for myself in a bar fight, so I'm not too concerned.

Amy, I'm on your side and am pissed at Susan and her double-D's. Cruel and unusual punishment to dangle a tasty morsel over the head of a tantalus like yourself. Please don't move to Ohio.

I know you've long held a seize-the-day, everyone-comes-along-for-a-reason attitude, but that has its limits. Friends shouldn't let friends date unavailable men.

I've been working on that longer e-mail you've been asking for – a reply to your partner question – it's on its way.

And so what if I've been spending a little extra time in the shower lately, if you catch my drift. A guy's got needs. At least I'm staying outta trouble.

September 10
To: Amy
From: Mark
Subject: All I want for Xmas

Dear Santa,

I feel like a new man.

No, that is **NOT** my statement of purpose in what I am seeking in a partner.

You asked about what I think I deserve. I don't believe that anyone "deserves" anything other than basic inalienable human rights. Life ain't fair and there's no use cryin' about it.

But as to what I want, that's a horse of a different color. No, that doesn't mean I'm into biracial bestiality. Oh geez, this is getting complicated, so here goes the wish list:

The woman of my dreams will:

- Be confident
- Have functioning ovaries, for future use
- Have mood swings well within the Richter scale
- Possess a predominantly sunny disposition and outlook
- Have what I call the Captain's Ball Factor (I imagine being invited to a swank affair on a large moored sailing vessel. The steward blows a shrill pipe and declaims our names as we make our entrance. And what I feel as all eyes turn is a profound sense of pride in the lady on my arm.)
- Have recent documentation of a clean bill of health
- Have a beautiful voice
- Not be a racist
- Be fully capable of monogamy (she's got a track record and a stated desire)
- Have impeccable hygiene
- Be passionate about something (unlike your criterion, I don't care if it's her job, a hobby, a cause, anything – as long as her eyes incandesce when she talks about it)
- Have had a relatively happy childhood

- Refrain from both clinginess and pushiness
- Have strong opinions
- Not have any chemical addictions
- Not be in recovery
- Have strong hands, soft hands
- Have a hearty appetite and an almost total absence of food aversions. Not finicky, she likes warm weather, cold weather, and she's game for pretty much anything
- Have a good laugh
- Have great skin (Ivory Girls of any race make me swoon)
- Be extremely well-educated or self-educated
- Have an energetic, sexy mom (if applicable)
- Love animals, and vice versa
- Be currently single
- Not have prior kids
- Not belong to a cult
- Laugh at my good jokes and forgive the bad
- Prefer butter to margarine, red wine to white, dogs to cats and hiking to treadmills
- Be equally at home in jeans or a cocktail dress
- Never ever use the phrase "Equally at home in jeans or a cocktail dress"

There. I did it. Know anyone who fits the bill? I'd stand on the corner, but I don't think I can fit all that on a cardboard sign.

Or, I could sum it all up in a word: Diana. Someone like her. We had everything. She was perfect for me. We were perfect. Except she was able to walk away. So I guess I'd add that: someone who won't walk away.

Love,
Mark

September 13
To: Mark
From: Amy
Subject: APB - CALLING ALL HAPPY HUNGRY CHICKS

Wow. Good job on the list. But don't discredit the shy girl with the tubby mustached mother and a fondness for treadmills and sauvignon blanc.

Just be open, is all I'm saying.

What we've established is that you want to be monogamous (we already knew this about you), you want someone who could have a baby (post-op trannies need not apply), and someone who, if bipolar, is well-medicated, and who is an easy audience and a confident, smart girl.

This really shouldn't be that difficult. Do you mirror that stuff?

I do worry about the paradox of strong opinions and absence of finickiness though. Those of us with strong opinions (and hands) know what we like.

But the "happy childhood" thing? Mark, I have yet to meet a person who would describe their childhood as happy. Most of us were insecure, confused and painfully aware of our ill-fitting corduroy hand-me-downs. I would concentrate on someone who's making a decision to have a happy/authentic adulthood. That's one of the problems I had with Jeremy, he would get scared when I would cry. Well tough titties, boys; we are highly emotional creatures and we get sad and scared and jubilant and if you can't take it, we've got that King Kong thing in the drawer.

I get the part about her being predominantly sunny. But women are taught to smile while held at cultural gunpoint. I think repression is the most evil thing in the world. Most chicks buy into it and it's criminal. My biggest pet peeve is walking down the street (hold on, it gets weirder) and some MAN (it's always a fucking man) talks to me with the same tone of voice you'd speak to an infant and says "Smile," or "Give me a smile, pretty lady."

Why? Maybe I'm thinking about the Armenian Genocide, or the kids who had to spend the weekends with Michael Jackson, or those Korean silk flowers with the plastic drops of rain glued on the petals.

My point is, I'm not in your movie. Then again, sometimes the man means well and just wants to share concern and when I feel that vibe, when it has a ring of caring, I do look up and grin.

I am really stupid and going out with Alex on Wednesday. He invited me over to play Scrabble at his neighbors. (I think this is normal peer date activity.)

September 16
To: Amy
From: Mark
Subject: The Tenth Trip is Free

Dear Dr. Amy,

You're good. Really good. I was bracing myself, thinking you'd give me hell for making such a long laundry list then having the giblets to ask for an unfinicky gal. Instead, like the best episodes of Fat Albert, I actually learned something.

Months ago I complained when you started a rant, "you guys..." but this time your aim is true. I see myself in your description of men who look for the nearest fire exit when a woman starts to cry. After getting your e-mail, I picked up my cardboard "Will Work for Good Woman" sign and scratched out the bit about a happy childhood and replaced it with "determined to have a happy/authentic adulthood." You're good.

Okay. Turnabout is fair play, so let's look at your list. One of the biggest differences between our paeans is the tank of gas factor. And yes, I'm talking about Alex. I didn't include it because even though I used to believe that long-distance relationships were for the birds (literally), I've since realized that all the times I comfort someone with my "There are BILLIONS of men on the planet" routine, that number gets cut down by a legion of O's when limited by an area code.

If you're lucky enough to find someone who rocks your world and makes you think, what's a little thing like an airplane to get in the way? Hell, it's practically an elevator ride with peanuts and a magazine. Cleveland's 2500 miles away and after a year of visits you'll have enough mileage saved for that trip to Bora Bora.

Every couple faces hurdles. Religious differences, infertility, clashing in-laws, layoffs. What's a little thing like relocation? If you're in love, how hard could it be for one of you to find a new job in a new city?

And if it takes a year of plane trips and courtships to seal the deal, then: A) that'll be a fucking romantic and sexy year of airport meet-n-greets, teary goodbyes, and beautiful correspondence; and B) you'll still have the rest of your lives to be together under the same roof. See Alex. Get to know Alex. Don't rule out Alex.

And don't forget the leaves of the Asian shrub, chewed as a stimulant or made into a tea. Q-A-T. That'll help you nail his ass on Wednesday.

Love, (8 points)
Mark (12 points)

September 17
To: Mark
From: Amy
Subject: All the Games

Maybe I'm just finding ways to distance myself from him. You know what I'm most afraid of (besides spiders and Anna Nicole Smith's voice)? I'm afraid that I am going to fall for this guy and then he's going to live his life and move.

Or we'll fall in love and he'll ask me to move. I am not going to move, Mark. I have worked so hard for the seemingly minor things that I have accomplished in this town. And I don't want someone to move to pursue me in a new relationship.

I want love to be easier than that, where I have my job and my community and he also has his job and community. I know it's so silly to have all these thoughts before we even play a neighborly game of Scrabble, but I can't break my own heart again.

– A.

P.S. Did you read correctly? It's Cleveland.

P.P.S. What's the weird herbology reference?

September 18
To: Amy
From: Mark
Subject: Needs

Qat is a good Scrabble word to know, as it's a Q without needing U.

So the Q doesn't always need a U. But what exactly is it that U need?

You've complained about not meeting quality men-who-are-really-men in this town. But now you want to hem in your radius. Okay, you're not ready to move now. Nothing wrong with that. But some day you might. Most people do.

For now – and yes, we're getting way ahead of ourselves, but this is about Dating Theory – for now consider that maybe he would move. Is moving for a new job really more acceptable than moving for love?

Moving for love is fine by me. As long as it's not moving for lust in love's clothing. That's why I'm saying if you spend a year of long-distance calls and visits, and you end up developing something solid, then he could come visit for 2 weeks or a month and get a feel for the town, and stay with you and get a feel for cohabitation, and he could check around for possible work, and then you would talk, and if he moved, it would not be this crazy impulsive thing, but a step in the forward direction. And like I said, that's fine by me.

Oh, and you should also know the currency of Poland for tomorrow. The Zloty. Big points.

– M.

September 20
To: Mark
From: Amy
Subject: Being in the moment

Well, we picked our tiles (it was couples Scrabble) and feigned interest in the board. Then we threw the game and went upstairs to his apartment. He put Sammy Davis Jr. on the stereo and we sat on the couch.

He's already half packed, so there were boxes everywhere. He offered me his paper shredder or food dehydrator. I told him I'd take both, so that I can make dried banana linguini and fondly think of him.

It's weird how when you're leaving, when someone is leaving, you don't waste time trying to be cool. We talked for hours about all of our fears, how we made all of these plans and our life wasn't going the way we plotted it out.

I told him about Dark Bill. He told me how the last woman he seriously dated had a daughter and an abusive ex-husband. He told me about how he came to Los Angeles to pursue a career as a film editor and he just couldn't get enough work. He said that he's moving because he has this job waiting with his dad's company in Cleveland. It's a family office supply business.

He's done everything right, studied film, worked hard, and yet his dream just didn't happen, so he's going to go write up account information for notepads about account information. He's sad. I'm sad for him.

This entire year his mother kept calling him from Cleveland saying, "Alex, you've got nothing to offer a woman, come work for your father." He is turning thirty and says he's done struggling (he was substitute teaching). We talked about how it's okay in this culture to be a financially struggling woman but a struggling man is just less attractive.

He admitted to falling for his last girlfriend because he would help her take care of her little girl. He brought over groceries and toys. He had never been a provider before and liked how it felt.

I understood everything he said. He liked feeling like a provider in the same way that I liked feeling like a devious teenager when I was with Bill.

Now all both of us had to do was create relationships that would let us feel those feelings. But he is moving to Cleveland to make money and I'm staying in Los Angeles and buying lingerie.

Talking with him was the easiest thing I've ever done.

About your question, I think moving for a new job is more acceptable than moving for love, because if it doesn't work out, you resent the job. But imagine it not working out and resenting the person? That's my biggest nightmare. Now you know.

I am aware of how pessimistic this sounds. I hardly know him, but I have too many feelings to ignore this. So I'm going to proceed under the umbrella that this is temporary, but that I'd be a fool not to get to know this person. Plus I've always wanted a food dehydrator.

Yours truly,
a.

September 23
To: Amy
From: Mark
Subject: Huddled Masses

Dear Amy,

>About your question, I think moving for a new job is more acceptable than
>moving for love, because if it doesn't work out, you resent the job. But
>imagine it not working out and resenting the person? That's my biggest
>nightmare. Now you know. I am aware of how pessimistic this sounds.

It's not pessimistic, it's chicken. If you make me start sounding like that smiley infomercial guy, "no risk, no reward," or like the meathead in the gym, "no pain, no gain," then I'll be the one doing the resenting. And now I may as well go all the way and jam-pack three clichés into a single paragraph. So here comes #3: 'Tis better to have loved and lost than never to have loved at all. I believe in that as much as I believe in anything.

That said, now it's MY turn for a tale of a half-empty glass (and before the night was through I drank that half, too). Last night I decided to stay home and watch a week's worth of TiVo. But just when I was getting comfortably numb I looked down to see that I had traded my sweats for jeans and boots had been yanked up over my socks, and my throat was still wet with a freshly sprayed hit of cologne. Apparently my body had decided to go out, but hadn't had the courtesy to inform me. So we (me and my sense of obligation to go out on a Saturday night) walked around the corner to James Beach, the friendly neighborhood weekend meat market.

On the walk over, my halves struck a bargain – I agreed to go out on the condition that I didn't have to speak to anyone, that I could just watch everyone else foist their moves.

It just pushed me farther into my shell. The thought of meeting someone new, of having to tell the same stories, to answer the same questions (grew up in Miami Beach... two siblings, both older... no, never married...) to grin and nod and feign interest, it felt overwhelmingly oppressive.

"I originally grew up in..." "My new boss..." "Have you seen the new..." "...been out here now for..." "Mainly we work with..."

I listened to snippets. I counted the number of men wearing hats indoors (didn't their mothers teach them anything?) – nine (seven in stocking caps, two baseball). I noted that three was the prevalent number of women per clique. And that each group of three women seemed to share almost identical height. Almost every guy left shirt untucked (I approve). This was very different than the Hollywood set. Cleavage was rare and made of flesh, not water balloons. Hair was colored naturally and whatever tattoos or piercings might have been out there were safely tucked away (unlike the men's shirts).

A few hours later, the women were drunker, eyes glassy, balance compromised. The men were louder. Someone had a piercing laugh. A bottle of Rolling Rock dropped and broke. At the far end of the bar, a creepy looking scarecrow of a man, German I think, was leaned against a pillar, silently watching all the people. He gave me the willies.

Then it hit me. I might as well have been looking at a full-length mirror. I paid my tab and walked home.

– M.

September 24
To: Mark
From: Amy
Subject: Enough is Enough

Mark this is awful. I thought we were just gonna giggle about dating and not have deep existential surgery. I'm glad you sent yourself home. You may or may not believe me, but right now I am quivering, just hovering over my computer and this tiny little voice is saying "You are so scared of not being loved and not being enough that you will go through all sorts of machinations to drown me out, all the logic in the world won't hush me up, and until you deal with me, you cannot pass."

I am afraid. There, everybody happy? I am afraid of being left and I am afraid of someone sticking around forever who bores me to tears and I am afraid of having to be the one who leaves.

How do I decide that I'm enough? Do I just do it? Just say it three times and click my heels together?

Alex and I have sat on his couch every night this week and I will say this, he is a bit odd for me. He showed me some strange films he made. Cut-out images of his parents superimposed over stock footage of fat chain-smoking tourists in Las Vegas playing nickel slot machines. There is an explosion and war footage and then his father disappears and he plays some Sammy Davis Jr. songs. His dad wanted to be a singer. The movies are sad. I didn't say anything. I can't even think clearly, because he's leaving.

He says that he thinks we're getting married. He says that he's the best thing for me and he hopes I realize that. Soon. Like in 48 hours. I tell him he's insane and that I will not follow through on a long distance relationship.

I can't stop thinking about how my life was with cowboy Jeremy. Everything was always on hold, I was in love with a ghost. Who did I spend the holidays with? Susan. Who did I cry to when I was lonely? Who brought me soup when I was sick? Susan Susan Susan. I will not fall in love with a ghost again. I said these things to Alex. He said he'd fly out with soup for me. Cute, but I'm serious.

The other thing is, the fact that he gave up on his dream is tough, but it's a drag and honestly, it's unattractive. When choosing between a broke guy still supporting his creativity and a stable guy longing for the days when he could make things, I'd take door number one.

This is what Alex and I do – eat take-out Thai food and talk and kiss for hours. I am driving him to the airport in two days. I think I have learned a lot here. As soon as I know what it is I'll send you a memo.

I couldn't be farther from the meat market. I'm at the 'long night of the soul' market. Good thing you took the cue from the German guy and split. A lone dude at a bar is only good in movies. In real life it's just kind of strange.

When Alex leaves, maybe you and I can go to James Beach together and chart the way folks hook up like sand crabs. Just for some laughs. I have a feeling I'm going to need a few.

A.

September 24
To: Amy
From: Mark
Subject: Option C

Ah, the broke guy vs. the stable guy. The bad boy vs. the boring man. Column A or Column B. The answer is always Option C.

I know it's almost impossible to believe. It takes the biggest leap of faith. You know all the party assholes who go through your wallet and medicine cabinet but are stellar in the sack. You see the manicured men with boring cars and respectable jobs and you can almost see a swarm of Zzzz's above their heads.

And the twentysomething girl says I guess I need to settle down but maybe one last joyride before I pick out a burial plan and design my own tombstone.

With C, you get everything. Fun and decency. Pizzazz and respect. There aren't a ton of men like that out there. But they're there. Trust me, Amy, they are.

September 25
To: Amy
From: Mark
Subject: Goodbye Cleveland

Ok. Back to Alex.

You had a very short list of criteria: under a tank of gas, passionate about his work, and I think you liked my item about having a predominantly sunny disposition.

I still believe long-distance (as a temporary state) can work. But not with Alex. Not with a guy who has given up on everything. Not with a guy who is already talking marriage. And most of all – any guy (or girl) who ever says, "I'm the best thing that ever happened to you" is always a pool of problems. Alex is drowning. And I refuse to watch you be his life preserver.

What I say next may make you think I'm only advising this out of my own projected bitterness, but I'm not.

Look at your list. Look at Alex. Look at the landing gear retract as his plane departs. And then don't look back.

Me, I have a moratorium on new people. There's this old Far Side cartoon where a boy raises his hand in the classroom and asks, "May I please be excused? My brain is full."

And that's me. I can't store any more favorite movies, childhood pets, cell phone numbers, birthdays, food allergies. Half the time I can't even remember anyone's name.

But I do miss those warm waves of mutual flirtation. So this week I dusted off my little black book (not literally; I'm not The Fonz) and made a few calls. Called up some old girlfriends, some near, most far. Luckily I'm still good friends with most. In fact, Diana once told me she was on the fence about me when first we met, but when she found out I'd kept good friendships with exes, that was when she decided to let me in.

But this week I wasn't looking for friendship or sex. I wanted to hear "I miss you" from someone who actually did. And I wanted to hear myself say it back. I was willing to listen to stories of new jobs, new boyfriends, family, travels, if at the end of that road there'd be a familiar silence where the two of us could just be, connected by our receivers, conjuring up fractured images of each other, layered memories. Phone love.

I got through to two. And I did get a fix. And like a fix, it didn't fix anything.

That fun night at James Beach you propose? Sign me up. We could both use it.

As long as I don't have to talk to anyone besides you.

Love,
Mark

September 26
To: Mark
From: Amy
Subject: Teevee in my Teepee

Took Alex to the airport. Don't even want to talk about it.

We said 'I love you' to each other. Can that even be possible after two weeks and two buckets of mee krob? And did I mean it, or did I just say it because I was wearing a long coat and it felt appropriate?

Now that he's gone, I think I meant it.

Susan called to tell me that she's fallen in love with a chef named Ed. Ed plays the cello and likes to wear vintage hats.

We had a little catfight, she says I fell out of her life over the past few months and she's tired of putting effort in and not getting it returned. I apologized and then cried a bunch about Alex and my car that needs a new transmission and my stinky job.

Then she told me something really important: "If you need to feel better, just say the word 'wigwam.'"

How can I top that? Wigwam. So now you know.

I tried to melt my brain and watch a lot of tv last night.

There were some great shows on, back to back bio programs (on different channels) about Julia Child, Liza Minnelli and Jenna Jameson. This is what I learned:

1. Marry a creative partner later in life. Work/play on projects together, be yourself.

2. There are always comebacks. Do your own make up.

3. Don't get gang raped when you're sixteen in Montana.

Love always,
A.

P.S. The phone thing is sweet. My weakness is old letters. I dig em up like a pig sniffing truffles and then I just feast on all the luscious declarations of boys gone by.

September 28
To: Amy
From: Mark
Subject: Throw me a line

Dear Amy,

Banner day. About an hour ago, I used my first line. And it flopped. (Bowing to the audience.) Thank you, thank you, you're too kind...

So I hafta ask. Do lines work? I have this hunch that somewhere in your closet you have a Trapper Keeper where you've maintained a collection of Greatest Hits (and Misses) – all the lines men have plied on you over the years. Would you mind cracking it open and sharing some gems? If you like, I can even promise never to use any. I think I learned I'm not the line kinda guy. And coz I know you'll ask, here it is. It wasn't actually a pick-up line, because I used it on a very old friend. It was a "Pretty PLEASE help me end a month of celibacy" line.

She's a fairly famous pop phenomenon now, with an unusual first name, so I'm going to refer to her as "Foxy," since that's what I usually call her. I've known her from way back in the day. She had a thing for me when I was spoken for. By the time that ended, Foxy was taken. By the time that ended, I was with Diana. And when that ended, Foxy and I were both single for the first time. But by that point we'd managed to develop a great friendship that's lasted almost eight years. So when I made overtures, Foxy gave me the "wouldn't want to risk ruining the friendship" speech. Damn.

The thing is, she lives 11 blocks away and yet we haven't seen each other in almost a full year. We've made sporadic attempts, but one of us is always busy. So about an hour ago I call her up, and here was my line, "Hey, Foxy, I've been thinking. And I realized that we can finally get it on! Since we never see each other anymore, I figure even if the sex ruins our friendship, it'll be no big loss!"

The good news is she laughed, and didn't take offense. And you already know the bad news.

Enough about me and my pathetic attempts. Tell me about other men's stupidity. Please.

Hungry for dirt,
Mark

September 30
To: Mark
From: Amy
Subject: Re: Lines

Hold on. I have to get my Trapper Keepers...

September 30
To: Mark
From: Amy
Subject: Line

Okay, one time in college (when I was spending an embarrassing amount of time drinking diet coke, sunbathing and stairmastering in the name of 'health') I was at the local frozen chemical fluff disgusting yogurt store off campus. While trying to enjoy my aspartame and convince myself that it really didn't taste like ant poison, a gentleman came up to my table and said, "You have really nice eyes."

Fine. That in and of itself is not a horrendous line, but if you're hitting on a woman in sweaty post-aerobic spandex at a yogurt store most well known for its negative caloric air pockets, then say "You have really nice thighs." Know your audience. And always flip it around, give us some originality.

Oh sure, the eyes thing is safe, but if he would've complimented my thighs, given my teeny tiny self-esteem at that point in my life, well, the gentleman may have gotten himself a sample of something that didn't taste vaguely like ant poison.

I once went to a party and a man approached me, blithering drunk and lower jaw hardly attached and said, "One of these days, I'm going to be a normal guy and you're going to be a normal girl, and then I'm going to ask you out on a date." He did and I went. I'm not sure who's stupid in that one.

A friend I was not attracted to finally got the nerve up to ask me out at a bar and he said, "I think you and I should give it a shot. You're a good girl. You've got moxie."

I told him, "I went to the free clinic and I don't have that." He gave me a blank look. We did not date.

I still think Bill's "I don't want to be your friend" ranks as either the stupidest or the greatest, I'm not sure which.

Then there was the man in New York who told me that when I wore a ski hat I looked like a small Mexican boy and he thought it was adorable.

Ohhhhh what about the guy who on our first date took me to karaoke and sang David Bowie's China Girl to me but then started improvising and singing "don't talk when I fuck you" directly at me. How bout that for a line? Is that a line?

An Irish guy I dated used to call me "his little distillery."

A tall red-haired man came up to me at the gym and said, "You're very sexy, would you like to go running in the sand with me? I know some great dunes. We could go now." It was Saturday night at ten o'clock. "No" I said, "I have a boyfriend, but thank you." Then he scowled and watched me for the next thirty minutes. I left and asked a gym employee to walk me to my car.

At Trader Joe's an Eastern European man looked in my basket and said, "You American girl is good. No eat fast food." I smiled and he said "Your teeth good, good teeth, good nails." I thought he was about to pull up my lip and gum me like a calf. "I bet you good other places?" Then it was gross.

A boy wrote me a note in college and it said, "Why don't you tell me some deep dark neon pink secret that's lying inside the pit of your soul. Or maybe just some small talk. I've got a secret, you're beautiful. Just thought you needed to be told it." Dammit Kip, where are you now?

An old boyfriend called and after a nice chat he said, "Look at me, I am missing yesterday." I guess I don't think that's stupid at all. I miss it too.

And one of my all-time favorites, "You have very dangerous curves." Jeremy whispered it in my ear in the first night we met. It progressed, the whispering, and after a few months he was doing it in Spanish.

A.

P.S. Do girls give you lines?

September 30
To: Amy
From: Mark
Subject: Whatever

Don't know if it was intentional, but that e-mail made me feel better about myself. I don't think I could ever say goofy shit like that to strangers.

I'm tired all the time. Work seems stupid. Lines seem stupid. I'm thinking about taking Dean up on his offer and heading out of town. I need a change.

If a girl's ever used a line on me, I didn't notice. Just seemed like some friendly person talking to me. I could use a good coma around now.

Yawn,
Mark

October 3
To: Amy
From: Mark
Subject: Where there's smoke, there's burning crosses...

Dear Amy,

In the span of the few short days since last I wrote, I've had a brief affair. An affair to forget. In fact, I've almost forgotten.

I was drinking in a corner booth at Jones. I don't like sitting at the bar – I feel nervous having my back exposed. I bought an order of calamari so they'd give me a table. This also gave me front row seats to a delightful redhead two tables over, also drinking alone. She had a slinky gold dress, lovely bare arms, and I figured she was waiting for someone. We exchanged five or six furtive glances.

When I got up to go to the side smoking room, she followed and bummed a cigarette then asked if I'd take a picture of her with her cell phone so she could put it on her website. "I have a few fans who love Nat Shermans."

I was baffled.

Turns out she's a smoking fetish model. (See earlier e-mail in which I proposed that there is a fetish for every noun in the dictionary.) Apparently there are men who get off on watching women smoke. They don't have to be nude or giving the old Lewinsky to a cigar. No, just normal smoking. These guys collect candid photos of women taking breaks on benches. Or freeze frames from movies with Sharon Stone. I was fascinated, I have to admit. She said some guys are so specific they only like certain brands, or cork filters, or watching women french inhale. I didn't want to be rude but I asked if she can support herself with this. She laughed and said I'd be surprised. There are magazines, videos, and her mainstay – the website.

She drank her next few Cosmos (apparently some people still drink them) at my table in the corner where we talked and flirted. I was kind of drunk and I impetuously leaned in to kiss her. She rebuffed me. And then smiled. And then surprised me. The bar is called Jones so what she reached for next was somehow apt as she vanished under the table. I'd seen this in movies but had no idea people actually do it.

By the time she came up for air – I had my eyes closed to avoid getting paranoid about who might be on to us – I didn't imagine she'd have more ammo in her bag of tricks but she did.

"Ooh. My roommate is going to love you." Her next sentence included the pronoun "she" and I relaxed a bit, then my heart started racing and I wondered if this whole thing were a joke and I was about to get Punk'd.

She gave me her number and vanished into the night. I drank coffee and ate bread for another hour until I felt ok to drive home.

I called the next day and she asked how soon I could be available, if I was free for lunch. I wasn't, but said I was anyway and cancelled an appointment, then met her a few blocks from her house at Koo Koo Roo. (Her call, not mine.)

She was dressed demurely in the daylight but still looked ravishing. Sober, her bearing had changed – instead of brashly forward, she was now familiar and warm, sincere. She told me about her childhood in a trailer park in Utah. Her story about the restraining order against her stepfather was as old as creation, but still I found it moving.

And then she paid me one of the highest compliments anyone can pay – she said, "Mark, I have to tell you, I meet people in this town all the time, but I never feel like I can be myself. There's something about you – you just seem so non-judgmental – you're the first person I've met in years I feel I can just be myself around." Wow. That is high praise. And I felt I deserved it, too, because I did look upon her warmly in the clear-headed light of day, and wasn't judging her at all.

And that's when it happened. That's when she shifted, and started being herself. And "being herself" meant this: opening her mouth and unleashing the most unmitigated torrent of racist bullshit about the women she works with (at her telemarketing job), how "they" smell, and, oh jesus, forget it, I'm not going to type any more of what she spewed even if it is all in quotation marks.

I lied and said that my phone was set on vibrate, then "answered" it and reported that I had to get back to the office and left in under a minute.

One hand on the steering wheel, I deleted her number from my phone with the other.

I had a nice few weeks of solitude going, and I broke it for **THIS**!?

I think I'm going to move to Cleveland.

– M.

October 5
To: Mark
From: Amy
Subject: Not o.k.k.kay

Woof. You and me boy are in the crapper. You've got some smoky bitch in a pointy white hat and Alex is visiting in a couple of weeks.

Again, first date theory applies. You meet at a bar in Hollywood when she asks you to take a picture of her and explains how she makes a living tonguing tobacco.

I am impressed. You stifled your hormones and didn't peel the foil wrapper after she exposed her ding dong self. You said she was very attractive. I think most men will slut around with a hottie despite her political affiliations. For a minute or two at least.

I'll admit to something. The Irish guy I dated? He was terribly handsome and sculpted metal things (he's the one who called me 'the distillery'). He threw a few slurs out at a Mexican restaurant one night and I tried to block it out. I knew, deep down, I knew that I would never be able to love someone who has this elitist world view. It was alive in him, you could feel it (maybe that's why I drank so much).

Anyway, it was brief, but I tried to make it go away. I tried really hard (that's embarrassing but it's true). It doesn't go away. A week before this incident while talking about relationships he said, "He who loves least loves best" (more exceptional world views). On the night of the slurs, I asked him why he broke up with his previous girlfriend of seven years and he looked me dead in the eye and said, "I turned and looked at her one night when she was sleeping and do you know what I saw?" (I wondered, did he see the woman who would wipe the drool off his face in the nursing home? Did he see himself next to her at their vacation home on Nantucket? Maybe he saw her the way she looked the first moment they met when they were still just beautiful strangers...)

"I saw cellulite."

We had dated for about a month before all these things came out. At one point he announced that he wanted me to grow my fingernails long and paint them. I told him I didn't like impractical vanity and the crud that gets underneath, which is another reason we never had sex, cause he refused to wear a condom. Plus he was uncircumcised.

No sleeping with bigots. We have successfully created one tenet we can live by, Mark.

Alex is visiting in two weeks. He says it's to see old friends. I don't buy it. Hate to sound like I think I'm the top banana here, but I think I'm the top banana here. I told him we could have coffee. What a joke. We'll be all over each other like a bad metallic dress.

Always,
a.

P.S. How long has it been since you've had sex?

October 6
To: Amy
From: Mark
Subject: Stag Partings

By Clintonian reckoning, it's been about a month and a half. I'm not missing it at all. I store sex like a camel. Why do you ask?

How old were you when you dated the angry Irish dude? I'm starting to worry about these guys as a whole. You described Alex, Bill and Mike as really sad people at various points. Your menagerie seems to have a lot of Sad, the occasional Angry, and when the maid comes in to dust this cabinet of curiosities, she really should also sweep out all the Aloof and the Ambivalent.

How do these guys even rate a date with you? If they're persistent enough and show sufficient interest, is that enough to get through your door?

If so, that's just sad and wrong. And I'm not talking about your pants. I'm talking about something far more valuable: your time.

You need to hire a bouncer. (I have one in mind...)

Tomorrow night's that monthly dinner party with my friends where the guys do all the cooking. I skipped last month, and am bowing out of tomorrow's as well. Too demoralizing to show up stag. Dean was cool about it, said he'd go stag, too, in solidarity. But I can't do that to him. They all say they miss my cooking. Just can't do the big room of couples thing right now. Is that ok?

Always,
Your Sparky

October 10
To: Mark
From: Amy
Subject: This is what it sounds like when the doves cry

Darling, do not think twice about the couples thing. Don't go. There are weekends when I can't even go to breakfast joints around town because of all the occupied two-tops who so clearly just fell out of bed and into the French toast, the same ones who are now spoon-feeding each other. It fucking kills me. Rips my guts out. I wanna be them.

The thing about the Irish guy was that he wasn't angry at all, he was grinning and articulate and adorable the whole time, until three weeks into it, when those things came out of his mouth like slugs (and he grinned while saying them with a little wink wink nudge nudge). I was 22 and dazzled by his wit and Mick Jagger lips (he was witty in other moments I promise) and we only dated for a month.

If I was in a court of law I would use "the aspartame defense." I may have incurred some temporary brain malfunctioning as a result of high-impact aerobics and the abuse of little blue packets.

Men don't walk into my life with badges declaring themselves maudlin grumps. They swagger in smiling and handsome, with all their secrets sewn into the seams of their pants. I walk in looking for the good and hoping the other person is doing the same, then we expose ourselves and moves are made accordingly.

Here are my thoughts –

Dark Bill was going through a midlife crisis. It happens.

Supermarket Mike I'm just making assumptions about. We don't know any facts about him except that he makes sci-fi shows and that he eats.

Alex, ahhhh, lovely Alex... Alex is in transition, listen if I was moving home right now to work for my father I'd be no peach. Don't you relate to him at all?

Okay, fine so you're a successful art consultant and can afford a night out at The Buffalo Club or the Little Door's vintage champagne, but what if you didn't have that job, and you really wanted to be an art consultant but had to work at the Souplantation and on that salary you couldn't even afford to take girls to the Souplantation. Would you take an opportunity to leave Los Angeles for a well-paying job?

This is a tough town honey, for men and women, and self-esteem is a hot commodity wherever you go. I'm not equating money with self-esteem, I'm equating a job that uses your skills and makes you feel proud (money is a natural by-product).

I think Alex's had been eroded. He is going to be fine, he's just sorting things out, and sorting is not always a happy process. You have to figure out what to do with the mismatched socks, then you have that red t-shirt that always bleeds into the whites and the gabardine slacks you have to dry clean, sometimes it's enough to make you wanna throw the whole load in and walk around town dressed in shrunken pink oompa loompa garb. I think Alex had thrown the towel in and is in the process of pulling it out.

How do they rate a date with me? They are funny and real and handsome. They come up to me at parties and say something that I find interesting, then they have strong veiny arms and have big full lips and I look at those and say, 'okay.' A few weeks go by and I see their victim side or their elitist side or their Eeyore side. And they see whatever side of me is icky and we stop dating.

The other thing your e-mail made me realize, it's not the sad guys that hurt you, so maybe that's why I've chosen them the last few times. They are just a steady buzz of oppression. It's the happy ones that sting. Lance never felt bad. And Jeremy was the portrait of fearless mirth. He'd take out the garbage and be whistling, it was like dating a male Snow White. It seems pretty obvious to me that these guys were happy because they were doing what they wanted with their lives.

Which brings me back to my criteria, someone happy about their job. I think it's that important, there's a shitload of self-esteem riding on that. Me want boy with good self-esteem. Maybe it has nothing to do with a job, maybe it's just a deep inner sense of self-worth. It's passion, and it's an underlying belief that you are in the right place doing the right thing.

You are officially the new bouncer. As my bouncer, when Alex comes to visit this weekend does he get into the VIP room?

Alex and I have been on the phone a lot. He hates Cleveland and has no idea what to do with all of his new office supplies.

You're the best,
A.

October 13
To: Amy
From: Mark
Subject: Still Crazy

I met my old lover on the street last night...

I was on Robertson, coming out of Storyopolis, looking in vain for an Uncle Wiggly book to give to my nephew. Less than ten yards away, coming out of the Newsroom Café, I see her.

Time stopped. All other faces, the passing cars, the trees in the courtyard, everything and everyone receded into a blur. But crisply in focus was Diana. I'd recognize her anywhere, even where least expected, since I thought she was living in London now.

She is. She smiled when she saw me, and she told me about her flat and her embrace was warm, and she didn't answer at first when I asked what she was doing in L.A. She said I looked good and I said the same, knowing it was the understatement of the century.

We were walking down the sidewalk, and I can't remember how much time passed, I remember thinking I needed to show her how well I was doing, I mentioned a few big deals I'd closed in the last few months, fitting this into conversation as non-sequiturs as I strove to make an impression. But she put her hand on my cheek and said how happy she was to see me, and my pretence melted, and all of a sudden it felt like a genuine moment. Better than that, it felt normal.

And then a car pulled up and she excused herself, she was on her way back to the hotel and flying out that night. Gently, she broke it to me she was here with her boyfriend, a South African producer she met in London who had business in Hollywood this past week. Somehow the way she said it she made me feel safe.

She apologized for not calling sooner, saying it was just a quick trip, and promising she'd call when she was back home. When she got into the car I wanted to duck my head down to see the face of the driver. All I saw were his hands. He wore gloves.

I don't remember driving home, but somehow I did. I couldn't stop seeing her face and hearing her refer to her new place as "home."

I made myself some dinner and listened to NPR. Went out to the movies with friends as planned. And all was right in the world.

Amy, I did it. Weathered the storm.

In line at the movies I said, "Hey, I ran into Diana today. She looks good, seems well." And my friends smiled at me. They could see I'd found some peace.

The air smells good today. I think it's going to rain.

Love,
Mark

October 15
To: Mark
From: Amy
Subject: What the Bleep?!!

Holy shit on an Agnes B. shingle – you ran into Diana on Robertson!!! The good news is you didn't crumble when she told you about the new serious boyfriend. Not because you had to put on a show for her but because it means that you really are over her. (You are only 'over' the person when you don't have to say 'I'm over the person.') Look out ladies, I think we've finally got Mark running on four cylinders.

Alex gave me a magazine subscription to 'Cleveland Monthly.' I asked him if he felt like being objectified this weekend, because that's all it would be. He said absolutely. I think it will be fine.

Last night I checked my answering machine from work and heard a frustrated flower delivery person at the gate. I froze and wondered if it was Dark Bill or Alex. I decided it was Alex. There were flowers on my doorstep fit for an opera singer, Miss America, Mariah Carey or... me? Spilling orchids and lupine and foxgloves, they all made it clear why these women turn into such haughty divas. When one is presented with a lactating garden of exotica, one feels positively royal. The card said "I find you charming. Thanks for spending your time with me. A."

My manager, Idina, came out of her apartment and said I should marry him (she also drinks a lot of bourbon and used to be a nun).

Susan is spending all her time with Chef Ed, my brother is moving in with the banker girl, and Shelley is going to marry Melissa in Hawaii. My single friends are folding like lawn chairs.

I don't know what to be for Halloween this year. Maybe I'll just wear the happy mask I've been wearing to work all week. Are you going to go out? All the girls will be 'in costume' i.e. naked. Hey I know, I'll wear my high school cheerleading outfit, carry a pack of Bartles and James wine coolers and be 'Glory Days.'

I'll cheer up soon. It's just, well, all this e-introspection.

xoxo
a.

October 15
To: Amy
From: Mark
Subject: Taking Stock

It's so funny you'd write me about e-introspection. I'd just poured myself a tall glass of grapefruit juice, ready to sit down and write you a reflective e-mail. Right before I fell asleep last night I remembered that it wasn't so long ago I was really pissed at Diana for having "caused" all this. (Yeah, I know, I also blamed you. And the crazy Italian neighbors. And the FDA, and anyone else who crossed my path.)

Today I woke up grateful that Diana caused all this. If it hadn't been for her swift egress, I'd never have learned that it's important for two people to clearly state their bottom-line goals. I'd never have learned that perfection on paper means less than damp twigs when sparks don't catch. I wouldn't have had these incredible adventures with alpacas and bigots and laundry (oh my!). And, most of all, scarecrow, I would never have met you, because I wouldn't have been at the singles table.

On a day like today I can't imagine being mad at anyone. Not at Addie (just being herself), not at Diana (who I've always thought simply deserves the best), not at Katya (who I pray is under medical supervision). And not at myself – who has stumbled and blundered and barked up wrong trees and given too much too soon and chased when I should have introspected and moped when I should have danced. Naah, not too shabby, the kid's done ok.

Ditto you and your own bad self. Sure you're about to get hurt again by Alex. It's in the cards (read carefully between the lines on that little one with the flowers). But it doesn't matter what I say. It will unfold how it unfolds, and all the while our single friends will continue to fall by the marital wayside, but so what. No need to rush anymore.

Maybe that's what I'll wear for Halloween. I'll go as a Slow Hand. And you can come with me, all dressed up like one of the Pointer Sisters (I vote for Issa).

Like the Right Rev Al Green says –

Love and Happiness,
M.

October 22
To: Mark
From: Amy
Subject: Time After Timing

Oh I hope some of your evolved world view rubs off on me. Right now I'm just tired and sore from kicking myself. Short version –

Alex came into town on Friday and we met for coffee at noon. He was sitting at a table wearing a suit with an espresso and a bouquet. Storybook guy. Anyway, he said he had a surprise and we got in his big Lincoln Rent-a-Town-Car and drove to Plummer Park.

I once told him I enjoy raw food so he pulled out a picnic of seedy organic treats and we enjoyed watching the Russian senior citizens play chess while drinking vodka out of paper bags. We stayed until almost dark when the transvestites showed up and began fighting over a shard of rusty mirror. Ah, romance.

I tried to make it clear without being too bossy that we were having a weekend affair, I wanted to tell him that even though the feelings would be great, it wouldn't be real. And that we could just enjoy it. Like a massage or a salesperson complimenting you, it would feel great, but it wouldn't really be real. I think what came out of my mouth was "We're not doing this again you know."

After lunch (and checking in with his father about some missing case of plastic rulers) he announced that he couldn't get a hold of his friend Scott so he "didn't really have a place to stay." I hated him. At the same time I felt responsible, at the same time I wanted him to hold me all night and never go away. (Oh God that's embarrassing to admit.)

Cut to Saturday morning – I forgot about promising my parents I would come over. The phone rings at eight; it's my mother. Alex listened while I talked in circles and then he wrote me a note that said, "We should just go, it would be fun."

My mother was jubilant. A real live man! In her house! With her daughter! She pulled me by my ear into the kitchen and said, "He is wonderful, look at the way he looks at you, he loves you. Couldn't you just like a nice person for once?" Then we ate smoked salmon sandwiches, heard about her latest head cold and left.

I thought the whole weekend was a success. Sure I'd cry my eyes out when he drove off to the airport but so what. Viva the handsome Cleveland Stranger. I was really impressed with the whole thing. Until Sunday.

"Alex, this weekend was great. Thanks for everything. I just want to be clear about what's going to happen here. It's hard for me to go back and forth with people. You have to start your life in Cleveland. And well. I live here." I was hiding behind geography.

"What are you saying?"

"I'm saying I can't do this again."

He looked at me like I had just called him a dirty name.

"You 'can't do this again'? I am not afraid of my feelings and I am in love with you. Tell me you're not in love with me. Tell me you don't have the same feelings!"

Whoa, now this is the worst torture ever, when a person MAKES you tell them you don't love them.

"I uhhm. I don't have the same feelings."

"You take me to your parents' house! Do you have any idea what that says to me?"

"It says I need to schedule visits with my parents Monday through Friday?" I didn't say that. I apologized for a long time. I didn't mean to send him mixed signals. I didn't Mark, I really didn't.

"You are an emotional al qaeda."

He hates me. I hate me. I was playing along, and I felt all in love and everything, but it was because I knew it was going to expire, first in two weeks, then in two days. From what I know about Alex I think we could be best friends, but not mates. That's what my gut says.

Sometimes I think all relationships are about timing.

I can't stop crying.

October 24
To: Amy
From: Mark
Subject: Evolution

Yes, you did send him mixed signals. But not about the parental visit. He invited himself, remember? That little note he jotted? He has foisted himself on you, and you've let him do so, even though he's far away, even though he's not passionate about his work, even though he tells you how you should feel about him, even though you have been acting just like that asshole from the Buffalo Club who told you from the get-go you'd only last a few months.

Yes, you should have known better. Yes, you could have made this easier on both of you. But no, it's not all your fault. He's flailing, as I said before, flailing in his failings, and you've let him cling to your buoys [insert boob joke].

My point isn't that I told you so. My point is that you told you so. Why bother making a list of criteria if you were going to toss it so swiftly out the jalopy window?

That wasn't rhetorical, and I'll answer it for you. You tossed your lists coz you went back into the man-muck too fast on the heels of Lance. You were sky-high over Lance. So stands to reason that Lance's baked meats have coldly furnished forth a depressing banquet of dark meat (Bill) and lily-white (Alex).

--

Ok, I'm back. It took me a while to find it, but I just found an old e-mail you sent me about Lance. Here's what you wrote – tell me if it reminds you of anyone, ok? (I'll give you a hint. There are two right answers...)

>He's had a girlfriend since he was ten, like for the last twenty years he's
>been in a relationship. I think that's sissy. You've got to have some time
>alone. How else do you get any perspective? What I am saying is, he was
>talking about children and vacation homes two weeks into it. He's one
>of those people in love with love, the idea of it. Like maybe I didn't
>even matter I just came around the corner after sink picture girl.

You have got to have some time alone.

Ok, my turn, all about me now, ok?

True to her word, Diana called from London. It was nice. No forward passes. No rear-windowing. Just caught up. Thing is, she kept saying, "Mark, you sound different." And I'd press her to be more specific. "I don't know. Just different."

Amy, you've seen more of me this year than she has (seen my viscera splattered across your screen, that is) – so you tell me:

Do I sound different than I did when we met almost a year ago?

Sometimes I think I've changed, and sometimes I think I still sound the same as the 12-yr-old boy getting ceremonially high in Fiji.

Much love,
Mark

P.S. I said I'd give you advance notice – I'll be in NYC for the next few days. Have to bid on some stuff for a few clients at auction. Not as glamorous as it sounds. In fact it's funny you assumed I make a lot in this job. I don't. Ask the Student Loan people. I'm bidding on stuff with other people's money. No matter how hallowed the halls in which I work, ultimately I'm still the hired help.

October 25
To: Mark
From: Amy
Subject: Inspiration Points

You are different Mark. It's like you stopped needing the relationship Band-Aid. Diana felt that, and it's an attractive quality.

Yeah. Alone time. Groovy. I'll do all those things the self-improvement books suggest, you know, organize my closet, decoupage, handle correspondence.

Wait, I think I've mastered correspondence. Maybe I'll take up Frisbee golf.

October 26
To: Mark
From: Amy
Subject: Blech

Just went out to get the mail.

I hate nothing more than Cleveland Monthly.

October 26
To: Mark
From: Amy
Subject: Love Letters

I take it back. More than Cleveland Monthly, I hate getting packages of office supplies. Alex mailed me an envelope full of notepads and then on the top sheet wrote, "This is not an invitation into my life, I just thought you were out of paper."

At one o'clock he left a message suggesting that he come visit next weekend. It's like he didn't hear our last conversation.

At three o'clock he sent me an e-mail detailing his most recent sexual encounter with some secretary who has a crush on him. It was so graphic and disgusting. He describes her pubic hair for an entire paragraph.

Honestly Mark, trust that it was a blink away from a Penthouse Forum letter. Then he started dissecting my relationship with my father, calling it "a dance of childish hero worship." He signed it saying that he was still in love with me and there is nothing I can do about that.

At five o'clock he sent me an e-mail saying he was coming to town next weekend, to "see some friends" and "did I want to get together?" I cannot believe this is happening. I have to deal with this, pronto.

October 26
To: Mark
From: Amy
Subject: Flying, crashing, burning

Okay, I think you are flying right now. I am flying right now. Shit I need your help. I gotta move on this. I need to terminate. Roto-Rooter style. Flush it down the drain. I need to respond now or I will not sleep tonight. I refuse to give mixed signals again. Oh cripes I am so wound up. Please sign off on this as the proper way of handling the situation. This is what I'm writing him...

> Dear Alex,
>
> I will not see you this weekend. I need to take care of myself and I don't think us getting together is part of that equation. My apologies for the lack of elegance (and previous jokes about objectification) but I'm really trying to be honest with myself and those around me these days. Best of luck with the office supplies and film work.
>
> Amy

What I really wanted to write...

> What kind of a stupid dick sandwich do you have jammed in your ear? Get a fucking life dude. Don't come to LA in some half-assed whiny attempt to eat In-n-Out burgers and become a barnacle on my apartment. That is fucking lame. And that letter with your sexual conquests in giant descriptive detail, here's a tip buddy, that's locker room poetry and not real seductive. I am now saying goodbye. Forever. Unless we are like at a car wash or something in Anaheim and you are visiting Disneyland and I am getting gas on the way to go pray at the altar of my parents' house. You are a freaking weirdo. Peace out. Good luck with your family, your therapy, and the rotting sense of robotism you are living in (which is why you get so repressed and weird). Later.
>
> P.S. Thanks for the fun times. There were some.

Too harsh?

A.

October 27
To: Amy
From: Mark
Subject: kwik

Am on the plane – this costs a fortune so forgive brevity – yes, am flying back a day late – will debrief in full when I get home. Go with the 1st letter, but I'm glad you sent me #2. It's ALWAYS good to get #2 out of your system. But don't send it.

Also, delete the "apology" sentence from #1. You don't owe him anything. And referring to objectification reminds him of your attraction to him and is a way your subconscious is trying to keep a door open. Mistrust this impulse. Delete it.

In case you're wondering, #2 only translates to, "I am still incredibly passionate about you – if you weren't deeply in my thoughts, I'd never have such strong emotions to express to you."

Be strong, simple and clear. No apologies. No regrets. Wishing him well is nice. Oh, and Alex finally did something to impress me. I don't think I could write a whole paragraph about bush. How much can one say?

This cost me $11.00. You owe me a Coke (in Tokyo).

October 27
To: Amy
From: Mark
Subject: Whoops, I did it again...

What is it with me and airports? As I was boarding the plane, I noticed an adorable woman in line next to me. We smiled but were quickly waved aboard. I looked at my ticket then squinted to make out her seat assignment. Would the Gods put us next to each other? I get so bored on that x-country flight. She seemed sweet. Maybe the plane would be empty and I could switch seats. We went up the same aisle, and then... she abruptly stopped at row 26, aisle seat. Me, I was in 28, opposite aisle two rows back. And the plane: bursting at the seams. Damn.

Something about that smile of hers got me in a punchy mood. Almost giggling, I wrote her a note and asked the stewardess to pass it. A few minutes later I got one back. Her name: Stephanie. The next note I sent was written on the back of an ad for magnetic shoe pads. Her next came scrawled on one for calf-high support stockings. We were working our way up.

When we'd exhausted the snake oil medical items from the in-flight catalog, I sent her the crossword puzzle, but I'd created my own clues and penned in the answers. Her next note wasn't a note – she bought me a drink (a rum-and-coke, not my usual, but how could I refuse?). The stewardess was an excellent sport.

I was remembering your silent date with Ted, and smiling as I grew more excited. And then came the blow. "Only 34 minutes," she'd inscribed on an air-sickness bag. She was getting off in Denver.

There was a pause before my next response, and she craned her head back to see if I were asleep or in the can. From the look on my face she could tell: I was in for the long haul to LAX. She sent me another rum-and-coke and asked how I'd feel about a layover.

Layover. What a word.

Turns out for $75 they let me change my ticket. Turns out she drives a grey Honda Civic upholstered in cat hair. Turns out Stephanie is a salesgirl at a department store. Turns out that when our conversation was stretched out to spoken whole sentences instead of written bits and scraps, my eyelids grew considerably heavy.

At least this lesson cost $75, not $100. (Lesson#418 stroke B: a cute smile is never enough.)

I was ready to head back to L.A. but had to weather one night in her parents' home (where she lives; they were away).

Her room hadn't changed since she was 13. Her bed was dominated by a giant rainbow pillow. Her favorite song is Genie in a Bottle. She offered me a SlimFast shake.

The living room windowsills were littered with the bodies of a dozen fat flies. They died a valiant death, attempting escape.

She asked if I wanted to watch a movie and I said yes, grateful for a two-hour reprieve in having to converse. I chose Clueless. Seemed apt. The tape wouldn't go in. "Oh that's right, I had to watch this," she said as she ejected a video and put it back in a case labeled "SCARVES."

Seems they give her training videos at work. This one is supposed to teach her many different ways of tying a scarf. It's supposed to help her sell not only scarves, but also more suits to business ladies.

I asked if it teaches the one where you use a really long scarf but leave a big hole in the middle – it's called the Isadora Duncan Donut. She said, "No, that one's not on there." Whoosh.

We watched the movie and she ate diet popcorn (why oh why is there such a thing as diet popcorn?). When she went to the bathroom, I seized the opportunity to go to sleep on the couch before she could offer me my choice of accommodations.

She woke me up in the morning with a glass of Crystal Light and an English muffin. I had about an hour before I had to leave for the airport to catch my flight. She sat down on the sofa next to me, wearing a fluffy lavender terry cloth robe, and she took my hand.

"Is there anything you want?"

"What do you mean?" I asked.

She looked away, then smiled and said, "You can have anything you want, you know."

"Anything?"

"Um, uh huh. Anything."

I sat up slightly on the sofa. "Are you sure? Anything?" She nodded.

"Then I want the Scarves video."

She was too confused to be hurt, and stammered something about how it wasn't hers, she had to return it to work.

"Then you shouldn't have offered."

"Isn't there anything else?"

"No. I want the Scarves video."

"Are you sure?"

"You said anything."

So, Amy, if you like, when you meet me for people-watching at James Beach, I'm happy to show you the side-knot or the windsor-twist or the chrysanthemum.

If Addie were around, I'd give it to her to enshrine with her bowling spray. But then again, I'm glad she's not.

Maybe Diana was right. Maybe everyone would have been better off if I'd spent this past year on the Island of Beautiful Women, or in a coma.

Cheers,
Your Frequent Flyer

October 30
To: Mark
From: Amy
Subject: Scarf Noose

Idina just asked me what I was howling about. I could not explain to her that my friend Mark had accidentally followed a full-grown mall rat off a plane, spent the night at her parents' house and then scammed her out of her scarf video, so I said, "Men in general."

That's one of the best stories I've ever heard. Did you even get excited in the pre-teen paraphernalia room? Tell me she had a canopy bed. I have one at my mother's house and every time I spend the night I feel like I'm sleeping under a Maxi Pad.

Environments are important. When I was in college I tried to make out with a guy whose room was wallpapered in Kathy Ireland posters, Kathy in a yellow bikini, Kathy in funny football gear with greasepaint under her eyes, Kathy in camping socks, it was awful. I don't imagine you have the same issue with the rainbow pillow that I did with Kathy, but it's a killer nonetheless.

I'm going to a Halloween party tomorrow night in Silver Lake with Susan and Ed. They are very sweet and trying to include me in the costume. So I'm going as Lisa Marie, Ed is going to be Elvis and Susan is Priscilla. I have to find some liquid eyeliner.

SO glad you are back. You were working in New York right?

xoxo

– a.

P.S. There is diet popcorn for the same reason there are flocked Christmas trees. Some people just like to pretend.

P.P.S. I am going to make you tie a scarf on top of my jeans around my thigh, Chachi Arcola style, only mine is going to be in the shape of the chrysanthemum. We'll see who's doing the people-watching and who's being watched (I mean with accessories like that...).

October 31
To: Amy
From: Mark
Subject: Pinky

I'm so pleased that my dead-end dalliance brought you a chuckle and momentarily tore Idina away from her bourbon and beef. I will tie one on for you any which way you like. But in my eye you are much more Pinky Tuscadero than Chachi. (And I have already been self-branded Ralph. Shit. I don't want to be Malph. Can we start over? This time I want to be the shoe. No, the thimble! Please!?)

I'm in an unfathomably happy mood today. Just got off the phone with Dean. We're going to meet up in your neck of the woods – West Hollywood – to watch the Halloween Parade.

Anyway, doll face, just have a great time tonight. I hope it's a great release with all your pals. And NO SINGING HEARTBREAK HOTEL!

Whoop, that's his MG honking, gotta fly. Two slaps on my thigh, then a finger snap, then a point –

Your little sister,
Leather

November 2
To: Mark
From: Amy
Subject: Trick or Trick

Hi –

I did my best Lisa Marie, stuffed bra, slick make-up, kind of eighties black shirt with shoulder pads. Susan looked really good in her black bouff wig and mini-dress (she was like, Priscilla in her twenties) and Ed went for the Depressing Elvis, but I think he was just happy to work his love handles into the costume.

Always the chef, he insisted on carrying a fried peanut butter banana sandwich. We'd only been there five minutes when he dripped Skippy on my blouse. I went into the kitchen to get a napkin and there, getting a beer out of the refrigerator, was a very familiar boy in a bolo tie.

"Who are you supposed to be?" I asked.

"The Sundance Kid," said Lance.

"Hmmm. Who's your Butch?" and out of the bathroom comes, no, not the Swiss Family Karen, but a new one, a beautiful Latin woman, wearing the requisite slutty Snow White costume from Trashy Lingerie. Yellow miniskirt, white thigh-highs, blue bustier. She looked at Lance and then walked into the other room.

"Your hair looks good," he said.

My hair? My HAIR? I could write a monologue about your balls and you're talking about my hair?

"Thanks. So... how's your mom?"

"She's fine. How's yours?"

"Fine. Line dancing." Huge awkward silence.

"So you look really good," he says.

WHY can he only comment about how I look? Why can't he just apologize, be normal, or be real or something. I mean, jesus, acknowledge our shared past already, some sort of admission that we once cared for each other, that we were fallible human beings.

"It's nice to see you Lance."

And then Snow White's breasts popped back in and I said something like "Have fun, don't eat too much candy." And walked away.

For the rest of the night I tried to channel Lisa Marie. I mean if you're Elvis' daughter you know how to handle tough situations like this. All I could think was, You're just taking care of business, Amy.

That's all it was. A little unfinished business. I had my heart broken by a guy with a virtual lazy susan of girlfriends who has trouble talking about things besides hair. This part of my life is now officially over. He made it very simple for me to resolve.

Love Me Tender,
A.

November 2
To: Amy
From: Mark
Subject: The Tippi Point

Dear Amy,

I'm not sure why you channeled advice from a woman whose marriage to the King of Pop lasted a mere 20 months. Unless you want to wind up on the Island of Lost Boys, I suggest you seek a wiser mentor.

Why was it nice to see Lance? Is that business really finished? He acknowledged nothing. You didn't tell him how you feel. You didn't tell him to go jump in a lake (remember – Sundance can't swim...). If it'd been me, business would seem even more unfinished.

Well, Dean and I were watching the parade, when I see something nothing short of genius.

A woman is standing in the middle of Santa Monica Blvd – she is the spitting image of Tippi Hedren. She is inside a phone booth. She pulls a little cord inside the booth, and this moves a stuffed seagull back and forth so it rams repeatedly against the outside of the booth. Tippi then shrieks in horror. Then she reaches down, picks up the booth, and marches another ten yards down the boulevard before she sets it down again and repeats her performance for the next throng of parade-goers.

Smitten, I jogged up the sidelines so I could watch again. Dean was laughing his ass off, "Dude, that's a GUY!" I was staring right at her and was sure she was a woman. Dean bet me fifty bucks. I reached out my hand to shake his when another hand shot out of the crowd and grabbed mine, saving me from the shake.

I turned to see her and she said, "Save your money, pal. That's Daniel Roberts – performance artist." Dean was choking on his own laughter. The woman punched me in the arm good-naturedly. "Don't feel too bad. He fooled Clinton once, too." My eyes went wide. "No, not like that," she assured me, "He just called Danny 'Ma'am' during a Q & A. It was great."

Dean, connected to me telepathically at that moment, vanished into the crowd not to be seen again. He knew from the way my eyes were beaming that I fancied this woman. Leah.

I actually recognized her. She wasn't in costume, unless you count the two cameras around her neck and the light meter. But that's her gig. I recognized her from the page of contributors in last month's Conde Nast Traveler which I read in the dentist's office a few days ago. She did an amazing photo spread about the much revered caste of transvestites in Western Samoa. (When I got home I googled her and learned she's also done over a dozen covers for Rolling Stone and Spin; travel and rock 'n' roll mags are the two sides of her photog coin.)

Leah is easy to describe if you've ever seen Bewitched. Remember how Samantha had that naughty twin sister, Serena? Leah looks very little like Sam, but EXACTLY like Serena. (I can't explain this – it's more than just the hair color.) She's 42, has a gravelly voice, vice-strong hands, and a killer stare.

I had an extra fifty bucks thanks to her, so I asked if I could blow it on some swank drinks for us both. She said she had another dozen rolls of film to shoot, but wrote down an address and told me to wait for her outside at around midnight, then warned me she might be a little late. And yes, she asked for my cell number so she could call if something came up.

I tried in vain to find Dean. Reached him on his cell and he'd already run into a few buddies and caught a ride with them to Cheetah's which was featuring a performance by our favorite dancer, back after a long hiatus due to complications that ensued when she broke into a celebrity's house and wore his clothes. Now she was back in action and Dean was psyched. But I more than happily took a raincheck.

I had a couple hours so I stopped in a newsstand and re-read Leah's mini-bio and checked out her photo spread again. She is really good. She gets right inside people. She holds nothing back. At least with a camera. The rest, we'll see.

The address was in Hollywood, just off the 101 near Barham. An unmarked white door with a bouncer who looked more than a little like Saddam Hussein. Leah called to say she was running late, and called one more time to apologize for further delays. It was 1:30 am when she showed. I was glad I waited.

Saddam opened the door for us and we walked up stairs into what turned out to be a private Egyptian social club.

Belly dancers swayed with swords atop their heads. Men stood and clapped and shrugged their shoulders to the rhythm. Men threw dollar bills over the heads of dancers as if they were dealing from a pack of cards. Music engulfed us. Tables were spread with mezza – dozens and dozens of tiny plates of every delicacy you could imagine. Men shouted. Women trilled. Dollar bills flew through the air.

She took my hand and led me to a booth which we shared with two other couples.

We ate some olives and talked about our travels. Compared notes on Fiji versus Samoa. She nodded when I talked about art stuff, but when I mentioned the combat classes her eyes lit up as this was a great passion of hers. So we talked about philosophies of attack and defense, metaphors from chess, scary anecdotes of close calls.

The music, the crowd, the everything was so seductive and overpowering, I finally leaned in and kissed her hard. She kissed me back, but then two seconds later she pushed me back. Not in a rude or rejecting way. I got the sense she just wanted to look at me. Which she did. Sizing me up. Then we smiled at each other.

I know I'm not a mind reader, but I'm willing to bet another fifty bucks that we were both thinking the same thing: "Hmm... at long last, a worthy opponent..."

She is whipsmart, a piercing presence, someone I could learn a lot from, but also embrace as an equal.

We're going out in three days. I told her I was picking her up and picking the place. She seemed to like that take-charge thing. So thank you, Amy, I learned that from you...

Happy Halloween Indeed,
Mark

November 5
To: Mark
From: Amy
Subject: Peace

Darling, Lisa Marie was channeled because I needed to be the daughter of the King. No one can fuck with the daughter of the King.

But there was nothing for me to 'say' to Lance. I forgive him for being himself, and that is: a guy in love with the idea of love.

I don't doubt that he meant the things he said when he said them. He doesn't have to acknowledge anything for me. There are no words that can change the way I hurt when he left, and there are no words that can alter my perception of it and the value I can see in our past relationship now.

What he does has nothing to do with how I live my life and how I choose to view the past. The important thing was that I saw him, I was strong, and I was myself, I was kind and honest. Flipping out on him would NOT have been myself, it would have been a little girl who thought that by having a fit she could convince someone else of her love, of her passion, and then she could collect the object she was wailing for.

I'm just gonna sit back and relax and let my lover come in with the tide. He'll wash up.

I wish Lance the best. I will always love his mom. And his red couch. We weren't about to build a solid relationship based on that (a fine Spring romance, though).

Is Leah Egyptian? Don't you have to be, to get into an Egyptian Social Club? And what the hell is an Egyptian Social Club?

November 6
To: Amy
From: Mark
Subject: Already over the hump

She's American, but her passport groans fat with extra pages. The Social Club is for elite Egyptians and the occasional friend – such as a photographer who knows the high and low places of Cairo, like Leah.

Last night I took her to the Santa Monica Airport. No, Amy – NOT an extravagant trip to Tahiti for our first date! There's a restaurant there that a chef friend recommended, called The Hump. He told me to drop his name with the chef, then refuse the menu. Which is what I did. Leah was pleased. We agreed not to make jokes about the restaurant's name as my first date choice. (Apparently "The Hump" is a nickname pilots gave to the Rocky Mountains on x-country crossings.)

The dishes arrived slowly, long pauses between each, and there were thirteen in all. It took five hours. Which was ideal as we had so much to talk about. There were NO pauses between our questions and answers, our stories and exclamations.

Ok, sorry, I have to tell you this part – even though I know you want to hear about the girl and not the food – but we had barracuda sashimi, and scorpion fish, and a shrimp tartare blended with caviar, black truffles and flakes of real gold atop a pedestal of daikon served with a giant fried shrimp's head. And then came the toast. The chef had slaughtered a snapping turtle just for the two of us. He drained the blood into a cup, mixed it with egg whites, port and cabernet sauvignon and... we toasted new experiences and drank it down. Later came the turtle itself, big fried morsels served with its gummy scales and some garlic chips. We each stuck a few of the turtle's tiny bones in our pockets as a souvenir. For the second time, I felt I could read her mind, and was certain we were both thinking, "This is a night I want to remember."

After dinner we walked up an outdoor flight of stairs to an observation deck where a mounted spyglass afforded a view of Culver City by night. And that's when we faced the real Hump. She said, "Mark, I'm only interested in something big. The whole package. Monogamy, marriage, kids, a whole life. If for any reason you don't see this as a possibility, as somewhere that this is moving, and moving forward, I need you to tell me now. I know what I want. And I don't want a diversion. At least not with you. My cards are on the table. I'm asking you to show me yours."

Leah's got some big old balls. But you know what? She wasn't asking for a commitment. Just a frame of reference. And it was the easiest question in the world to answer. "Leah, I want the same things in my life. I'm not out looking for a good time, for more adventures. You are definitely someone I could see myself getting serious with."

"Well, ok then," was her only reply. And it didn't come up again.

On the drive home, I deleted over 50 names from my cell phone. Each and every one I'd collected in the past nine months. And I have a new pledge. Two weeks from today, I am going to print out my list of criteria. And if any of the big ones are unchecked, I will not let things progress farther with Leah.

Amy. This is the first time since we met that I think you and I have both found a kind of peace and solidity. Do you feel it, too?

Love,
Your Mark

P.S. Please don't give me shit about the snapping turtle. The things are vicious.

November 8
To: Mark
From: Amy
Subject: Snapping Pictures/Turtles

TURTLE STEW!!!!!! EWWWWWWW!!!!

You sure do like the zany exotic stuff. Ever just have a piece of steak and fries? We'll call them frites if you like that better. Once when I was a kid at my grandparents' house in South Dakota my uncle caught a snapping turtle and I watched it sit in a cardboard box for three days. If only I had known to make a smoothie with its blood and some white zinfandel I could've seduced little Tommy Campbell down the block.

This is important. Tell me what you like about Leah. I get that she's assertive, she attractive, she's worldly, all lovely qualities. Was the date natural? Were the stories from her heart or her scrapbook? Just stuff to 'vet' as you would say.

I think she sounds cool. I wonder what's making her want to settle down now. Very impressive the way she laid it out there and didn't ask you to mind read.

You, my love, need to be careful with that mind-reading trick. It's a faulty apparatus and you're better off asking, honestly, even if it sounds hokey, "Is this a night you want to remember forever?" and then she'll say "Yes" or "No, I was just thinking that the new moisturizer I got really is making my face microdermabrasion smooth." You guys do seem right in sync.

Today in the mail, a cookbook from my grandmother, 'Light Cooking For Two.' Which is good because when I do light cooking for one I'm always a little hungry after.

xoxo
a.

November 9
To: Mark
From: Amy
Subject: Hola Compadre

Yahoo! Susan just called and said she's throwing me a birthday party at Ed's house. I want the theme to be 'Quinceñera.' And even though I am not a young Hispanic girl, I will wear a ruffly dress and knock the shit out of a piñata.

You and your new lady friend should come.

November 9
To: Mark
From: Amy
Subject: Clean Thoughts

All right, I should have included this in the last one.

All this alone time really has me thinking. Mostly about sex. I am developing a theory. If water is a symbol of renewal, and renewal comes in the form of an orgasm, then is a bath a clitoral orgasm (reclining, open, soft waves) and a shower a vaginal orgasm (erect, pressure streaming in from one direction). Essentially, in a Freudian world view, would a shower be more mature?

I think about these things when starting my day.

November 9
To: Amy
From: Mark
Subject: Deep Thoughts

Orgasm is a renewal? Not in my neck of the woods. Round these parts, it is a brain-cell devouring zombie with a soporific mickey chaser. But hey man, enjoy the research. Sorry. The Big "O"/Little Death is a sore subject today.

What do I like about Leah? Why don't I just send you a picture? I don't have a digital camera. And even if I did, I'd be too intimidated to whip it out in front of such an accomplished photojournalist.

So instead, since they say a picture's worth a thousand words, I've allotted myself exactly that to transliterate my snapshot of the pulsing heart beauty who herself has snapped and shot every notion I ever held of what could be possible with love in this lifetime.

I know that you know that I have only just met the woman. So you know that she and I do not yet have any memories or shared stories. I can't color in each pixel of her wry smile with our earned anecdotes.

I snapped this shot of her last night:

I parked high up on a canyon access road. I brought us drinks. You can see the bottle of Stoli and the ginger beer splayed just behind the jaunt of her bent right knee. Half a lime still lies, a still life simple on the side of the truck. There on the canyon access road I for the first time found myself face to face with a more than worthy partner in crime. Two who are as far from virgins as two can be now plunked down in a place where nothing exists except firsts yet to happen. Our first fight. First road trip. First morning entwined. First flare of jealousy. First dinner party. First gallery opening. First fuck. Because this picture is made of words, you can see more of her than her well-worn boots or her silver and leather wristband. You can see the perfume of her throat, the thirst of her mouth, the gravel in her voice that rubs me smooth as a cabochon tumbler.

--

She just called – I told her I was painting a portrait of her. She said that was funny, because she was on her way to the Getty, and could I meet her there? I hooked her up with Bob (no, not THAT kind of hook-up) and Bob's arranged it so Leah can shoot a few rolls in the Getty Garden.

So I gotta get outta here – I didn't make it to 1000 words, but hopefully you get the picture...

Oh shit, I left you hanging with that bit about the big O being a sore spot. For now I'll just say that my pistons aren't firing quite right, but I think maybe that's a good thing. I should probably explain that, but I gotta go.

– M.

November 10
To: Mark
From: Amy
Subject: Mark's Anatomy

WHAT DO YOU MEAN YOUR PISTONS AREN'T FIRING RIGHT?

Mark, do you have boy vaginismus?

(No flowery descriptions either. Spill the beans without all the curlicues.)

November 11
To: Amy
From: Mark
Subject: Fluffer Wanted

I mean: we talk, then kiss, then kiss and kiss, then things get seriously hot and tectonically heavy, and I've ripped off her pants and I've yanked down my own and I've unwrapped a glove, and...

Ok. I know the speech. It happens to lots of guys. Well, it's only ever happened to me once before. And if you must know, it's now happened with me and Leah not once, not twice, but yes, three times, three dates in a row. She, of course, has been super cool about it, even though sex is clearly a deal-breaker for her, she senses everything's gonna be alright. Me, I'm panicking, and that can't be helping matters.

I even considered faking one so she'd think all was well. (Yes, secret's out, men fake orgasms, too. At least I have.)

So since the coal-shovelers below decks are on strike, the Captain in his Bridge has had extra time to pontificate. I am overtired, we've been out and up all night so many nights in a row, so maybe that's it. (Yeah, not bloody likely. I was out all night with other gals. Was never an issue.)

Naah, there really are only two big candidates I can think of. One is about fear. The other is about love.

Fear: Remember I told you I googled her? I didn't tell you everything. According to various blogs, tabloids and fan sites, Leah has been with members of seven of the top 20 major arena bands in the world. In one case, the lead singer, massive sex symbol. She also was the center of a scandal involving a member of the Jordanian Parliament – this was about 14 years ago – and it got a lot of press at the time (the guy is worth about three Steve Forbeses and a Bloomberg). I even found a topless photo of her with a member of Spanish royalty snapped by paparazzi somewhere in Santorini.

So I'm in way the fuck over my head. I am sexually intimidated for the first time in my life. What moves do I have that she's yet to experience?

Love: Amy, you said it yourself, Leah and I are so in sync. We seem to be on the same trajectory, our cannons pointed to the selfsame azimuth. This is the real deal, the whole nine enchiladas. I wish I had that white dress from Turkey – I just know it would slip perfectly over Leah's shoulders and come to rest, flawlessly, as she comes to rest in my arms after one of my last three failed attempts to mount her.

I know I need to relax. Actually, the last time we tried to joke about it and we had a few drinks, I mean a few EXTRA drinks, so I'd loosen up and not get so overwrought about either my excitement at this pairing or my terrors of stumbling in the footsteps of the past. But the extra alcohol didn't help any...

Everything else seems so right. She seems so sure about me. Her candor blows me away. Nothing I do or say makes her flinch. We play this game where we try to scare each other away. We tell each other the worst things we can think of about ourselves. But I can't make her flinch. She sees something in me.

Please give me advice, Amy! I need it bad right now! (And could also use the advice.)

Very fondly,
Mark

November 12
To: Mark
From: Amy
Subject: Leah Likes You

Oh my God. This is awful. I mean, it will go away, but here you are all attracted to each other, and there's some meanie weenie fairy in Orgasmland.

I'm sorry. I'll try and be more, uhh, ah forget it. All I can tell you is this, I have been on the receiving end of this and it's a weird place to be. And the male, oh okay it was Jeremy, would apologize until his voice was hoarse which made it even more awkward. The best thing (I know this sounds goofy) is to ignore it. Just play, don't give a shit and well, you know how to whistle.

Think of it as your body's way of stalling, drawing out your courtship. Susan used to try and get me to sneak Viagra into Jeremy's morning oatmeal. I couldn't do it.

The other weird thing about my experience (trust that I am a healthy sexual adult), I loved him so much I didn't care. I cared, but I'd still take the guy if he was a stump. The less he fixated on it, the sooner it would come back. It would always be available when we weren't in Los Angeles, but once he was in the West Hollywood grid... maybe he was experiencing the same things you are with Leah? Whoa. I never thought of that. Maybe I'm going to learn something here.

So you're sort of intimidated by her, and by her past, and it gets translated into your groin. Hmmm. If I wasn't close to you I'd think that this was some kind of Hallmark card excuse, but you're telling the truth and all these previous chicks were no sweat.

I think this is just about getting to know her more and feeling confident that you're the only apple of her eye (might be a little residual Addie). Play play play.

I'm going to go to Olivera Street now to get some crepe flowers to put in all the female guests' hair. The party is going to start around nine. We are thinking of getting a ranchero band (I have always preferred ranchero to mariachi).

Oh and I'm wasting my twenties not having sex.

November 14
To: Amy
From: Mark
Subject: Cue Etta James

Wait, when was/is your party? Did you tell me and I spaced? I could've sworn you told me your birthday was November 18th, no?

Maybe you were right about residual Addie. I caught myself feeling anxious during the daytime these past two weeks, wondering where Leah was, and who she was with, but having the restraint not to ask her. You are only a stalker if you ACT on these thoughts. I think it's normal for everyone to have them. Right? Dean agrees. He told me, "No one I know who's worth his salt isn't a jealous person."

It took me a minute to work out the double-negatives, but then I got it. Why is that? I mean it sounded convincing when he said it, but could it possibly be true that being jealous is a POSITIVE trait? Maybe it is (if it doesn't get out of hand; see "stalker" above). Maybe it's the other side of monogamy and nidification (a new favorite word: it means nest-building). And I also think you're right about my body wanting to stretch out the courtship. Me and Leah seem to be on a kind of fast-track. But my body needed to differentiate this "two people old enough to know what they want" from "Mark's lack of impulse control as he goes cannoning out of the gate."

Yesterday we went to Pie 'n Burger in Pasadena and ate some pie and burger. We talked about kids and pets and religion and politics. Then we walked through Huntington Gardens. And out of the blue in a thicket of bamboo she turned to me and said, "Mark, I've never felt this way about anyone before." I was speechless. She pulls no punches this one. She kept walking. I caught up.

I was glad the paper warned of rain. It didn't. But I had my coat. Which I spread on the leaves behind a maintenance shed. Our clothes more on than off, Leah and I finally came together. Houston...

You warned me not to attempt to read her mind. But I swear I think I know what she was thinking, and that it was the exact same thing that I was thinking. Hey, happy almost birthday.

At Last,
Mark

November 15
To: Mark
From: Amy
Subject: Hey Jealousy

Yes noodle head, my birthday party is on the 18th at Ed's house, 1284 Abington Place. You do not have to get me anything, you do have to show up. And don't forget your beloved Leah.

As for sex in public places. Good for you. Maybe you have geographic penile dysfunction like Jeremy.

I've never cared for the jealousy stuff. My stance is, if they're looking for something else then they don't have to look far. Los Angeles is crammed full of interesting beautiful ladies, I can't dislike anyone for that. I'm a big fan of women supporting each other and jealousy doesn't fit into that equation for me. If a guy's going to wander he's going to wander. My being snappy and whiny about it is not going change things. I don't understand relationship jealousy. I think it's something we learn from daytime tv. I feel more akin to the bonobo monkey (that's right, the one with the biggest clitoris, for more information see Natalie Angiers' book, WOMAN).

Bonobos do it simply for pleasure, they do it all day long and it has nothing to do with reproduction. (Bonobos are also big on the monkey orgy scene and that I cannot relate to because I am just your average middle-class white girl and I like my repression and J. Crew.)

I have sex the way I bowl. It's for fun, it's relaxing, it's healthy. It is not competitive or about claiming the title. Oh sure, every woman wants to feel wanted, wants to feel like the most desirable creature on earth, but if the guy's smart he'll figure that out.

If the girl's even smarter she'll deem herself that and then we all win. I like the alpha approach and then I like to slide into the bonobo phase. Bonobo umbrellaed by monogamy. Can a girl get some of that?

Love,
A.

November 15
To: Amy
From: Mark
Subject: Today's special

U2 can be a Bonobo...

The dysfunction wasn't geographical. It was egotistical. And self-protective.

The magic wand that waved my magic wand back into being was Leah's phrase that she'd never felt this way about anyone before. And I believed her.

Later on, I confided this to her. I told her that I'd been subconsciously worried that I was just another one of her conquests or adventures, another stamp in her passport. And she looked at me, dead to rights and said, "What makes you think that isn't exactly how I've been feeling? Mark, you don't think you've made women feel that way before?" That was an eye-opener.

Like obituaries and ads for early bird specials, Leah and I are inextricably on the same page.

I feel so special I should ride on the Short Bus of Love.

– M.

RE: the 18th, me and the missus will be there with maracas on.

P.S. I'm a couple days early of the two week mark, but I went ahead and printed out my "criteria" list like I said I would. Leah literally matches EVERY item on the list (except she prefers treadmills to hiking). I think we can let that slide.

November 17
To: Mark
From: Amy
Subject: ?

I'm. Uhmmm. Mark? I feel like I'm going to throw up.

Hold on, I have to breathe for a second.

Jeremy just called from a pay phone outside of Phoenix. He is coming to Los Angeles and he wants to talk.

November 19
To: Mark
From: Amy
Subject: Royal Flush

I just got home. My tiara is still on and I think I slept on a quesadilla, but other than that everything's fine.

The party was a beautiful mess of old and new friends, nachos, piñatas, tequila and lace. I hacked the purple taffeta bridesmaid dress off at the knee (don't tell Geoff or Melinda), added a tiara and a red crepe paper flower behind the ear, and all was bueno.

I was dancing, throwing back el modelos with Shelley, karaoke-ing on the rented machine and doing a fantastic version of "Besame Mucho," thinking, Gee my life and pals are swell, when Susan brought me my cell phone, her charcoal-cherry-lined lips pursed.

"It's Jeremy."

Of course it was. I couldn't really breathe. It was eleven-thirty and the party was at full tilt. I took my phone and went into the bathroom.

"Hi."

"Hi."

"I'm right by your house."

"I'm not at my house."

"Oh. Where are you?"

"I'm at my birthday party."

"Oh shit. It's your birthday."

"It's okay."

"Where's the party? I mean. Can I come there?"

I gave him directions and then I just sat on the toilet and felt stupidly and strangely alive, like every cell in my body was awake. I was here. I was at IT.

On the front porch I sat and did breathing exercises until he pulled around the corner in his new truck.

He walked up the street, gently took the crepe paper flower from behind my ear and hugged me. It was tumbleweeds, familiar frames falling into each other, not magnets at all, just tumbleweeds crossing the same state line.

"You smell like a mall," he said.

He smelled the same way he did when we were fifteen, sage and beer and soap.

"You smell like you."

We laugh and sit down out in front of the party. We talk for a long time about what's going on in our lives. I tell him about my job, my family, my ridiculous e-correspondence with you that keeps me sane. The whole time we're talking thoughts are passing through me like waves, thoughts linked that had never been so truly linked before such as "I love this man so much" and "We are really truly not meant to be together."

He tells me about his most recent hiking trip and how he's going to buy some property and build a yurt. I see him clearly for the first time. He is a man afraid of telephone lines, repulsed by freeways and 7-11's and stationary lives. He is a man who is happiest when sleeping outside. He doesn't give a fuck but he lets you know it on paper made of thick white stock like him.

I see him for the first time. We could've talked for hours but I had to stop.

"Jeremy why are you here?"

"I just wanted you to know. I'm getting married... and I loved you. I always loved you. Even when I... Well, I did. That's all. I really did."

I nodded.

"She's a biologist. We're going to do organic sustenance farming. You'd like her. You guys are very similar."

The only houseplant I have ever had is moldy bread.

Then we hugged and said goodbye.

You missed a hell of a party.

I feel lighter than air, I am walking on Devonshire cream and yet I have never felt more real. How could it have taken this long for me to let go of a dream? How could it have taken me so long to admit that my dream was really to be able to trust that I am and will continue to be loved.

It's all real. I guess I needed him to say it to me more than I thought. I am in love with the world. Today I leave the tiara on, Sparky.

November 19
To: Amy
From: Mark
Subject: In absentia

Dear Amy,

I missed your party. I suck.

Of course I have an excuse. But not a fun one. No gallivanting off to play with peacocks at the Playboy Mansion's new Neverland branch. No.

Simply put: Leah and I had our first fight. And it lasted hours. And if we'd shown up, we would've been major downers on your special day. It was shitty timing, but totally unplanned. I am sorry.

So you say you are in love with the world? That is exactly what you said about Addie. So what does that mean? With Addie it sounded like you meant, "Open to all experiences, faithful to none."

How long were you away from your friends while you spoke to Jeremy? Did they worry about you? Do you think Susan and the others were inside crossing fingers and lighting candles and holding thumbs, wishing that Jeremy would ride up on a white horse and whisk you away?

I wish I could say I totally understand it when you say that you just know in your bones that you and Jeremy were never meant to be. That's what Diana told me way back when.

I accepted it. Accepted it as gospel, like 2+2=4, like green means go and yellow means accelerate, like Jews eat Chinese food on Sundays. I have no idea why. I'd be lying if I said I understood. I just accept. And go on from there. So you're on the inside, and I'd like the inside scoop.

How do you just KNOW that? About someone with whom you were so intimate and so much in love?

Leah spent the night for the first time last night. We tried to make up around 4 am and got into trouble in medias sex. The crazy Italian neighbors. Pounding and cursing and threatening to call the cops. Did I mention they have a young daughter? Have I told you about Leah's glass-shatter pipes? And that the walls are made of soap film?

I think Leah's still a little pissed at me. (Not to mention the neighbors.)

I told her I'd make her dinner tonight so I'd better jet to the market to get some stuff.

Sorry again I didn't make it to your party, Amy. It sounds like you took excellent care of yourself.

Even though it didn't happen for Bev, in your case age is definitely bringing ever more wisdom.

I'll tell you about the First Fight another time.

Happy Birthday,
Mark

November 21
To: Mark
From: Amy
Subject: Come in Orson

Okay. One at a time. Sheesh.

1. In love with the world like Addie, no. Remember me? Bonobo with a side of monogamy? What I mean is, I let it sink in on the porch at my birthday. I let it sink in more than I even did when we were together, that Jeremy did love me. When I let that hit me it was powerful and freeing. I, Amy, am infinitely lovable. This in turn makes me love my postman, it makes me love Idina and her smoky bourbon breath. I love my red slippers, my pink and green lamp, my friends, my cereal and my computer. It is painfully easy. And in this recognition I am transfused with the possibility that I could love, for real, like with my heart and with my secrets, just as I am. Nobody needing to change me. Just as me. Today.

2. How long was I gone? I don't know, forty-five minutes. Were my friends hoping I would be whisked off? Honey, homey don't play that. My friends were hoping for me to be happy. If you look around, your friends will not be blinded by romance and they will have a little more insight than you. (I believe Susan said, "Actions speak louder than words. Jeremy has been wind-bagging from Yellowstone Park for a month now. You are not getting your needs met. Move on, dumdum.") Which brings us to...

3. How did my friends and myself KNOW it was not meant to be? Did you or did you not hear me when I explained that his dream home is a YURT. I like supermarkets with fancy salad bars, I enjoy a fine magazine stand, and positively love wood floors. I like whatever that nifty word for nesting is. He enjoys clan of the cave bear. The variations are so dramatic that neither of us would be happy sacrificing one for the other. I can't even live in the suburbs, Mark.

4. Number three does not mean I was not in love. I have been in love many times and though there is no scientific evidence, the secret theory I hold deep down is that every person you've ever loved you are inextricably, innately, biologically bonded with for eternity. Despite the fact that I am a serial monogamist and can't get past the year-and-a-half mark. So though I loved him, we were not meant to be together. Our other life passions outweighed our attraction.

5. You have not discussed Leah's sexual theatrics.

Always,
A.

P.S. You are forgiven for not coming to my birthday party. I would've felt the same way I felt when I saw my third grade teacher at the supermarket. Utterly confused and displaced. I think of you as the Orson to my Mork – the voice in the ether that helps me understand this mixed-up world and my mixed-up heart and that mixed-up thing wearing the panties. I also love unavailable men.

November 23
To: Amy
From: Mark
Subject: The Asshole Song

Nanu, Nanu –

What the hell is wrong with me? Do I strike you as the self-destructive type? Isn't it obvious from my e-mails that I want things with Leah to work out? And, in general, for LIFE to work out? So I ask you: what the hell is wrong with me?

Leah's not talking to me. Not because of fight #1, but because of fight #1 + fight #2. And I shouldn't call them fights. It's insensitivity #1 and insensitivity #2. Believe me, when I tell you how idiotic I've been you're gonna wanna take back all that sensitive guy stuff you used to say to me.

The plan was to take her out to dinner at a sweet Greek place halfway between Leah's place and Ed's. Charming garden outside. (She has noticed that I always pick restaurants with patio dining so I can smoke after the meal. At this point she is restraining herself I can tell, rolling her eyes and shifting her chair a few inches upwind. She's not ready to ask me to change for her, and I'm not ready to change for her.) It's romantic, their lemony chicken drips meltingly down the back of your throat and the owner's wife's cousin supplies her with a rare ouzo variant that is complex and meant for sipping yet still packs a wallop. Needless to say, I got punch-drunk.

After the meal, I nodded to the waiter and mouthed the words, "We're ready now."

Leah saw this and asked what's up. The truth is I had special-ordered this incredible baklava made with lavender-blossom honey. But to Leah I shrugged and smiled and said, "Nothing." The courtyard was deserted. Just us. And that's when I got up from my seat and got down on one knee and softly said, "Leah..."

Her eyes went as wide as a desert sky. Her lower lip dropped.

And then I continued:

"Sorry. My shoe is untied." And then I tied my shoe. And then she cried. I thought it was funny. It was not. To say the least.

She walked out. I wanted to throw cash on the table and run out after her, but I didn't have enough so I had to wait for my plastic to process. By the time I got outside, I could just make her out a couple blocks away, still walking. My hands were shaking as I waited what felt like hours for the valet. I cruised up next to her and apologized.

"This is crazy! You can't walk home! Can we please just talk?" Two blocks later she relented and got in, slamming the door.

We drove in silence for about fifteen minutes. And then we started talking.

Our first fight. Fighting isn't always a bad thing. In fact, I've always believed that fighting-style is the single most important determinant of a relationship's potential. Any two fools can kiss and coo and neck at the zoo and pick out china patterns, too. But how do you handle conflict? Do you pull your punches, or go below the belt? Dance around with distracting footwork, or pummel relentlessly? That's where the future of a relationship lies.

We did ok. It wasn't the most civilized fight. It did get a bit nasty. But halfway through I realized – wow – this is my first fight with anyone in over a year – not since Diana – in other words, I haven't really cared about someone and felt that deeply invested until now.

And you know the rest of this story. It was too late for your party. Back at my place we attempted a physical patching up. Leah channeled her residual anger into the most intense love-making, and she was howling at the top of her lungs, when again we were quashed, interrupted by Italian curses and pounding on the wall – Faccia de merda! Vaffanculo! Puttana! Caccati in mano e prenditi a schiaffi! – and all was lost. Ruined.

Fight #2. The next day I prepared a six-course meal for her. Spent the whole day cooking. I'll spare you the menu. Suffice it to say it was elaborate. After dinner, I gave her a present. She unwrapped it:

A ball gag. (A really fancy one with fine red leather straps.) I told her it was a gag gift. She started crying. Shit.

I apologized profusely, explaining that I'm not into that stuff at all, I was just appropriating something from that scene in order to increase our pleasure, since then we wouldn't have to worry about the Italians and we could stay focused on the matter at hand.

(Ok, not my exact words.)

She sobbed and said all guys are shit, that her last boyfriend had seemed like such a great guy then forced her to do terrible things (she never told me what, and I had the wisdom not to ask). She said I had seemed like such a nice guy, too. She left about twenty minutes later, still crying. Haven't heard from her since, and she didn't respond to my e-mail.

So I ask you yet again: what the hell is wrong with me? And also: will you still be my friend, or are you going to abandon me now, too?

I probably deserve it. I feel as clueless as the March Hare when after he attempted to fix the Mad Hatter's watch with a slather of butter, he defensively exclaimed, "It was the BEST butter!"

"Fine red leather straps." My God, I'm an idiot.

No excuse,
Dark Mark

P.S. Your secret theory about two people who have once loved being forever bonded reminded me of this poem, but I can't quite remember – I'm going to look for it...

November 25
To: Mark
From: Amy
Subject: 'I Don't Know' is not an answer

Mark, what's Greek for fucking moron? You're lucky YOUR nuts weren't wrapped in phyllo dough, topped with syrup and baked. This is a woman who made it very clear from the beginning what she is looking for. I know you didn't mean to be, but what you did felt cruel. Why did you really do it? You better own up to that.

I would have dumped you on the ball gag.

There is nothing pretty, erotic, funny or charming about a device used to insulate a woman. But that's just me. Jesus, I'm getting steamed just imaging it. Why did you really do that?

Let's see here, why is Mark acting childish and cruel to the lady he claims to be really crazy about? Are you trying to destroy this relationship, or make her feel small? Because that's what those two actions say to me.

I am concerned. Your "I'm not willing to change for her" comment strikes me as odd. It's not so much change as to make the other person as comfortable as possible. I mean, would it kill you to not smoke after the meal? You gotta give a little. Always err on the side of the lady, did mom not include that in the don't kiss and tell lecture?

I have a theory about people and their little 'jokes.' Here it is... **THEY ARE NOT JOKES.** Somewhere deep down you are communicating. When Ted took me to a titty bar on Valentine's Day he was communicating something, something like, I like **LOTS** of titties. Wearing the safe "joke" hat, he told me this. Later he just came out and said it in plain English. Okay, so he said 'rock star phase.' I understood.

Figure out what your joke is really saying. (I do want to get married, I don't want to get married, I want you to shut up and look like a Hawaiian luau pig, whatever.)

Please let this mull about in your brain and get back to me.

Me. I am still in a fine mood. Marla the bartender and I were talking and I said, "I don't hate men."

She said, "Sure you do. Men are pretty hateable. But then you're pickin' the wrong ponies. You gotta find one who adores you. One with a good bullshit detector. Nothin' finer than a man who can call you on your shit. That's when you really fall in love with him, cause you respect him.

"I waited seven years for Frankie to come along, and that man was worth it. He's still a pain in the ass, but he's worth it. Keep your eyes out for the right soul. He's out there. He's not what you imagine, what you think. God's smarter than you and all your 'thinking,' and He's gonna send him to you. He is out there."

She's a smart woman that Marla.

November 25
To: Amy
From: Mark
Subject: Dog House

Dear Amy,

I agree. "I don't know" is not an acceptable answer. My love-mobile does not sport a Handicapped tag, and I can't hide behind a chromosomal abnormality (XY), plead the fifth, insanity, or my childhood made me do it. I will own up. I already did, to myself, and now to you.

The honest truth: my two idiocies were completely unrelated. Not a pattern. The second one is the easiest. It was totally premeditated, and it was just a joke. Sometimes a sex toy is just a sex toy. In this case, I really did believe that it would be a fun thing for us – to be able to enjoy the sweaty entwinement without having to deal with eviction – I can honestly say if the roles had been reversed, I would not have been offended.

She had a bad association, and that was it. She is a provocative person, not shy, very self-possessed, and it never occurred to me that I'd touch a raw nerve. But if she had opened it and we'd had a great laugh, you and I would never be having this discussion. I feel terrible it made her feel that way, but my yardstick is always the Golden Rule, and like I said, if it had been done unto me, I would have thought it was funny and titillatingly playful. To read into it that I want to silence her is absurd. I adore her strength and her opinions and I have zero interest in a yes-woman or a geisha-girl.

But the first one is not so easy. I had to think about it. A lot. It was NOT premeditated. I was a little drunk, and that means uninhibited. And what I felt then and there was that I wanted to marry this woman, I wanted to create a new life with this woman, and not in some silly impetuous horn-dog throes of impulse kind of way.

I looked into her, and saw a beautiful complement to my own values and aspirations, and I saw a person I could learn from, and could imagine growing old with. And I wanted to propose to her then and there. More than that, I wanted our new life to begin immediately – I wanted Monty Hall to appear and slide open Door #3 and there would be our home, a dog, our circles of friends united, everything.

And then I chickened out. No ring. It's only been one month. It seemed somehow disrespectful to suggest marriage after a month.

"Take it slow," I heard your voice say in my ear. And then I made that goofy, no, hurtful joke. And I deeply regret it.

So there. Now you know. And although you didn't ask me to, I want to apologize to you, too, Amy. I know I let you down.

Love,
Mark

November 26
To: Amy
From: Mark
Subject: Sexual Urgency

Dear Amy,

Ok, found it. "Sexual Urgency" is the name of the poem I was looking for, by Rumi. It's about how whenever two people come together in love, an entity is born – your associations bear progeny – and because this spiritual result will last forever, you must be extra careful before going to join forces with someone. You knew in your bones that this coming together with Jeremy was a bad idea. But with Leah, I no longer have any doubts.

See I've now been redeemed. I picked up a dozen roses today and I was on my way to Leah's house, but when I got to my truck I found Leah, wearing roller blades, in the midst of leaving a note on my windshield.

Once again, even after my two-day marathon of stupidity, she and I were back on the same page. She said nothing, waiting for me to read the note.

"Dear Mark, I haven't been so upset and angry in a long time and then it hit me. You can't feel those feelings unless you deeply care about someone. At least I can't."

[Weird, huh? That's almost the SAME thing I wrote you a couple days ago about how it actually felt great to have my first fight in a year!]

Her letter continued, "I know you didn't mean to upset me. And I do forgive you. Mark, I am in love with you."

For once I was succinct, and simply said, "Me, too."

I don't know where yet, but we're gonna go away somewhere fun for Thanksgiving. We have both suddenly realized we have a LOT to be thankful for.

Love,
Mark

November 28
To: Mark
From: Amy
Subject: In Love At Last

I'm going to stick with "no woman laughs at a ball gag." The visual is just too Silence Of The Lambs-y. Your Golden Rule thing (that you would consider the gift "titillating") confirms a stereotypical gender classification for me; you are a man. You consider toys that look like hockey goalie equipment titillating. If it's not pretty or lightly funny (I'm talking like bunny rabbit ears, a pink tutu), keep it out of the bedroom for AT LEAST the first few months. You don't need anything the first few months, anyway.

I'm glad you two made up. Perhaps you should come to Thanksgiving at my parents' house. You could give my mother the ball gag. OH MARK, she just wails and jabs and sticks 'em in like little poison darts.

"Sure would be nice to have someone besides our immediate family at the table."

"Don't you ever meet anyone nice, Amy?"

"What happened to Alex? He seemed like a fine man."

"The day I married your father I was a virgin."

This is just five minutes through the front door. I am a rock. I choose peace. This is not my real mother. My real mother is Priscilla Presley and she doesn't care if I'm married or single. This is the mantra I silently whisper to myself while my mother coos at my 22-year-old cousin's bridal shower invitation and then shows me the plastic plates with the pansies and the 'nut cups' that she will be using for the luncheon.

Anyway, wish me luck.

Amy

P.S. Ed dumped Susan. Says he "fell out of love." Susan says she doesn't want to go to Dollywood anymore. Now she wants to go to the Amazon to visit those women that chop their right breast off so that their rifle can lean better.

November 28
To: Amy
From: Mark
Subject: On the road again

Hey you. Second e-mail I've written you from a plane. On our way to San Miguel de Allende for four days. Got a great last minute deal. Leah says hi. She's drinking a can of bloody mary mix and she has a red moustache. I've been telling her all about you, about us, about this past year, all the way from 0 to 20000 feet.

I finally got her a gag gift that made her crack up. While she was waiting at the gate I went to Cinnabon and bought her two cinnamon rolls. I wrote on the box, Dear Princess Leah. She wore them on the side of her head for about two seconds and laughed. Then we each took a bite and spit it out (nasty!) and boarded the plane.

Happy Thanksgiving, Amy. Next year, let's do Thanksgiving together, minus the nut cups. Let's start our own tradition, what do you say?

– M.

December 1
To: Mark
From: Amy
Subject: Corny Cornucopia

That is the sweetest thing I have ever heard.

Here's to next year pilgrim,
Amy

December 6
To: Amy
From: Mark
Subject: Revenge

Earlier I said fighting-style is the best predictor of a relationship. But the two gauntlets that must be run before you can say you've found a compatible match are: TRAVEL and SICKNESS.

Thanks to Montezuma's legion of bacteria and one absent-minded night when she forgot to brush her teeth with bottled water, Leah and I have now survived both.

The three of us are back in L.A. now: Leah, me and Imodium AD. I kept her hydrated, searched high and low for the scented candles she requested (picture me: "Por favor – candelas perfumados? Candelos sentidos?" while I made a gesture of striking a match and sniffing. My mime and Spanish skills suck. But a nice English-speaking shopkeeper got me what I needed). So we had a few great days of travel and a few lousy ones of sickness.

Our last night there, she was conked out so I went for a walk. In the central plaza, the Jardín, boys wearing their best walked clockwise while girls in their finery walked counter-clockwise. Men sold paper flowers, balloons, cotton candy and grilled corn rubbed with limes and chili powder. The promenade lasted two hours.

I sat in the middle, nibbling the corn while I watched for pairings. Several smiles were exchanged, but no phone numbers. The pinwheel kept spinning. And I thought of us, you and me, going around in our own waltz. A smile here and a nod there. But mostly a lot of walking, the soles of our shoes inscribed with the story of our collective love lives, circling while the sun sets.

A new year is coming. May the merry-go-round stop and land you in strong, worthy arms.

Much love,
Mark

December 7
To: Mark
From: Amy
Subject: Green-Eyed Lady

Hmmm. You're watching sexy Latin young things flirt and I am thumbing through Cleveland Monthly. (Did you know that they're having the Great American Rib Cook-Off in May?)

Susan is on a belligerent "fuck you Ed" mission, so we went to a bowling birthday party last night. Some client she did graphic design for. Anyway, she went to the bar to talk to the client and a short dark-haired fellow asked if he could bowl with me.

He was cute in that next-door-neighbor-kid-that-I-used-to-baby-sit kind of way. We bowled. I enjoyed the fact that he refused to give me his name. "You can call me Kingpin," he said. Turns out Kingpin is one hell of a bowler. College league.

He was sweet, but trying so hard to be entertaining. It was painful. Like watching an episode of kids' Star Search.

[Note to self: wit is the salt of conversation, not the food.]

I went to the bar to find Susan and she was making out with a tall blonde guy in a booth. He offered me some tequila, I declined, Susan had a shot. I noticed that he couldn't keep his eyes open. Tiny red fluttering slits. Then he said, "Hanks for coming to my urthday. I'm Yake."

Susan piped up, "We worked together on the Vickers project."

"Yeah," said Yake, "what a shitbag job, more tequila."

The waitress brought him four more shots and then he started sucking Susan's neck instead of limes.

This is where it gets awful. Susan insists that we go to the next bar. She wants me to get to know Kingpin while Yake fishes for her tonsils. Because I am a good friend and she is post-breakup tender, I say "Yes." But I really just want to go home to my surrogate boyfriend, aka the electric blanket.

We go to The Drawing Room. Kingpin and Yake meet us there. Kingpin asks for my number. I give it to him. He leaves. Then I sit and stare at the bartender's big boobs for an hour while Susan and Yake practically mount each other on the pinball machine. Boobs bartender hollers last call and I drag Susan to my car.

"Can you drop me off at Jake's house?"

"Who's Jake?"

"The client whose birthday party it was."

I sort of laugh and feel sad and say sure. I pull up to some apartment complex mid-Wilshire district, then she looks in the mirror and says, "Can I borrow your blush?"

It's 2:30. Jake/Yake was piss drunk, and unless she is rouging her labia majora like a 17th century courtesan, he will not take notice of the blush. I'm just saying, don't waste my blush.

I was so rotten. I told her she should ask me for something she'd actually use, K-Y, a condom, fur-lined manacles. Then she told me to "take off my 'Johnny Judger' t-shirt," got out and slammed the door. No blush.

I am an asshole. I am sad. Maybe I was jealous?

Am I jealous of a meaningless birthday booty call? Mark? Was I mean or honest? I thought she could handle it. I thought I said it because I wanted her to think clearly about what she was getting into.

December 9
To: Amy
From: Mark
Subject: In the gutter

You jealous? Spare me. Strike it from your mind. If all you'd wanted was a ball, you could have had Kingpin and nine of his friends lined up and waiting for you.

I'll stop. But if memory serves me right – you liked Bill's paranomasiac (punning) ways.

You're being silly. If you were in the mood for sex, you could have drawn upon the Drawing Room's vast reservoir of able-bodied hominids.

Want to know the real deal?

Cheap sex is dangerous because from a distance it looks like the beautiful, meaningful bonding of love. Someone peering in your window couldn't tell the difference. And a little part of you peering out through the window in your heart can't tell the difference either – because it REMINDS you of real love, of everything possible in this world. But cheap sex isn't this real love; it just reminds you of it, and therefore makes you sad, abysmally sad. Because now you're not only far away from love, you are REMINDED of how far away you are.

In Hebrew the word for holiness is kedushah and the word for whore is kedeishah. It's just a simple vowel, and I think that's the point. They share the same parts and points of union, but they are light years apart.

I'm glad you went home to your blanket.

Love,
Mark

December 10
To: Mark
From: Amy
Subject: Kedeishah kedeishah kedeishah (Ho Ho Ho)

Yeah. Me and my blanket. It keeps my legs, groin and tummy area all warm and cozy, almost sizzling, but then my chest and head are totally neglected. (So really it kind of IS like a boyfriend.) Then I accidentally left it on, so I woke up sweating and remembered the time Richard got drunk and peed in the bed and blamed it on me, so which is better – electric blanket or boyfriend? You tell me.

Enough silliness, I need some advice. Kingpin called today and asked me to go to the movies. He really is a nice smart guy. Should I go out with him? I just want to stay open for the right 'soul.'

Like Marla said, he won't always be what I imagine. Could he be a guy who calls himself Kingpin?

xoxo
a.

P.S. How are you and Leah doing in the sack?

December 11
To: Amy
From: Mark
Subject: No Jokers or Penguins either, please...

Addie didn't have a cell phone and you gave me hell... meanwhile Kingpin doesn't even have a real name?

Well, he does, but it's the same name as an obese, no-necked Batman villain.

Amy, the kid is in college. Lots of smart, nice guys in college. Way too young for you.

As to the sack, Leah's so skilled, she could write a book. Actually, her vagina is so skilled it could write a book, hold the pen, dot the i's. I'm a lucky guy.

I'm trying to arrange a gallery show of her non-rock photos. That's gonna be my Xmas present to her, if I can pull it off.

– M.

December 12
To: Amy
From: Mark
Subject: Blast from the Past

Dear Amy,

Ran into Beverley in the courtyard yesterday. She'd been in Paris for the past month. Said she'd had no luck. She seemed different. Higher strung. Or maybe she just had her breasts lifted again.

Out of nowhere, she told me that her father was a soldier in the SS. Nonchalantly, like "My dad was a carpenter." Not with pride, nor shame. And then immediately, without segue, she asked, "How would you like the best blowjob of your life?"

I am seriously thinking of quitting smoking.

God help us all,
Mark

December 13
To: Mark
From: Amy
Subject: Drowning Not Waving

Okay, you might as well know right now that I ignored your advice. I kept talking to Kingpin on the phone and finally agreed to a movie last night.

He BOWLED in college, Mark, he's not IN college.

Kingpin picks me up, he's got Def Leppard "Pour Some Sugar On Me" on his stereo, really loud. He is driving a black Mercedes. I assume the song has been cued up so that he can make a few jokes and headbang to it in an attempt to entertain me. I am right. I smile. Not entertained, but smiling.

We go to the Grove. On the way down I holler over the ben a wen wen wen wen woa woa, "HOW OLD ARE YOU?" He looks confused.

"I'm uhhh... I'm hmm... I'm 34."

He takes me to the pseudo-Balthazar and we are chatting about what we do for a living. He is in advertising.

I say, "Hey, when we were in the car, you took a minute when I asked you about your age. What's really going on, Kingpin?"

"Well. I just, the thing is... I didn't know how to answer the question, I'm 34 today."

"Today is your birthday?"

He nods. I screech dolphin style. Then I pretend to go to the bathroom and ask the waitress to bring us a piece of birthday cake with a candle. The whole restaurant sings. He is uncomfortable. Then he says, "I'm getting together with some friends at St. Nick's tomorrow night to celebrate. You should come."

I am amazed that this guy chose to gamble on spending his birthday night with a virtual stranger. I mean, what if I was a total bitch?

Think of that. For the rest of your life you have to remember your 34th birthday as the night you spent with that bitch.

During the movie I try to focus on the story but kept getting back to the fact that it is his birthday. I didn't want to kiss him or date him again, but Jesus, it was his birthday.

After the movie we got into his car and he unwraps a piece of gum and all I can think is, "This is his pre-kiss gum, this is his fresh mouth flag and he is waving it to my nation."

"Would you like a piece of gum?" he says.

"No. Thanks." That is my nation arming all of its borders with anti-aircraft cannons.

He turns up the Leppard and begins to sing and bang his head, proving what a silly fun-loving guy he is. I smile. It is his birthday.

At my door he goes in for the kiss and I retaliate with the giant bear hug. I try and restrain myself from giving him a head noogie.

He asks if we can get together tomorrow night (WHAT was I supposed to say?).

I say "I'll call you."

Back to the electric blanket,
Amy

P.S. Do you think Leah does Kegels?

December 15
To: Amy
From: Mark
Subject: Blast from the Past, part II

Do them? I think she invented them.

Amy, do you realize that not once since we've known each other has either one of us said to the other: TOLD YOU SO. I guess that makes us a couple of class acts.

That said, TOLD YOU SO.

You and me've had some shitty birthday luck, huh? No more dating people with cartoon character monikers. PLEASE!?

So...

Diana called. Despite the breadth and depth of the Atlantic Ocean, she had caught a whiff.

"Are you seeing anyone?" she asked.

"Yes."

"Are you in love?"

"Yes."

"I'm really happy for you."

"Thank you. I am, too."

When Leah arrived for dinner, I wanted to tell her. I felt it would be a beautiful proof of my love, my emotional availability, my earnestness. But I didn't.

Instead, I lifted her up into my arms, kissed her on the neck, and buried my face in her hair for a few minutes until finally I released my grip.

"What was THAT for?"

I smiled, took her hand, and led her into the other room where dinner was already waiting.

I wish she lived with me, but my place is too damn small.

Love,
Mark

December 16
To: Mark
From: Amy
Subject: Ex-Mass

I'm glad you didn't mention Diana's call to Leah. It could've gone two ways:

1. Wow Mark, (insert sarcastic voice) that's really BIG of you to tell your ex about your present life situation. (It can be offensive, like why wouldn't you tell her.)

2. Wow Mark, (insert touched voice) I mean so much to you that you're telling major people in your life about me.

Either way, it really isn't important for her to know, so you did the right thing with the head muffle and all.

The holidays are ridiculous. Everyone is crumbling. Dark Bill called and wanted to go get a coffee. We did. It was a disaster. I asked him on the phone if he was ready to be friends.

Then we sat there and he looked at me like he was hungry. Like he was going to eat my hands. It was awkward.

He asks me, "Are you seeing anyone?"

"Yes," I lied. I thought of Alex. Alex had been important. I had been seeing Alex, so I just inserted Alex.

I didn't sucker-punch him; we haven't been romantic since the summer. He then told me how insensitive I was. It was insane. I guess we can't be friends.

The other bummer, I got rid of my electric blanket after reading that they promote bad Feng Shui. Then my furnace broke. I thought about Bill and his central heating.

Target was out of space heaters. Empty shelves. I started crying on the manager's shoulder. "Please... please don't make me go over to my ex-boyfriend's house... please." He found one in the back for me.

I came home, turned it on, wrapped myself up in a blanket and passed out. Then I woke up to the smell of something burning. My blanket looked like a retarded Girl Scout's marshmallow. Did I almost light myself on fire like an Afghan woman? Was this a subconscious cry for help, a hysterical moment of protest and frustration at my mundane romanceless life, or did I just fall asleep in front of the heater?

My mother asked me what I wanted for Christmas yesterday and I said, "A pap smear."

She ignored that and started gushing about all the holiday parties I should be going to and all the nice new fellows I could meet in the next few weeks.

What are you doing for the holidays? My parents' house has central heating...

December 18
To: Amy
From: Mark
Subject: Home

Dear Amy,

I called my mom last night and told her all about Leah. I love my mom but we almost never talk about stuff like this. In fact, Leah's the first person I've told her about since Diana. She sounded happy and suggested I bring her home for the holidays. Why hadn't I thought of that!? I immediately went online, found tickets and called Leah. She was in Joshua Tree in the middle of a photo shoot with a speedmetal band. The reception was terrible, but at least I made out her answer: "Miami Beach? Are you kidding? Yes!"

So I – sorry – WE will be home for the holidays.

As tempting as your mother's cakes and cookies and the presence of central heating sounds...

Love,
Mark

December 20
To: Mark
From: Amy
Subject: Mark Goes WeeeWeee

Oh God you're "we-ing" and I am a minute away from Weird Aunt Amy mode.

Dear Santa, I'd like a peasant blouse, a hemp elastic waistband circle skirt, Birkenstocks and some large geode jewelry. I would also like a subscription to Kitty Cat monthly, and a Laura Nyro record. Don't forget that Guatemalan fabric fanny packs make great stocking stuffers.

I'm going to start practicing Weird Aunt Amy catchphrases to use at holidays.

Brother: When are you gonna get a boyfriend?

Me: Oh Kevin, a woman without a man is like a drunk fish watching the Tour de France. Anybody wanna French braid my armpit hair?

Have a wonderful time with Leah and your mom. I bet Miami will be a wonderful place to be in December.

December 21
To: Mark
From: Amy
Subject: I'm a Genius

I just came up with a brilliant idea! Shelley is coming to my parents' house for Christmas. Bless the gays, each and every one.

Finally, someone to drink beer with my dad.

Love,
Amy

P.S. Are you guys going to be in Miami for New Year's?

December 22
To: Amy
From: Mark
Subject: An invite in the St. Nick of time (minus the nicotine)

Sorry this is so rushed. We leave tonight.

Listen, sorry I didn't think of this myself earlier, but Leah had a great idea – she suggested I invite you (or you plus one) to Miami Beach to spend New Year's with us.

Wanna do it? Last minute deal kinda thing? We totally have room for you (and yours) in the house. Think about it. I'll be on e-mail in Miami, so lemme know.

Oh – I never told you what I'm getting her for Xmas. The best gift I could think of. I've always kept this secret to myself, that one day I would meet a woman for whom I would quit smoking. So Xmas Eve, I'm giving Leah my last pack and my beloved Zippo. And I mean it.

I am a man who is not at all scared of commitment.

– M.

P.S. we-count of this e-mail: 2.

December 23
To: Mark
From: Amy
Subject: Christmas Fantasy

That is really sweet and would be in line with most of my male/female relationships. The last time we hung out was at a wedding in February and then I spend Christmas with you, your mother, and your new girlfriend. Yeah. Sounds about right.

Thank you so much for extending the offer but Shelley is coming over tomorrow and we have to get on the freeway so that I can go fall asleep in church.

Bringing an outsider to holidays is key. I'm going to take Shell to Five Crowns, the local bar where twenty/thirtysomethings go drinking on Christmas Eve. I usually skip the Christmas reunion scene, but instead of shivering at how all the people I went to high school with fall into two categories (bloated and happy or beady-eyed and competitive), I'm going to just enjoy hanging out with my new friend in my old hometown.

Wouldn't it be fun to run into some mistletoe and Tiger Doyle? Last I heard he was in Georgia. (Shit. Secret's out of the bag. I kept tabs on the guy I had a crush on in preschool.)

Tell Leah I think she is ridiculously considerate and kind.

I'm glad you're kickin' the cancer sticks, but do it for yourself. If it's Leah's present it's void, or worse, it's a decision to resent. Do it because you like you and you know you like you better with white teeth and the ability to run stairs without an inhaler. When in doubt, harness your vanity, it will inspire when other things fail.

I care about you Mark, and want you in one unstinky piece. I'm sure Leah agrees.

Always,
Amy

December 25
To: Amy
From: Mark
Subject: Cold Turkey and Some Mistletoe

Merry Christmas, Amy!

I woke up this morning in my childhood room to the sound of running water and the sight of Leah in a body stocking. Needless to say, it was a very merry Christmas indeed. She drew me a bath and we slipped and slid, and all this before 8 am. Official wake up the parents time.

Sticklers for tradition, in my family we always open stockings first. Of course, I was already a step ahead, having recently unwrapped Leah. Next we gather around the tree, sipping egg nog and eating matzo brei (it's an odd family, sue me) where we exchange presents. Leah got me possibly the BEST crossover art/food gift: this golden rare book called Les Diners de Gala by Salvador Dali full of decadent photos and drawings of Sal and his wife's surrealist dinner parties, food sculpted into intricate lobster towers and animals eating themselves.

There I sat in my fairly normal home, with a book-window into an extraordinarily eccentric home, with Leah, imagining our future home which will have a foot firmly planted in each of these worlds.

It's all too good. Everyone's getting along with everyone. Even my Dalmatian Rorschach is crazy about Leah. You even like her, sight unseen.

But today's darling is definitely Mark. I never knew quitting smoking would earn me so much lavish loving, praise and adulation. I am a rock star. With the lung capacity of a shrimp. But that's changing. Leah says she can hardly wait for the oral-stimulation-cravings to kick in...

Tell me all about your Xmas. I picture Shelley Indian-wrestling your dad while your mother festoons the tree with Spaghettios. Am I close?

Ho ho ho,
Mark-o

P.S. I wasn't going to mention this, because it's probably nothing, but it's way too late in the game for me to start censoring myself, so: I'm probably totally wrong and over-reacting, but when I told Leah you weren't coming for New Year's, she seemed... relieved. Now I feel stupid I even said anything. For some silly reason I really want you two to like each other. I don't know.

December 25
To: Mark
From: Amy
Subject: Ask and You Shall Receive

Leah is totally normal (and therefore, may not be the girl for you). If I were there I would be the third fourth and fifth wheel, creating a terrible lopsided apparatus incapable of forward motion. She would be pleasant and have to ignore the fact that she wanted to ravage you ALONE in your childhood bedroom instead of playing charades with me. I would have to ignore the fact that she was ignoring that fact, everyone would drink too much and be sexually frustrated.

Now, are you sitting down?

Shelley and I went to church. I drooled on my hymnal until my dad punched me in the arm. We went home and ate "a Neiman Marcus ham." My mother reminded us of the retail pig no less than every ten minutes, then Shelley and I went to Five Crowns.

The bar was packed. I said hello to the Jenkins twins. They are both married and their husbands work at their father's car dealership. Laura is pregnant and Lisa is a schoolteacher. My lab partner from biology sophomore year gave me a hug, we ordered drinks and then Tiger Doyle walked in.

Did you hear me? Tiger Doyle walked in.

I told Shelley and she said, "If you don't go say hi to him I'm gonna tell your mom that you got her present at Rite Aid."

"Give me a minute."

I was trying to think of something charming to say and trying to get the lab partner out of the bar stool next to me when a voice said, "You still have those Mr. Potato Heads?"

I froze. Shelley smiled, stood up and provided an empty seat.

Tiger's divorced, works at a bank, wants to travel to South America, still likes macaroni and cheese. He is driving up to Los Angeles on Thursday to take me to dinner.

There really is no place like home for the holidays. Oh my gosh, what if I actually have a date on New Year's?

Wait. I just realized that Thursday is New Year's. Mark, I have a date with Tiger Doyle on New Year's Eve.

Amy

December 27
To: Amy
From: Mark
Subject: Happy Yellow New Year

You are lying. No you are hallucinating. You totally manufactured this out of your imagination. Borrow a cell phone camera immediately and take a picture of Tiger holding his driver's license up to the camera so I can see his name clearly, and then attach it as a jpeg to your next e-mail. And then, when I receive the photo – which will probably be a close-up of a Marmaduke comic strip, I will use it as evidence to have you committed.

I can't believe you ran into Tiger Doyle and are spending New Year's with him. Can life really be so obscenely perfect?

Quick question – I don't think you really got my Leah question. Sure, I understand the thing about her wanting me to herself on New Year's, but the confusing thing is, THEN WHY did she suggest inviting you in the first place!? That was HER idea!

That's the part I don't get. Was she just being polite? Was it a test? I'm still confused. But on the plus side, I'm still not smoking. I am acutely aware of it. It has become an action:

"What're you doing, Mark?"

"Can't you see? I'm not smoking."

December 29
To: Amy
From: Mark
Subject: Cheating

It's 4 am, and I feel like I'm cheating on Leah. I literally snuck out of bed, carefully climbing out from under her arm, tiptoeing to my stepfather's office to use his computer to write you.

We had another fight four hours ago, and this time it was definitely not my fault. I was writing you an e-mail, which is now totally lost, because Leah came up behind me in a bathing suit and got angry that I was writing to you instead of going for a midnight swim with her. Her exact quote: "You two have been at this a whole year now, why don't you just get a room and get it over with?"

That's verbatim. Where did this come from? I suddenly feel like I don't get women at all. We've been having such an amazing time. Something is going on.

Anyway, I got super defensive, insisting everything is just platonic with you and me, and then I got really mad at her, for putting me on the defensive. I called her insecure. I asked her where was the confident woman I fell for. She was really pushing my buttons because clearly I had pushed hers without meaning to.

Where does this come from? I hate conflict – as I've mentioned before – and it's almost the new year and I just didn't want to be having this fight. So I pushed the button to save the e-mail to you as a draft, but my stepdad's computer is different and somehow I ended up erasing it.

She swam by herself while I went to bed early; sometimes my whole body and brain shut down as a way of avoiding chaos.

When she slid into bed, she was all sweetness, stroking my hair and telling me she was sorry. I'm so confused, Amy. What is going on? I wondered if she'd been reading our e-mails. She would never do that. But even if she did, so what? Haven't I only said really nice things about her?

Utterly baffled,
Mark

December 31
To: Mark
From: Amy
Subject: Suspicious Minds

It makes Leah nervous how close we are. That's understandable, sometimes it makes me nervous how close we are.

You know why she suggested inviting me. She wants to like everything you do. If you wanted to watch Pearl Harbor all weekend while eating diet popcorn she'd wanna do that too. She's in love with you, dumdum. Patch things up. Explain to her that we are, you know, whatever we are. Friends who talk about everything. Who can't spend more than two days apart, online. Whatever.

The fact that I am having dinner with Tiger Doyle tonight is romantic karma madness. I have not spoken to him in twenty years (his father was made partner at his law firm and they moved to a larger home shortly after the potato head party). I mean, we used to see each other in high school at dances and parties, but we never talked. Not like the way we did when we were five. Oh God, what are we going to talk about?

I had to call and ask him if I should get dressed up. He said, "Why not?"

See. I told you I'd have somewhere to wear the dress. I feel like I bought this thing a million years ago.

Your Pink and Sparkly Wishful Purchase,
A.

P.S. The best New Year to you.

January 1
To: Amy
From: Mark
Subject: The Stroke of Midnight

It's not fair. I remember once writing you that no one ever said that life is fair. It isn't.

It wasn't supposed to end like this.

I haven't slept, so I don't feel like writing you all the details about what happened last night. The only good news is that at least I figured out what's been going on in Leah's head lately. So, mystery solved. But at what expense.

She told me she wanted to spend New Year's alone with me on the beach. We did. After the sun set, she gave me a present. I unwrapped it. It was a box of my brand of condoms. It rattled. I opened it. It was empty. Except for a note: "Let's do it." She proposed to me. Not marriage. She wanted us to start trying to have a kid.

I guess she'd been planning this for a while which is what put her on edge the last few days. Anyway, I was taken aback, and that seemed to terrify her – it wasn't the reaction she was expecting.

I told her that I very much want to have children some day and that I think we'd have beautiful kids and that she'd be a great mother. She cried. I did, too. But I still didn't grasp the situation.

She started undoing my pants and I asked her what she was doing. She got upset again. I asked her, did she mean let's do it now?

Yes. That's exactly what she meant. "But, Leah, we've only known each other two months. I'm crazy about you, but it's been two months!"

"Yeah, and I'm 42, Mark, how much more time do you think I have?" I didn't have a comeback. I guess I hadn't thought of it, that's the simple truth.

Never before had I been so aware that I am not a woman, and no matter how many I know and how much I've learned from our letters this past year and from my life, I can never hope to understand certain things.

She reminded me of our conversations, how we both want big things, and I said I don't take any of that back, but that I never meant two months. I said can't we just wait a little longer?

"How much longer?"

I tried to answer, then realized I couldn't, couldn't come up with a number, and she needed a number.

She said she felt like I was testing her, and how many more tests did I have in mind?

I don't think that I'm like that. But am I? Is the "honeymoon period" just the sugar-coating on a serious little pill called "compatibility testing"? How did this all happen?

I told you a long time ago, I firmly believe that no couple has ever had a productive conversation when one of them was in fight-or-flight mode. Well, we both were, and it got nasty. She accused me of having led her on and wasted her time. I said I felt blind-sided, rabbit-punched.

When finally she stormed away, waves crashing dramatically to frame her exit, I sat in the sand and all I could think about was how much I love her. By the time I came to and went after her, I couldn't find her. She wasn't at the car. I drove around up and down the streets, but couldn't find her anywhere. I was a wreck.

At 6 am I drove home, the sun was rising, and she wasn't there. Her cell phone was there with the rest of her stuff so I had no way to call her. She had a small purse, nothing more. I had never felt so helpless in my life.

In the morning my mom asked where Leah was and I said she was out for a jog. My mother could sense something was wrong. I went and hid in my room all day. About 5 pm I got an e-mail from Leah saying she'd flown back to L.A. – she couldn't bear the thought of flying for five hours next to me, knowing I was not ready to have a child with her. She asked me to make sure I brought back all her stuff.

I offered some lame excuse to mom and changed my ticket so that I'm coming back tonight on a red-eye. I've got to get some sleep but I can't sleep.

Help me, Amy. I'm sorry to have said nothing about your pink sparkly reunion with Tiger. Please forgive my one-trackedness. How many life cave-ins can happen in a year? If I had an insurance policy on my heart, I'd be filthy and miserably rich.

January 1
To: Mark
From: Amy
Subject: New Year New Creepy People

5, 6, 7, 8, and BREED!

Wow. I'm sorry honey. I am. Though in a weird way, I understand. Leah was upfront from the beginning. She wants a relationship and a baby. You want a life not spent hopping to the tick tock of the clock. Right?

Leah is a fool. A fool with a plan, but a fool nonetheless. You two had so much in common and yet she refused to respect process. As a photographer, she should be well aware of the necessity of process. I am sorry you are sad my friend. How about this generic idea to put things in perspective: we are all exactly where we are supposed to be.

Would you like to compare pain to boredom – my New Year's Day highlight was going to three supermarkets with Susan to find black-eyed peas.

But Amy, you wonder, what happened with the glorious Tiger Doyle?

Ahhh, yes. The wunderkind of preschool lust, Tiger Doyle came to the door, wearing jeans. The first moment was awkward squared.

"Hi. Happy New Year. Why am I the only one dressed up?"

"It's fine. You look really nice."

Everything he is wearing has a label on it, Nike t-shirt, Levi's, Hat with Volcom logo, jacket with Quicksilver logo, I notice that his socks have a Tommy Hilfiger symbol. The man looks like he's going to NASCAR.

Okay. Letting it go, moving on, I walk out my front door towards his car, of course it is a giant white SUVehicle. Every time I see these things I imagine Ford developing a new one and naming it 'Ennui.'

Ennui, the latest SUV, fits a family of four. Hey, do you guys wanna go for a ride in the new Ennui? It just drives in a circle over and over again, soccer practice, high school, piano lessons, church, soccer practice, high school, piano lessons, church.

"I don't know LA very well," he says, "so I made us dinner reservations at the Century Hotel."

What??? A fucking hotel? Are you mad? I let it go. At least I won't run into anyone I know while wearing my prom dress.

"Super."

At the hotel restaurant, it's that goofy scene: set menu, mostly old people. I remember why I usually stay in on New Year's, when the waiter in a foil hat blows a horn at me and asks me if I'd prefer steak or sea bass.

We have some wine, and then Tiger begins to talk. Really talk.

"I divorced my wife last year. It's been hard. I mean, we met in college, probably got married too early. She wanted to go back to school, I wanted a family. So I let her take night school classes at the community college, 'Chinese History from Yao to Mao.' She wrote a paper on the Tang Dynasty and then she slept with her professor."

"I'm sorry," I say.

"Yeah. Well. I couldn't compete with Dr. Ping."

I tried to drive the chat back to the present, told him how I'd been in Los Angeles since college, how much I loved the city despite the celebrity nonsense. He says he'd never live in LA, too far from the beach, too much "garbage." I admitted to liking garbage. I asked him about the job in Atlanta.

"Well, I guess the best thing about that was the secretaries with southern accents."

Then he said, "You know what my template of the perfect woman is? A ballerina. Delicate. Feminine."

I think about my dress for a moment and wonder if I am these things. I wonder why it matters so much, to me and to Tiger.

"Well," I say, "I think that females start to fall into two categories, it's wifey vs. good woman."

"What are you?" he says

"Maybe a little bit of both." He nods and looks uncomfortable.

We finished dinner and then went to the bar to wait for the stroke. At midnight we hugged and kissed on the cheek, same as our sandbox, circa 1980.

When leaving, the valet slammed my dress in the big white SUV door. It ripped a little at the hem and there were some nasty grease smudges, but it didn't matter. I was tossing this dress out along with the insane notion that I'd found my soulmate at five years old.

If we could sedate Leah, she and Tiger might be a real match.

xoxo
a.

January 2
To: Amy
From: Mark
Subject: Dropping off

When I got to my truck in self-parking, someone had written in the dirt, "I WISH MY WIFE WAS THIS DIRTY." I knew it wasn't Leah. She would have used the subjunctive.

I drove straight to her place to drop off her stuff and see where she was at. She tends to explode, then quickly calm down, so I was hoping for the best.

It was 7 am. I knocked lightly. No answer. So I left the bags with a simple note saying I was at the café down the block. I sat there and caffeinated for a few hours then came back at 10.

Still no answer.

Just as I was about to leave, she opened the door.

I said hi. She said thanks for dropping off the stuff. I said no problem.

She said have you given it more thought. I said can I come inside so we can talk.

She said have you given it more thought. I said all I know is I need more time.

She said the one thing she didn't have was time. Then she closed the door.

I don't think Tiger would like Leah. She is more kickboxer than ballerina. And I know Leah wouldn't like Tiger, for the same reasons you closed the door on that daydream. Provincially closed minds are as infertile as untilled soil.

Love,
I don't know whether to sign this e-mail "Heartbreaker" or "Heartbroken."

January 5
To: Mark
From: Amy
Subject: We will be fine

Don't you think going to her house at seven am was a little dramatic? I mean, if the woman wants to have a baby she's got to be well-rested. I just think you should have called first. Saved yourself the theatrics. Anyway, it seems to be... over?

I'm sorry, Mark.

Hey – did I tell you that on New Year's Day, Susan and I had a major come-to-jesus?

I told her I didn't mean to hurt her feelings that night when I dropped her off at Jake's. She said she wished she would've stayed in the car and fought with me instead of going up to his eighties coke pad apartment. Black leather as far as the eye could see. Duran Duran albums on the wall, framed. And (shocker) total whiskey dick.

As for Leah, if she was 'the one' you would've had kegs of sperm breakin' down her ovary door. You know it, too. You didn't feel it in your guts, so now you're wondering why you didn't HAVE the guts to tell yourself that. You are also wondering if you made a huge mistake, as in "Hey, if you happen to see the most beautiful girl, that walked out on me, tell her I'm sorry, tell her I need my baby..."

You are sweet, Mark. Dramatic, but sweet. I understand, though. When Alex and I broke up, I sat in his rent-a-car while he told me that he loved me, and his face was so full of conviction and determination that all I could think was, God, I hope I feel this passionate about somebody someday. I really do. Even if I get kicked in the chops, to feel all the things he is claiming to feel, all that fire in the sky. I want to feel that way about someone.

Upon further inspection it became obvious to me that a large portion of Alex's feelings were about what I meant to him. I meant Los Angeles (he insisted he could court monthly from Cleveland), I meant the possibility of not having to continue working at the family paper products company (he wanted to find part-time weekend film projects). I was a link to keeping his dreams alive.

Without dating me, he had no business coming back to LA all the time, unless he really invested in his career, and he was not going to do that, which is why he was leaving in the first place.

To me, he meant losing my messy single girl ways of leaving a half-eaten yogurt next to my hair dryer.

I know that these things may or may not be true, but this is how they felt, and until I can find someone who can handle, no wait, enjoy, all the not-quite-matured parts of me, and vice versa, then I will wait.

What does (or did) Leah mean to you?

Me. I'm making macaroni and cheese tonight. Realized something else with Tiger Doyle – I like dating, I just hate getting to know people.

Your Friend,
Amy

P.S. What did you think that you had to "talk" with Leah about, when you went to see her?

January 6
To: Amy
From: Mark
Subject: Bookends

I don't know if you're right. That my unwillingness to spermatazoically budge is an indicator that she's not the one. Can't it just mean I'm sanely unimpulsive when it comes to creating life? I still believe if we'd had another, I dunno, six or seven months before she broached conception, it would have made a vas deferens.

Diana wasn't ready to do the big stuff. Her excuse was reasonable: her age. So she dumped me. Now, almost exactly a year later I meet an incredible woman with whom I connect on every level, and she wants it all, but wants it too soon, prematurely. I can't reason with her. And so I must leave.

I am willing to take skyscraper leaps for love. I'll move to another country, change jobs, put finances on the line. I will move mountains with a demitasse spoon. The biggest rewards demand the biggest risks. But I will not roll the dice with an innocent human life.

Leah can. She has that much faith in me, in us. She thinks I am using this as an out.

Amy, you have called me a Guy on numerous occasions. In the end, is that all I am, yet another protoplasmic lump afraid of commitment? Am I just another scared boy?

– M.

January 7
To: Mark
From: Amy
Subject: Baby Boy

Possibly. We're not sure yet. But you are not into her BECAUSE she needs the hyperspeed stork. That is part of her, and her values. It isn't part of yours. At the end of the day, it comes down to values, and lips and eyes and biceps and breasts – but values too.

I can't write. I just went to the pharmacy. Something terrible has happened.

January 7
To: Amy
From: Mark
Subject: ???

What happened? Don't leave me hanging like that! Please write ASAP.

January 7
To: Mark
From: Amy
Subject: Ritual

"What happened?" The Valentine's decorations are up and you and I are approaching our anniversary, a year from the day that we decided to act as AA-style sponsors to each other in our romance addiction. Or whatever it is.

Mark, I am going to take some serious action. Tomorrow I am going through my apartment and I am dumping everything given to me from a past man friend. I am going to clear out some space for someone real. Someone new.

January 8
To: Amy
From: Mark
Subject: Reassurance

Dear Amy,

I'm confused. What happened? Are we talking about something physical or emotional?

Today I called Diana. I asked her the same questions I asked you two days ago. She was really amazing. For the first time since the breakup, it felt like we were real friends. She told me not to feel so bad. She said she knows me and knows I'm not the commitment-phobic kind. That my only "problem" is that I am a responsible human being. And that this is indeed a tragedy, but not every tragedy has to have a villain, and that in this case there is no bad guy or girl. Just plain sadness.

She was thrilled that I quit smoking. What do you call the opposite of "collateral damage"? My lungs' new lease on life is definitely an unexpected bonus of knowing Leah.

It felt great to talk to Diana. And even better, it felt great that I had no nostalgia, no desire to get back together. Only an enjoyment of what it is about her that I admire – she sees the world clearly, simply and compassionately.

Always,
Mark

P.S. I will only admit I am addicted to love if you promise to wear one of those tight black dresses and carry a big electric guitar, like in the Robert Palmer video.

January 10
To: Mark
From: Amy
Subject: I love me

What happened, oh Man-With-Man-Like-Lack-of-Response-to-Cultural-Novelty-Cues, was that I went to the store to get toiletries in January and had to face an aisle of shiny hearts and Valentine's items. Pink candles, mugs with cupid, the whole bloody gold-doilied shebang.

A year ago I didn't care as much, but after spending all this time analyzing my relationships with you, I feel more rudderless than ever.

I had a good cry and then decided that being single is fine. It is more than fine, it is where I am and because of that it can be nothing less than great. (The fake-it-till-you-make-it school of behavior.)

To commemorate the year, I made a funeral pyre of the man-gifts:

1. Miu Miu pumps (Lance)

2. Vintage AC/DC t-shirt (Ted left it here)

3. Pocket Rocket vibrator (don't ask)

4. A set of screwdrivers (Jeremy)

5. White silk nightgown (Alex)

6. Pink cotton underpants that say South by Southwest Music Festival on the ass (Dark Bill)

Then I called up Cleveland Monthly and told them to cancel my subscription. That felt good.

xoxo,
Amy

P.S. "Responsible human being." Fine. Why can't you just admit that you found her demanding demeanor a turn-off? One day it's about taking the trash out, the next day it's about kids, you just didn't wanna wake up and wonder who stole your 'nads.

January 11
To: Amy
From: Mark
Subject: Time in a Bottle

No word from Leah. I'm reduced to listening to sappy love songs which seem to seep in through the pores of the wooden walls. Jim Croce is singing, "If I had a box just for wishes and dreams that had never come true, the box would be empty except for the memory of how they were answered by you."

Well, that's sweet and all, Jim, but if the box is just for wishes and dreams, what the hell are memories doing in there? Don't you have a basket of memories, or a carton of nostalgia, maybe a vase of remembrances? Jim, face it: the box is empty. You've got the memory, but it's not in the box.

And your box is empty, too. But will throwing out the artifacts also sweep away all those cobwebbed memories? Only time will tell. For now, I say good for you, Amy.

In the spirit of Charlize Theron's breasts: onward and upward.

January 12
To: Amy
From: Mark
Subject: Frozen Butterball

Been ten days since I've heard from her. Another week without cigarettes. I feel hollow and ravaged and I miss her so much (Leah, not my cruel brown leafy mistress).

I want to call her, I want to write her, I want to show up with garlands of pearls hand-collected from oysters at the bottom of every one of the planet's oceans. But I have not and will not. Out of respect.

My monthly dinner club meets tonight. The theme is "Paris in the Thirties." I'm making macaroni and cheese.

M.

P.S. I wonder if she's already looking for someone else.

January 15
To: Mark
From: Amy
Subject: Cheesy goodness

I don't know if throwing the stuff out will usher in a new groin, but it was hard for me to do. I think it means that as long as I kept the stuff, then I was still attached to the possibility of those guys, of them changing or even of me changing for them.

When I put all that stuff on the table, I looked at it and wondered, "What happened this year?" and then I told myself the truth and that is, I DON'T KNOW.

What I do know is that these things that stripped me, elevated me, electrified me, left me a little thinned-out and gave me new wrinkled raspberry scar tissue. I can let them go out the window.

And I can be sure that I am better today because I am clearer, but not colder. All that pride that I swallowed has made its way into a shiny glow reserved for infants. I guess that's how love works: you expose a little more of yourself, you can be sheer and fragile like a pale pink dress and know that being trampled is part of it but not the end.

Now if you'll excuse me, I have to go find my meds.

I think you should write Leah a letter and then bury it out in the sand where you first met Addie. We're putting them both to bed.

You don't care if she's with someone else, because Leah wasn't the woman you wanted to be with. The woman you want to be with doesn't give you ultimatums. (Or if she does, they give you an erection.)

I have a friend who wants to set me up this weekend. Should I go?

Tell me what you think or I won't be your friend.

Your favorite,
Amy

January 17
To: Amy
From: Mark
Subject: Broken

Yes, you should go on the setup.

You just made room in your life and your heart. So why forego the Jell-O now? The worst thing that happens is I get another great story from you. Another letter from the frontline.

Either way, I win. And you, you've got nothing to lose.

Me, I've been walking along the beach once or twice a day. Seems like all I see are mothers and babies. Toddlers on the boardwalk. Each pair of eyes looks up at me in accusation: You failed her, Mark. I feel crushed under the wheels of their strollers.

You're right. Maybe I secretly do love ultimatums. I can't bear the thought of Leah missing out on her life dream. She deserves to have her prayers answered. I know she does.

Can't take it anymore. Why don't I just do it? Take the plunge. What's the worst thing that could happen?

Unless I hear otherwise from you by the end of the day, I am going to go over there tonight and propose.

No pressure.

Mark

January 17
To: Mark
From: Amy
Subject: Talk About Ultimatums

GREAT IDEA!!!!! Offer to spend the rest of your life with someone you've known for two months because... de wanna widdy biddy baaaaby.

You have told me that this does not feel right to you.

HALT. LISTEN TO YOUR HAIRY MAN HEART.

I know you love Leah, but she is not the last woman on the planet. Get out of scarcity thinking. Write me back ASAP and confirm that you are not at Robbins Brothers buying a giant ring made out of 24K FEAR.

January 18
To: Amy
From: Mark
Subject: All that glitters isn't guilt

I ignored your advice. I went over to her place and made a pitch. She should be sainted. She didn't want a man who was merely capitulating, caving in out of guilt. She told me to go home and think about it. Said I was talking too animatedly, it seemed too much like a whim.

I protested. But she held firm. By the time I got home I realized she was right. And I already knew you were right. I just couldn't help myself.

I'm struck by how profoundly I am moved by guilt. People talk about Catholic guilt, Jewish guilt, Japanese mothers ply with it, too. It seems like guilt is hard-wired into every culture.

But it's a lousy reason to have a kid. This situation with Leah was and is a nightmare.

I think your setup date is tomorrow or the day after. Please tell me everything. I want you to just forget about this whole situation of mine. I want to know every detail of your date. Because this tunnel of love/roller coaster ride is CLOSED FOR REPAIRS UNTIL FURTHER NOTICE.

– m.

January 19
To: Mark
From: Amy
Subject: Tripping

Just so you know, I'm going out with Scott tonight. He is a friend of Marla's boyfriend.

Also, just so you know, I don't believe in guilt. Guilt is manufactured in a small town at the pit of your stomach. Just take "I Don't Want To Take Responsibility For My Own Wants and Needs" Lane, make a right at "If I Do This People Will Like And Accept Me" Avenue and you'll be at guilt.

a.

P.S. I will come back with a full Scott field report.

January 21
To: Amy
From: Mark
Subject: Return to Sender

I wrote a long e-mail to Leah. She wrote me back a haiku. In seventeen syllables she politely asked me to leave her be while she moves on.

R-E-S-P-E-C-T. I found out what it means to her.

Next time I get the urge to drive over there or write her, I'll e-mail you instead (and actually wait for your reply).

Scott was the night before last. Check in with me soon, so I know he wasn't an axe murderer. Or that the two of you aren't out cuddling alpacas. I hope you either got off or got off Scott-free.

Your eternal cheerleader,
Sparky

January 21
To: Mark
From: Amy
Subject: Repelling

Scott was about as interesting as pumice. Oh, wait. Pumice has texture.

I think retelling a boring date is more torturous than the date itself, so I'll just say that anyone who dresses in four colors of sand and talks about geology for more than two glasses of barbera should be tenured and well paid for their love of sediment.

We sat down at a wine bar in West Hollywood and Scott described himself as "a real rock hound." I asked if he preferred classic or contemporary, Led Zeppelin versus the White Stripes. He looked at me like I said something in Latin, then told me all about sand and gravel and mica and erosion.

I know, I should be open, learn something, be fascinated instead of trying to be fascinating, but Mark, he was talking about gravel.

He was tall, with sandy blonde hair. I kept hoping that he'd let out some sort of wild streak. Not a chance. This guy is all about magma and related topics.

He seemed interested in me, I told him about my job, my fire-breathing mother, my occasional inner-channeling of Lisa Marie Presley (perhaps this was too much).

Things were going well. I thought, So he's a bit boring. I could learn to love the rocks. Go to rock shows. Hang out in Arizona. Get a shovel. Did I tell you he was handsome?

I told him it was my bedtime, he ASKED ME to stay for another drink. I declined. He told me he hadn't had this much fun in ages. I drove home thinking that maybe there could be a little something here worth excavating, despite how boring the first hour and forty-five minutes were. Gravel Boy was turning me around.

Now it's been two days. No call. Was he lying when he told me "this was the best time ever"? I can't think about it. Why do I care that the boring rock guy isn't calling? I'm swamped at work and I've been so grumpy.

I haven't seen the pretty gay boys at the gym in weeks. I need to stairmaster with the Schneiders.

But seriously, why would he say that?

January 24
To: Amy
From: Mark
Subject: Rocky Road

Dear Amythyst,

A rock hound who drinks Barbera? Are you sure his name wasn't Huckleberry? Doll, you have to dust off that old sedimentary list of man-criteria. You said you wanted a man with a burning passion about Anything. Not Anything that you, too, happen to find thrilling.

Ahh, grasshopper, so you say you wish to know why men say they will call and then do not. I ask you, are you prepared to receive the sacred and carefully guarded answer? Fold your legs on this cushion and I shall tell you:

Just coz.

Coz you didn't spark his tinder into flames. But like most guys, he's not a fan of confrontation. So he blew smoke (where there's smoke there's not always fire) up your pretty little ass, and erased your number from his phone.

But wait, don't leave just yet. There is more. Much more. Fact is, there are MANY reasons. Men are simple creatures, but we do not live simple lives. Much can intercede between the digit and the dial.

So how about this? Let's switch positions. You stand and I will kneel and ask forgiveness.

Your job: take my confession, be my intercessor. I have a lot to apologize for. A lifetime of undialed numbers...

True, I usually say, "talk to you later" or "see you later," both of which are vague enough to be defensible in a court of law. But I won't get into heaven on a technicality, so here goes.

And so, I am very, very sorry that I never called you back:

- Bernice, because you freaked me out ironing your stepdad's trousers.
- Tonya, because we met online and when you showed up you bore no resemblance whatsoever to "Tonya." Why start off a potential relationship with a lie? It didn't even cross my mind to call.
- Sarah, ditto.
- Israeli lady who showed up with her Bichon-Frise and whose name I've forgotten, double ditto.

- Jessica, because I told you I was taking you to a charming French bistro and you arrived in sweatpants.
- DeeDee, because you spent a full hour complaining about how hard it is to find a decent guy, and our date lasted exactly one hour.
- [Celebrity – name withheld], because I frankly felt you were out of my league, and I got the distinct sense you only went out with me to have a laugh at my expense and I felt a little rotten about myself when I got home.
- Kathy-with-a-y, because you said absolutely nothing but, "Cool. What else?" for the entire date. And when I asked you questions you said, "Nothing much" or "I don't know" and then "But what about you?"
- Kathi-with-an-i, because I didn't realize 'til halfway through dinner that you look exactly like my mother. So I kind of freaked.
- Gillian, because I met you at a bar and you had huge fake breasts and five-inch heels and a rawhide micro-skirt, and when you tipped the bartender I saw your purse was full of ones, so I knew you were a stripper even though you told me you were a physician. My jaw dropped three months later when I saw you on the cover of Los Angeles Magazine's Best Doctors issue.
- Leila, because I invited you to drinks and after ordering two glasses of champagne you insisted you were starving and when I said I'd already eaten you told me that was ok I could watch and then strong-armed me into buying you dinner.
- Cathy-with-a-c, because after our third date when I tried to kiss you goodnight, you turned away for the third time in a row and I figured you wouldn't grieve if I never called.
- Dina, because when you asked me about religion and if I'd be willing to convert, I knew I gave the wrong answer and was pretty certain you weren't interested.
- Judy, because the day after we met I got this huge new contract at work, threw myself into it, and horrible as it sounds (I'm sorry), you just didn't make enough of an impression and I totally forgot.
- The Aussie anthropologist, because you're the one who did the Skull Kiss. Enough said.
- Cora, because you were lovely, but I'd just been dumped, and was too afraid of getting rejected again. Truth is I kept hoping you would call.

- Trista, because you were so excruciatingly emaciated that I actually felt sad looking at you and when you shook vinegar on your salad it looked like your wrist might break.

- Tina, because you were so cynical and kept telling me you knew I wasn't going to call and you made such a huge deal of your bitter certainty, I decided to prove you right.

- Priya, because you asked me four times, "Are you sure you're not gay?" and the first time I thought it was funny, but by the end of lunch, I was annoyed.

- Stace, because after you spent the night, my watch went missing. And two furious weeks later when I found the watch (it had fallen behind the sofa), I was way too embarrassed to call and explain why I hadn't called. You were totally hot and I blew it.

- Bree, because I found out you used to date Dean.

- Talya, because Dean told me something about you he probably shouldn't have, and which I'm too embarrassed to write.

- Sylvia, because I met someone else two days later whom I liked better, and I didn't want to lie to you, and I didn't want to tell you the truth.

Tail-between-my-leggedly,
Mark

January 26
To: Mark
From: Amy
Subject: Sure I Can

"Blowing smoke up my pretty little ass?"

See, if everybody stopped subscribing to guilt... well, then no one would go home for holidays, airfares would dip, ham sales would go down, we would crash the economy. All right everyone, keep up the subterfuge.

So, then, the list of reasons that you didn't call women back has no rhyme or reason. This is good to know. Reassuringly random. Rock boy hasn't called, maybe he [insert one of the 23 reasons you didn't call those ladies back].

I just got an invitation to another wedding. The good news is the groom, Ben St. Sure (that's his name, I swear), is a friend from high school. The bad news is, I had a fling with his older brother at their law school graduation party.

At first I was worried that they wouldn't invite me (fooling around in the laundry room is grounds for future social event dismissal) but they did. More bad news, I can't remember his name. All I remember is Ben's grandmother saying what a cute couple we made, a band that played Rod Stewart covers, and the smell of dryer sheets and champagne.

How do I find out his name? He was a really good kisser. Oh God, if I have to find a yearbook that means I have to go to my mom's house. Could I just call him Mr. St. Sure?

January 29
To: Amy
From: Mark
Subject: The Closure Makes the Man

Dear Amy,

You get to the wedding early and look at the place cards. That was an easy one. I'm also a big fan of the enthusiastic, "Hey you!" Play your cards right and you're in for a little cling-free bounce and snuggle.

So Leah wrote me an apologetic e-mail. After a month of blaming me for leading her on with big talk about starting a family, she found herself thumbing through her little black book. She recognized the juggernaut of her desire to have a kid, and soberly realized the pressure she'd put on the shoulders of a young relationship.

I think she's overstating things; it takes two to screw up a tango. Still, I'm relieved to again hear the voice of the Leah I'd loved, and to know once and for all that the Leah I knew was neither a honeymoon confection nor a product of my wishful imagination.

That said, the lines have been drawn. And that is that.

Over and out,
M.

P.S. Will you don the ripped purple taffeta?

February 1
To: Mark
From: Amy
Subject: Barney is Dead

The purple taffeta is not in any condition for wearing, not that it was before either. It has been given to Goodwill (the dry cleaner couldn't get the salsa stain out after my birthday party).

Are you and Leah going to continue to be 'friends'?

I tend to think of that notion as one party assuaging their own guilt. So I'm not a big fan.

Ben St. Sure just called, to tell me that after I fooled around with his brother at the graduation party, his brother went back to Fresno and e-mailed him a photo of a hickey I administered. Ah, technology.

A girl can't even tramp around and get away with it anymore.

February 2
To: Amy
From: Mark
Subject: Shadows and Fog

Oh that was YOUR love bite? That e-mail went around my office, too. Nice. Your broken capillaries are famous, Amos.

Leah's haiku still stands. One day, perhaps we could be friends, but it's a statistical improbability. Speaking of which:

If Punxsutawney Phil sees his shadow today, it will be another six weeks of my winter of discontent, taking me to the Ides of March, when my heart's liable to be stabbed from behind on the steps of the Senate.

If only I could fit him with a little groundhog blindfold...

Happy G-Day, pal.

Furrily yours,
Mulligatawny Mark

February 4
To: Mark
From: Amy
Subject: Trouble is Okay

Glad you liked my slutty e-mail photo. As for Mr. St. Sure, his first name is Joseph. Joseph St. Sure.

I couldn't help it, I had to figure out his full name. So yesterday I drove to my parents' house.

It was about five and no one was home, so I started digging through all the Reader's Digests under the panty-liner bed. Where the hell did my mom put my freshman yearbook?

In walks Betsey (my mother) wearing her three-tiered line dancing skirt and rhinestone "DANCE" brooch, obviously returning from another evening at Denim and Diamonds in Anaheim.

"Amy, what are you doing?"

"I'm trying to find my yearbook."

"Why?"

"I just want my yearbook. I have to find out the name of a guy I made out with."

"They're in the attic. How about a salmon sandwich? I've got coleslaw."

"Mom. I really just need the yearbook."

"Well that's tough, cause I'm not going up in the attic in my cowboy boots, so you're going to have to wait."

ARRRRRGGGGGG. I have to wait. I cannot navigate my way alone through the city of unmarked boxes and dust.

Half a salmon sandwich, scoop of coleslaw and three butter cookies later I get her into the attic.

"How could you not remember the name of the guy you made out with?" she says.

I shrug.

"Oh Amy."

And I got ready for her to chastise me. I got all buckled in for the 'When I married your father I was a virgin' speech, I'm ready, I've got my mantra ready, I choose peace now... and then she... she... she starts laughing? My mother (who never laughs) is laughing?

"You are so funny. Running around always looking for excitement. Always looking for trouble. But then I suppose a certain amount of trouble's okay."

I am so confused. My mother just said, "A certain amount of trouble's okay."

Plus, she is LAUGHING!

"The day I met your father I was done for. One blind date, he walked to the door and that was it. I knew it was all over for me. He was the most handsome man I'd ever seen. He borrowed a friend's car to take me out and I loved him that second. I loved him when he was eighteen and drunk and catching rattlesnakes at fraternity parties, I hated him when I was twenty and on Valentine's Day he sent me roses with another girl's name on the card but I loved him when he carried my books and I loved him terribly when he wrote me letters from Viet Nam. Then I loved him when he came home from Viet Nam and ran around with a bunch of beach bimbos. I loved him when you and Kevin were born and I love him today when he sits in that chair and falls asleep with the apple core on his shirt. Nothing you can do about love."

Hmmm. So I hear.

February 4
To: Amy
From: Mark
Subject: A Prayer in a Fun House

What are we doing, Amy?

Maybe all we're looking for is a pair of mirrors in the shape of eyes.

And in these mirrors we always look pretty, handsome, smart, sharp, the belle and the beau of the ball.

Your mom's right. Nothing you can do about love.

February 5
To: Mark
From: Amy
Subject: Blind Justice

All right! Enough of our namby-pamby love stuff. Back to the brass tacks (or brassy and tacky, as was the case last night).

I went out on a date with an entertainment lawyer who refuses to read menus. He proudly explained to me that he didn't have time to read menus and that he always knows what he wants anyway, so why waste his time.

He then asked the waitress for a plate of spinach with a side of prosciutto. The waitress explained that they didn't have prosciutto, they had what was on the menu.

He tore into the waitress, all about how he was the paying customer, and how she should go tell the chef to bring him the closest thing to steamed spinach and prosciutto.

I got up and explained that I had to use the ladies' room and then drove home.

February 5
To: Amy
From: Mark
Subject: Jones

No, not the bar where the smoking fetish racist inhaled.

I am jonesing for a cigarette. Forget girls. I miss Nat Sherman.

Why are there people like that lawyer on the planet, Amy?

If I had been at that restaurant last night, I would have shouted to you for the first and only (I hope!) time in my life, "You go, girl!"

But if you ever tell this to anyone I will hunt you down and give you a ball gag with fancy red leather straps.

February 6
To: Mark
From: Amy
Subject: No Fumar Homeboy

It was hideous. On the way home I kind of laughed. I think a year ago I would've sat through dinner gritting my teeth, but if I've realized anything, it's that my time is valuable.

Do the same thing with the smoky treats and keep your no-smoking thing going. Your time is valuable. The more foreign garbage you choose stick in your lungs, the less time you get to e-mail me. Also, I still believe in the vanity angle. Wrinkles, wrinkles, wrinkles. I remember you being a tan fellow. You are striking a balance, embracing your inner Redford while eschewing your self-imposed Harry Dean Stanton.

Do you have any dates lined up?

February 7
To: Amy
From: Mark
Subject: Bite your tongue

Dear Amy,

Please do not badmouth Nat Shermans! Even though I know it's over, I still love them!

It'd be like you saying something nasty about Diana. That too is over, but I still love her.

So leave them be! And don't worry. I won't smoke and I won't appear on Diana's doorstep with a box of platinum, diamonds and utter foolishness. True, a few years from now, after she's had a chance to roam the globe, who knows what might happen. But if I ever do meet her again, hopefully it will be with fresh breath.

Defensively yours,
Mark

P.S. I am dateless. And I feel fine. No regrets about deleting those fifty numbers. You?

February 9
To: Mark
From: Amy
Subject: Soundtracks

Of course I feel fine. I am committed to not acting like my singleness is a tumor, remember?

I am a little lonely, though. I think it's good to admit that.

Oh sure, listening to Otis Redding doesn't help, but I'm one of those people who really likes to enhance her feelings with props.

I have candles, soft pink light bulbs, the strangely well-manicured self with no one to discover it, and soul music talking about being down so low.

I know all those dorky chick books will tell me to embrace my inner beauty and have some 'special alone time' to loofah myself and then do some Wiccan ritual calling upon my feminine wisdom and channeling all the love in my heart and letting it fill me up and blah blah blah, but the truth is, tonight I just feel kind of lonely.

It's not really special alone time, it's specially lonely time. But I don't know, maybe that's okay too.

If I had put on Sly and the Family Stone this would've been a different note.

February 9
To: Amy
From: Mark
Subject: Happy Ending...?

When I asked, "You?" I meant "You... have any dates lined up?" not "You... feel fine?"

But I get the picture, and the musical accompaniment.

So. I ran into Leah at Urth Caffé. Her knees familiarly touching the knees of an attractive gentleman who looked well-off enough to be my client. (Art consulting, not self-defense.)

She looked genuinely happy, and I was going to leave it at that, but she saw me. Some expression flashed across her face, but it was so quick it didn't have time to register.

I imagined she was maybe uncomfortable with my seeing her with someone else so soon after our parting. I wanted to tell her not to be, that she's someone who knows what she wants, and God bless her for that. Then again, you wisely warned me against trying to read someone's mind.

I can honestly say I am happy for her. In love, timing is everything. The heart wears no watch.

Peacefully,
M.

February 10
To: Mark
From: Amy
Subject: Oh, the heart wears a watch, all right, and a cell and a two-way pager

1. You think Leah was uncomfortable? Duh. She was shocked to see you. That's what happens when you freak out on a guy and then you see him a few weeks later at a public place of caffeine and commerce.
2. Just because the dude is rich doesn't mean she's got the easy baby oven popping out the baby cakes. What are you "happy for"? That she's got another guy to have coffee with? Okay then. That's all you can assume.
3. I'm just suggesting you be honest about your experience and your feelings, oh Postmodern Zen master. Two weeks ago you were on her doorstep proposing. It must have hurt a little, and don't tell me there isn't part of you still creeped out by her Uterus Mission Statement dating style.

Sounds like denial to me, but peace out,
a.

February 10
To: Amy
From: Mark
Subject: In Leah's Defense

I am happy because I want her to have all the happiness I wasn't able to bring her.

No, she didn't creep me out, ever. I wasn't ready at two months, but I'm the one who made the mistake of not asking enough questions, or not the right ones.

I appreciate what you're saying, Amy, but this time around I think I just needed you the way a drunk needs a streetlamp: more for support than illumination.

Love,
Mark

February 11
To: Amy
From: Mark
Subject: The Cute Meet

I know what our problem is, Amy. I think you were on to something back when you wondered whether Lance actually loved you, or just loved you to that soundtrack.

You and I want to star in a romantic movie. Cinematic entrances. It's why you hate (and why I grew to hate) online personals. Where's the great Meet story? I drive with Joni Mitchell by day and Tom Waits by night, and it's their L.A. I experience.

We know the scenes by heart. The tearful goodbye at the train station. The perfect romantic gesture. The overcoat at the door with nothing underneath. The trip to Paris montage. The rose petals on the bed. And then we audition actors to play the romantic lead.

Does life have to be a story? Can we let go of this need for the Cute Meet and the Ride into the Sunset? I think if we're ever going to be truly happy, Amy, we have to learn to let go. And open ourselves up to the unexpected, the unrehearsed.

February 11
To: Amy
From: Mark
Subject: Spinning Cupid's Bottle

Almost forgot. It's that time again. Dean has again invited me to the secret Kissing Party. And I am inviting you. Now that you've heard all those Dean stories, I think it might amuse you to meet him in person. Bring along Susan. And Marla and Shelley. We can merge our worlds. End the electronic divide. It will be silly fun. Wanna come?

February 11
To: Mark
From: Amy
Subject: Party of Two

In response to your theory about wanting our lives to be romantic movies, that is the most horrible and accurate statement you have ever come up with (although the nekkid trench coat doesn't turn me on and I have a country chick singer/Rolling Stones soundtrack in my movie).

I say we don't go to the kissing party, though. No siree, no lost souls swapping spit for you and me. This year we will not pay homage to black lace panties or men with veiny arms. We will toast what it is we have created together, and that is intimacy and carpal tunnel syndrome.

Thank you for this relationship. Look at you, Sparky, you actually made it for a whole year. I would have lost money on that bet.

But my goal was to learn to be more open to real people and real relationships, and I would like to celebrate that by getting together with you on the fourteenth. What do you say?

February 11
To: Amy
From: Mark
Subject: Splendid

A. –

I accept. Heartily. But it's Ladies' Choice. You name the V-time and the V-place and I will V-there.

So it's been a year. Hope you'll still recognize me.

We have so much to celebrate. You used to keep reminding me to slow down, and look what I did. Spent an entire year dilating myself in slow motion to accommodate this new person: you.

Zip me the 411 and I'll see you soon.

February 12
To: Mark
From: Amy
Subject: Spirit(s) Guide

The night after tomorrow. Eight pm. We'll go see my old friend Hector. He's at the bar at Vermont. Wear your Intellectual Marlboro Man outfit and I'll recognize you.

This is going to be fun. It would be weird if I brought my laptop so I could write to you instead of talking, though, huh?

Wow. I probably shouldn't be telling you this, but I'm excited and nervous.

I can't believe I just told you that I'm excited and nervous.

February 14
To: Amy
From: Atom Kirkossian
Subject: FROM MARK – NOT SPAM!

Remember when we were waiting for our drinks and I got up to go to the bar and you told me to sit down, that the waitress would bring them, but I insisted and you thought I was nuts? It was a ruse. I saw this guy at the bar (the bald Armenian with big hoot owl glasses) using a BlackBerry, and thought it would be fun to send you an e-mail from the middle of our – our what? Our night out? Our one year anniversary? Valentine's? Or we don't have to call it anything at all. It's just, well, I'm so used to talking to you this way, and when I saw him there I couldn't resist. Or maybe I'd just feel awkward looking you in the eyes and telling you you smell good. Maybe by the time you get home and read this I will already have told you. That I'm excited and nervous, too. That I'd come to think of you as black and white, words on a screen, consonants and vowels, and had completely forgotten how utterly beautiful you are. And in that dress... Alright, he's getting pissed so I'm heading back over, drinks in hand, really looking forward to the rest of tonight. Before signing off, I just wanted to say hi to the Amy I've been writing all this time, who's sitting about fifteen feet away, no idea what I'm up to with the bald owl, thinking I'm totally nuts. Maybe I am. But I'm damn glad to have company. – Mark

----

Sent from my BlackBerry Wireless Handheld

Amy Turner

Amy has written for French rock 'n' roll magazines and performs her own essays at various theaters in Los Angeles. Her one-woman show "Turner Gets Off" was praised by the *LA Weekly* for its "effervescent stage presence and self-deprecatory humor." Now living in West Hollywood, Amy was most recently a staff writer for the NBC series *Studio 60 on the Sunset Strip.*

Mark Van Wye

In Miami Beach, Mark walked his first date to the door then shook her hand good night. Three weeks later she dumped him because he was too shy to kiss her. At Amherst College he founded the comedy group *Mr. Gad's House of Improv,* briefly dating one of the comediennes until he surprised her with a visit to her parents' home where he vomited on the rug and on their dachshund, thanks to a tainted hot dog. A decade later he received an MFA in Playwriting from Smith College, an all-girls institution, making a great first impression by being cast as the incestuous child molester Uncle Peck in *How I Learned to Drive.* His photo appeared on the poster all over campus where it was scrawled with the word "asshole." He never knew if it referred to him, Uncle Peck, or men in general. Currently Mark lives, cooks and writes in Los Angeles, where he serves as Director of Development for King Cole Productions.